Look for these titles by *Erin Nicholas*

Now Available:

No Matter What
Hotblooded

The Bradfords
Just Right
Just Like That
Just My Type
Just the Way I Like It
Just For Fun
Just a Kiss

Anything & Everything
Anything You Want
Everything You've Got

Praise for Erin Nicholas's *Everything You've Got*

"*Everything You've Got* is a touching story of love, forgiveness, and acceptance. It really is everything rolled together with a few steamy moments that will knock your socks off. I would move *Everything You've Got* up on your to-be-read pile and enjoy this romance with a smile."

~ *Sizzling Hot Book Reviews*

"*Everything You've Got* by Erin Nicholas is highly recommended, for if the handcuffs don't get you, then the always-good owner of Camelot bar will tempt you with his good looks and sexy charm. Loved it."

~ *Fallen Angel Reviews*

"A cute and sexy story that proves that being yourself is the best medicine."

~ *Night Owl Book Reviews*

Everything You've Got

Erin Nicholas

Samhain Publishing, Ltd.
11821 Mason Montgomery Road, 4B
Cincinnati, OH 45249
www.samhainpublishing.com

Everything You've Got

Print ISBN: 978-1-61921-113-1
Digital ISBN: 978-1-60928-956-0

Editing by Lindsey Faber
Cover by Scott Carpenter

First Samhain Publishing, Ltd. electronic publication: March 2012
First Samhain Publishing, Ltd. print publication: February 2013

Dedication

To anyone who's ever been bullied or made to feel like you're less than you are—I know kick-ass boots don't fix everything. Then again, they can't hurt.

And to everyone who helped make this book happen (finally)—PG, Sky, Meg, Stella and Lindsey—and the readers who loved Sabrina and Marc but knew that Luke needed a story too (thank you!).

Chapter One

Kat Dayton could generally get men to do whatever she wanted when she wore her kick-ass boots.

But Luke Hamilton wasn't like other men.

She'd been wearing her kick-ass boots around him forever and he had yet to do what she really wanted—make a move on her.

So, tonight she was going to also need handcuffs. And a blindfold.

Marc Sterling looked from the silver rings dangling from Kat's fingers to her face and back to the rings. "Those aren't very subtle."

"Screw subtle," she told Luke's best friend. "It's his birthday, he's being stubborn and crabby, and none of the other ideas will work."

"Sure, forcing him to show up should put him in a party mood."

"It's a surprise party. The whole premise is forcing the guest of honor to show up," she pointed out.

They had been debating with the rest of their friends how to get Luke to the surprise party for a week. Luke stayed at the restaurant he owned with Marc until midnight every night. In addition, he'd been in a bad mood for, oh, about two months now. And it had been getting progressively worse.

So he was less than agreeable to most suggestions in general and fun, social ones in particular.

His bad mood had definitely made Kat less than jovial.

Because he was pining for a woman.

And this was not just any woman. It was Sabrina Rose

Cassidy Sterling. Kat's best friend. Marc's wife.

Well, maybe he wasn't *pining.* It wasn't like he'd stopped eating or sleeping or even speaking to or spending time with Marc and Sabrina. In fact, his relationships with both of them seemed completely normal.

But he had been downright surly at the wedding and reception and he'd been...brooding ever since. He'd been a workaholic before, but his time in the restaurant was about greeting his guests and supporting his staff however they needed him. He'd been out and about, talking, laughing and clearly in his element. The hours in his office at his desk were always after the restaurant closed. Now it seemed he spent a lot more time in his office and, though on the surface he seemed normal when he was in the main areas with guests, Kat knew him well enough to notice he was less than happy and satisfied.

It couldn't be a coincidence that Luke's grumpiness had started at Marc and Sabrina's wedding.

Marc took the cuffs from her, passing them back and forth between his hands. "You know, on second thought, this is a great idea. This might be the one thing that could get him out of his funk."

Kat had seen that look on Marc's face before. He looked mischievous. She didn't like it. "What does that mean?"

"I'm just sayin' that birthday cake and confetti aren't the first thing he'll be thinking of when you come at him with handcuffs."

"There's going to be confetti?" Kat asked. "That's a little cheesy."

"Not the point."

Kat propped a hand on her hip. "Okay, what will he be thinking?" She knew exactly what Marc was thinking, but she wasn't at all sure Luke's mind would go the same direction.

"You, him, a pair of handcuffs. He'll be thinkin' this is the best birthday ever."

Damn right he would. The thought snuck up on her, but right on its heels was *If I had Luke Hamilton at my mercy for even ten minutes he'd think it was the best frickin' day of his* life.

Wow. She really wasn't sure where all of this was coming from. She'd been around and single in sexy boots for long enough that if Luke was interested he could have done something about it by now. She had no reason to think that he'd be interested in her rocking his world—birthday or not.

Still, given half a chance, she wouldn't mind giving it a try.

The worst thing that could happen would be she'd lose one of her best friends.

No, worse than that would be him not being rocked by her attempt.

That would be *way* worse.

And was definitely a possibility.

They'd kissed once in college. It had gotten hot and heavy too. Then they'd been interrupted—by Sabrina, of course—and Luke had never even mentioned it again. And he certainly hadn't ever tried to pick up where they'd left off.

Stuff like that was a little tough on a girl's ego, frankly.

"So," Marc was saying, "with a surprise party you have to find a way to bring the person to the party—which we tried by having it at our house. Or you bring the party to the person. That's the new plan. We'll bring all the stuff here and have it in the party room. You're in charge of keeping him away until we're ready."

"Oh sure. He barely leaves this building." Luke worked fourteen hours a day, seven days a week. It wasn't healthy, or necessary. They had a fantastic staff. But The Camelot was his dream. There was no place he'd rather be.

"Then keep him in the building but out of the party room," Marc said with a shrug.

The party room was off the main dining room and had huge doors they could shut to block the party planning. Provided Luke didn't decide to go check why the doors were shut. Which he would. Luke knew every bent fork, bruised banana and scuffed tile in The Camelot.

"How will I possibly do that?"

Marc swung the handcuffs in front of her face. "Be creative. Get him in his office—then keep him there. Somehow. Be creative. We'll need about twenty minutes to get all the stuff from our house over here and set up."

"You said 'be creative' twice," she pointed out. Her heart was already pounding even as she was coming up with an excuse not to do it.

"Creative is fun," Marc said with that grin she hated. "Creative is memorable."

Did she want this night to be fun for Luke? Of course. And memorable? Sure. Would *she* like to be those two things for him? Definitely.

Did she need to use handcuffs for that?

She sighed. Admittedly, she'd like to.

It seemed that her imagination had quite easily taken handcuffs plus fun plus memorable and come up with a few scenarios.

"You really think this is a good idea?" she asked. Marc was the only person in the world who knew how she felt about Luke. He also knew that she didn't think Luke returned her feelings.

"It's a perfect idea. He's been moping around here for weeks."

Yeah, moping was a better word than brooding. "I'd just be cheering him up then?"

"A hot girl who wants to handcuff him? Cheerful is a mild word for it."

"But it will be *me* handcuffing him."

Marc gave her a wink. "You're the only one who should do it."

She really wanted that to be true. "You promise I'm not going to fall on my face with this?"

"Tell me something," Marc said instead of answering directly. "You are a go-for-it girl. I mean, you do what you want, you don't worry about what people think, you're sure of yourself. Why haven't you gone after Luke?"

"He was hung up on Sabrina," she said without meeting Marc's eyes. There were things behind the bravado everyone saw that even Marc didn't know.

"Uh-huh. I bought that initially. But you and I both know that Luke knows that Sabrina belongs with me."

Kat sighed. That was the complication. She did believe that Luke felt Marc was the right guy for Sabrina. Which took her one decent excuse away and made her face the fact that maybe Sabrina hadn't been what was keeping Luke from being with Kat. Finally she said, "Maybe he doesn't want me."

"He's a very, very smart man, Kat. Of course he wants you."

She rolled her eyes. "I appreciate the sentiment. But I've been right here all along. Why hasn't *he* made a move?"

Marc tossed her the cuffs. "Maybe you should ask him that."

She looked from her friend to the cuffs.

Maybe she should.

And if he told her the truth and it wasn't good, well, she'd just never be able to face him again.

"If I end up looking like an ass, I'll kill you," she told Marc.

He laughed. "I'm not worried."

She raised an eyebrow—the one that she'd pierced specifically because she could raise it like that. "I'm serious. If this flops, I'll blame you. Then someday you'll come to my office with terrible stomach pain and I'll know it's acute appendicitis. I'll know that it could burst at any moment and slowly poison your system, but I'll tell you it's heartburn and give you antacids and send you home to suffer. Slowly and painfully."

He cleared his throat and seemed to be trying to hide a smile. "I had no idea you were so vindictive."

"You haven't made me look bad before."

"Got it."

"And you still think I should handcuff Luke?"

"You should definitely handcuff Luke."

"I have a blindfold too."

Marc gave her that damned grin. "That's my girl."

Luke didn't see her or hear her approach, but he *smelled* her. And he didn't care why Kat was behind him when she got that close.

He opened his mouth to tell her he knew she was there but suddenly her arms came around his neck and something covered his eyes. Instinctively, his body stiffened before her hot whisper touched the skin on the back of his neck.

"Hold still."

He smiled in spite of having no idea what she was doing. "Kat, are you actually blindfolding me?" he asked as he felt the cloth over his eyes tighten slightly.

"You knew it was me?"

"Of course. I know your body spray." He felt her surprise in the way she suddenly froze.

"Oh." She cleared her throat.

That made him grin. "Now what?" He was up for anything involving Kat, frankly. He'd been on his way to find her. He was also smiling for the first time in almost two months.

Because ten minutes ago, his best friend had given him his birthday present—Marc had told him that Kat had feelings for him.

It was like sunshine had broken through a dark, cold day.

Sappy perhaps, but that's how he felt.

Two months ago he'd watched her with another man at Marc and Sabrina's wedding and had wanted to put his fist through the wall. Kat made the first move. Everyone—every male anyway—knew that. If she wanted someone, she let them know. Not only had she not given Luke any indication that she felt more than friendship for him, but she'd brought another guy to the wedding that would have been the perfect place to turn *their* relationship into more. If she'd wanted that.

He could admit the whole situation had made him into an antisocial ass over the past months. But tonight things were going to change. Marc had said the magic words—Kat wanted him.

And now she was blindfolding him.

Yep, this had the makings of the best birthday ever. And he wasn't talking about cake and confetti.

"You have to leave the blindfold on, okay?"

Taking it off hadn't even occurred to him. "No problem."

"Really?" Again with the surprise.

"A hot girl and a blindfold? I'd be an idiot if I wanted to take it off."

He heard her chuckle softly. "Thanks. So you're good with this?"

"Very good." It could only be better if she were the one in the blindfold. All kinds of images were racing through his mind as it was.

"Come on." She took his hand and they started forward.

The Camelot, his restaurant and dream come true, was the place he spent most of his time and he knew every inch. He even managed to keep from stubbing his toe on the wingback chair near the arched doorway that led into the short hallway of offices.

After they'd stepped into his office, he heard the door shut and the lock click.

"A hot girl in black leather, a blindfold, a private office with a locked door on my birthday. My expectations are rising every minute."

"Black leather isn't all that uncommon for me," Kat pointed out.

"True. But the rest... Well, it's understandable that I would be expecting more than something like—oh, I don't know—a set of DVDs for instance."

There was a stunned moment of silence and he imagined she was staring at him in shock. No, she was probably frowning.

"How did you know?" she finally asked.

He chuckled. "A good guess. I hope it's *Burn Notice*." It was their favorite show. They discussed the current episode every week.

And he would love the DVDs. Just like he'd loved the first three seasons of *House*, another favorite, she'd given him last year and the boxed set of *Seinfeld* the year before that.

He liked to think she gave him their favorite TV shows to prove that she was paying attention to what he liked because she cared. But this was Kat Dayton. If Kat wanted or felt something, everyone knew it. Instead, she had to come up with an annual gift for a friend. Period.

"You think you're pretty smart, huh?" she finally asked.

"Sorry," he said with a shrug. "I know how much you hate being predictable."

She really did. She wore black all the time, preferred tight, fitted clothes, loved boots and had a number of piercings. She also used dramatic eye makeup and body paint and her short dark hair was styled and colored differently almost every day.

"I might still have a few surprises left."

He felt her move in closer and heard her rustling in her bag.

"I can't wait."

"Not nervous at all?" she asked.

"Definitely not what I'm feeling." He was feeling...intrigued. Excited. Amused. Optimistic.

She had feelings for him and he had her undivided attention. There were only a few ways—a few very specific ways—this could get better.

It was common knowledge that when one sense was removed the others became stronger. He felt like he was completely tuned in to every move she made. There was a soft metallic *clink* and the air around him grew warmer as she leaned in.

"Were you predicting this?"

He felt her hands slide down his left arm to his hand and he took in a deep lungful of vanilla. Then he felt cold metal around his wrist followed by a *click*.

No way.

"Handcuffs?" he asked. He lifted his arm and found his left wrist connected to the arm of the chair.

"Handcuffs." She still leaned close. "So, if you have different expectations of a birthday involving a blindfold, how do you feel about one with handcuffs?"

He grinned. "Kat Dayton wants me at her mercy? I'm liking it a lot."

"I'm...flattered." That had sounded more like a question.

He chuckled. "Being the first guy you handcuff? Me too."

There was a pause and he felt her straighten away from him. "How do you know you're the first guy I've handcuffed?"

"I've heard about your strip poker games, your skinny-dipping...somebody would have definitely been talking about being handcuffed."

"I played strip poker *one* time with Greg Matthews and skinny-dipped *one* time with Travis Nelson. Here I thought I was dating gentlemen."

"You did not. You've known these guys since third grade," Luke said with a grin.

She blew out a breath. "Well, you know that both of them likely did some embellishing. You probably shouldn't base your expectations on what Greg and Travis said."

"You're right. I should definitely find out for myself." Even without exaggeration he knew that a few minutes with Kat, skinny-dipping or otherwise, would be better than a whole season of *Burn Notice*.

"Find out?"

"What a great kisser you are."

He heard her little intake of air. Okay, so maybe he had some surprises for her too.

"You want to..." She cleared her throat. "Did you just say you want to kiss me?"

He chuckled at that. He'd kissed her once in college and he hadn't been able to completely forget it. Even though he'd tried when it became clear that she didn't want to do anything more about it. He wanted to kiss her again. Tonight. Now.

"Definitely. And you have to give me what I want—it's my birthday."

He held his breath, waiting for her to laugh, or say *you've got to be kidding me*, or something similar.

"They say the memory is the first thing to go as we age," she said softly.

He heard the hurt in her tone and reached instinctively with his free hand, snagging her fingers as she tried to move away. "I remember the kiss, Kat. Vividly and often. I'm just teasing you."

There was an excruciatingly long pause. He'd told the truth. He thought about that kiss. A lot. More and more all the time. Like the more she kissed *other* guys. Like he'd seen her doing at Marc's wedding...

He loosened the hold he had on the arm of the chair and forced himself to relax. She wasn't kissing anyone else tonight. He had to focus here. There wasn't another guy with her tonight. He didn't need to worry about being an ass to a guy he'd known his whole life, like he had at the wedding. All the guy had done was agree to be Kat's date to the wedding. He really hadn't deserved Luke's glares or refusal to engage in conversation or the beer down the leg of his pants.

Anyway, she wasn't kissing anyone else tonight.

Finally he heard her pull in a slight breath just before she asked, "Does Marc still have his appendix?"

He frowned. What the hell did that mean? "I'm, um, sure he does."

"Okay, good."

She pulled free of his hold but just as he was grabbing

blindly, she leaned in and put a hand on each arm of the chair.

That was better.

"You ready?" she asked, her breath on his cheek.

"Is anyone ever really ready for you?" he asked.

"Aw, you say the sweetest things." Then she touched her lips to his.

The contact was relatively chaste, and the heat and want that washed over him was completely out of proportion. But one taste and he had to have *more.*

When she started to pull back, Luke reached up with his free hand, cupped the back of her head and opened his mouth.

She didn't even hesitate. She groaned as she leaned into the kiss, meeting the stroke of his tongue with hers. The next thing he felt was her straddling his thighs and climbing onto his lap.

From there everything went crazy. Her hands went to his hair, holding his head still. His hand went to her lower back, pressing her closer. His hips lifted and her pelvis pressed down, pulling moans from both of them.

Then her hands went to the front of his shirt while his hand moved to the back of hers. She unbuttoned buttons while his hands slipped under the stretchy fabric of her blouse and onto bare skin. Goose bumps broke out under his hand and she shivered as he ran his hand up her spine to her bra and down again.

And then the song "Be Our Guest" from Disney's *Beauty and the Beast* erupted from her purse.

Kat tore her mouth from Luke's. He felt her panting against his lips.

The song continued. Because it was Kat's ringtone for Marc.

"Ignore him," Luke said gruffly, once again cupping the back of her head and attempting to bring her forward.

But she pushed against his chest. "Hold on. I have to talk to him."

Luke pulled the blindfold from his eyes. “It’s Marc. He’s got nothing interesting to say.”

She slid back and off his lap. “Let me just—”

“Put him off,” Luke said firmly. “Then get back up here. We’re not done.” Damn the handcuffs. Suddenly he realized they weren’t as great as he’d first thought. He couldn’t grab her as she was backing away.

She met his eyes and for a moment she froze. Now, without the blindfold, he could see it in her eyes—everything had just changed.

They had kissed. Really *kissed.* The kind of kissing that involved so much more than only lips. The kind of kissing that led to other things. The kind of kissing that changed friends into much, much more. Not the kind of kiss that had anything to do with *done.*

That was a just-getting-started kiss.

She grabbed her phone and quickly typed something in. A message to Marc, Luke assumed. Hopefully something like *leave us the fuck alone.*

Then she tossed Luke the key to the handcuffs. “I can’t believe we just did that.”

“It’s about damned time,” Luke returned, unlocking himself.

“What do you mean?”

“It’s about damned time you did that. Or something like it.”

Eyes wide, she propped a hand on her hip. “Me? What about you? You haven’t showed up on my doorstep with handcuffs either, you know.”

“When would I have done that?” he asked, stretching to his feet. “When you were dating Greg? Or when you were dating Travis? Or when you were dating Matt? Or when you were dating Derek?”

Kat’s other guys had been driving him nuts for a long time. Especially when they told skinny-dipping and strip poker stories. But those were the guys Kat chose to be with.

"So you were content to sit around and wait? You must not have wanted it too badly," she said.

"I didn't really have a choice, did I?" he asked with a frown.

"Some kind of guy code or something?"

Luke tossed the cuffs, key and blindfold onto his desk and strode toward her. She backed up until she was against the door. He put a hand flat on the door by her ear and leaned in. "You're not like other women, Kat."

"Thank you."

He gave her a grin and a nod of acknowledgement. "You know exactly what I mean."

"Do I?"

She did. He could tell. But he said, "If I had asked you out, you would have said no. Because you always say no when the guy asks without encouragement."

"I don't know what you're talking about," she said, focusing on his shirt collar.

What a liar. "I had to wait for the signal that you wanted me. You don't always ask the guys out, but you do always make it really clear when you want a guy to make a move. The guys flirt, throw out hints that they're interested, but no one officially asks until you make it clear you want it. If they ask and you haven't given the signal, you shoot them down. Even I had to follow the rules."

She swallowed hard and Luke wondered if she was surprised that he knew this. She liked control. She liked getting people—especially male people—to do what she wanted. Which was why she chose men she could boss around. They tended to be younger than her, but even if they were older they were totally into her before they even got to buy her a burger.

He was totally into her. He wasn't easy to boss around, but they could deal with that when it came up.

"You've been paying attention," she finally commented, looking up and meeting his eyes.

Yep. For years.

"And waiting," he said.

"And when would I have given you the signal anyway? When you proposed to Sabrina the first time or the second time?" she asked.

He winced. Right. He knew Sabrina had been an obstacle. She was Kat's best friend and he'd had a...complicated relationship with her for years. They'd been friends, they'd even been lovers once, Luke had bent over backwards for her, he'd been her protector, her haven, her rock.

But he'd never been her true love.

"I was never really hers and you, of all people, knew it," he finally said.

His feelings for Sabrina had always been hard to explain. She'd needed him. That had been more powerful than her loving him for a long time. But she'd exhausted him.

Now he was done with all of that and Kat was the perfect choice. Kat didn't *need* anyone. Which meant he wouldn't go crazy trying to figure out how to meet those needs. And he wouldn't fail at it.

"But you wanted to be hers," Kat said softly.

"I wanted..." The life Sabrina was now living with Marc.

That realization had hit him when he'd first realized his best friend, the man who was practically his brother, was in love with the woman *he'd* intended to marry. He'd also realized it wasn't losing Sabrina that hurt, but the idea that he still had to wait for the woman that was right for him. Sabrina clearly belonged with Marc.

Luke loved Sabrina. Like he should love the woman his best friend was married to. Like he should the woman he'd grown up next door to. Like he should a very close friend.

But not like he wanted to love someone someday.

Not like he might be on the way to loving Kat.

"I wanted her to be happy," he finally said. "I thought I could make her happy. I was wrong. And now she's happy with Marc. Completely."

"She really is," Kat agreed. "Completely." She emphasized the word, meeting his gaze directly.

"I know." And he did.

Kat just looked at him for a long moment. Finally she nodded. "Okay."

He breathed in a sigh of relief. His relationship and feelings for Sabrina were important issues to resolve before they could move on to the issue of *them*.

"Now what?" Kat asked. "Sex?"

He loved that about her so much. There was no guessing, no games. Kat was straightforward in everything.

"Definitely sex," he told her. "But everything else too."

"Everything?" she asked with wide eyes. "Like wh—" Her reply was cut off by a shriek as the door behind her swung open without warning, pitching her into the hallway—and Marc.

The only other person with a key to Luke's office.

"Whoa," Marc chuckled looking from one of them to the other as he set Kat back on her feet. "You two okay in here? Nobody's answering my calls."

"You're interrupting," Kat said, straightening her skirt.

"I'm thrilled to hear it," Marc said.

"So get out," Luke told him.

"Can't. I need you out in the dining room."

"No way," Luke said. "When I leave this office it's only to go home. With Kat."

"Again, thrilled," Marc said with a grin. "But there's something you have to do before you can leave."

"Handle it," Luke said through gritted teeth.

"This has to be you," Marc told him.

"Dammit, Marc. I don't ask you to do this. Ever. This time I want you to handle the restaurant."

The Camelot was Luke's life. He didn't mind staying, he was doing what he loved most. Until now. Now he wanted to leave early—well, early for him—with Kat. It was unprecedented and both his friends noticed.

Kat's eyes were wide. So were Marc's.

"Why don't you check on whatever's going on in the dining room and then we can leave together?" she offered.

"I'd rather do what we've been doing."

"Which is what, exactly?" Marc asked, eyebrows up.

"Discussing our love lives," Luke said smoothly.

"Is that right?" Marc answered. "I wasn't aware either of you had a love life."

"Hey, I date," Kat said.

"I said *love* life, not sex life," Marc told her.

"Hey," Kat said again, swatting Marc's arm. "What is with making me out to be the town slut?"

"Not slut," Marc said. "Girl to hang out with, without any strings attached."

She started to protest, then must have realized that wasn't completely inaccurate. There were no strings in her relationships.

"Well, there are strings now," Luke said. "And we're both about to have a love life."

"You're getting a girlfriend?" Marc asked with a smirk.

"Yep. Terrific gal. You'll love her," Luke said.

"And Kat's getting a boyfriend?"

"Guy who's crazy about her."

Marc chuckled and Kat rolled her eyes as she took Luke's hand. "Let's go. Dining room."

Luke sighed and followed her into what could only be his surprise birthday party.

The crowd of people who loved Luke was large and enthusiastic about celebrating the day of his birth. Kat barely had time to wipe the lipstick smudge from his bottom lip before he was surrounded and carried away from her.

She took the moment and space to take what felt like the first true, deep breath since she'd approached Luke with the blindfold.

Wow.

Her life had totally changed in the past thirty minutes.

Luke Hamilton had kissed her. He'd *kissed* her. And he wanted more. Sex—oh, thank god he wanted sex—and more. She wasn't *exactly* sure what that meant except that he'd said he wanted strings attached. He'd called her his girlfriend. She took another deep breath. Luke Hamilton always knew what he wanted. He always had a plan.

Apparently *she* was now what he wanted. She was his plan.

Watching Luke work a room was something to behold. He moved and smiled and talked with a natural, easy grace and sincerity that made every person feel like *they* were important and that he had all the time in the world to hear their stories. It was impossible not to like him, not to want to be near him.

She'd watched it for years. Even before owning The Camelot, Luke drew people. He wasn't easygoing or laid back. He was driven and determined. He didn't like when things didn't go according to his plan. He was a problem solver. He'd point out what needed to be done and then jump in to do it. But that was what people liked. They liked knowing that someone would always take charge and do it right.

Marc had more charm and humor to his style. They balanced each other out. Where Marc wanted everyone to be happy and smiling, Luke wanted everyone to take responsibility and get stuff done.

Together they could accomplish anything.

Her phone rang and she answered it without looking, her eyes on Luke. "Dr. Dayton."

"Tom Martin's in the hospital."

It took Kat only two seconds to focus on the phone call instead of Luke's butt. "*What*?"

"Tom Martin was just taken to the hospital by ambulance."

The voice on the other end of the phone belonged to Nancy, the nurse who worked with Kat in the Justice medical clinic.

"*What?*"

"I'm on my way to you. Don't move." Nancy was on the other side of the room. Ten seconds later she was right in front of Kat.

"What did they say?" Kat asked with trepidation. "What happened?"

"Jeff didn't give me details other than the fact that they picked him up and he's unconscious."

Kat closed her eyes and rubbed the spot in the middle of her forehead. Jeff was one of the volunteer EMTs in Justice. He was also Nancy's son-in-law. He probably shouldn't have told Nancy even what he had, but Nancy was one of Tom's health-care providers. Health-care privacy acts kept information from people who didn't need to know it. Nancy and Kat needed to know this.

Just then Nancy's phone chirped with a text message. She looked at it, then up at Kat.

Kat braced herself. "What?"

"Julie found him unconscious on the kitchen floor and called 9-1-1," Nancy reported, referring to Tom's wife.

"Shit," Kat said softly.

"Let's go into the lobby."

The restaurant was closed, the lobby empty when Nancy led Kat to one of the wingback chairs by the window.

"Breathe," her friend ordered.

Kat tried.

Nancy's phone beeped again.

"Taking him in for CT scan. Still unconscious," Nancy read from the screen.

"Arm weakness and a headache," Kat said. "That was all he had this morning."

"I know."

"He was laughing and joking when he left. He told me he liked my new belt and he gave me a hard time about my golf game."

"I know."

"His blood pressure was within normal range."

"Right."

"He'd been working in the yard just before his arm started bothering him."

"Yep."

Kat looked up at her nurse and friend. "I missed something." Her stomach pitched as she said the words out loud.

"You don't know that," Nancy protested, straightening and putting her hands on her hips. "There are a dozen causes of arm weakness and headache."

Kat had to make herself breathe normally as she pressed her hand against her stomach. "I thought it was his rotator cuff."

"It could easily be his rotator cuff," Nancy said with a frown.

"It could also be..." Kat actually felt her voice wobble.

"You don't know that," Nancy insisted. "And this morning could be unrelated to tonight."

Of course it could. Kat knew that. Tom was a healthy, active sixty-seven-year-old man with a dry sense of humor and a generous streak. He had the reputation for buying the most Girl Scout cookies in town and having his Christmas lights up before anyone else. He also had the best garden in Justice and worked hard in his yard, which could have hurt his shoulder and caused a headache. Hell, there were twenty possible reasons for a headache today.

Including built-up pressure in his brain.

Kat slumped back in the chair and rested her head back against the wall behind her. "Crap, Nancy. He had a stroke. The day he saw me with symptoms."

"Katarina Dayton," Nancy scolded. "You don't know that. And even if it's true, it isn't your fault."

But it might be.

Early detection of stroke allowed early treatment. Oftentimes very effective early treatment. But there was a small window of opportunity.

Nancy's cell phone chimed with a new text message and she looked down with trepidation.

"Crap," she said softly.

Kat sat up straight. "What?"

"Brickham just got there."

Awesome.

Dr. Henry Brickham was the senior partner of the Alliance Medical Partners, otherwise known as AMP, a group of physicians serving Alliance and the surrounding communities, including Justice. He had also been Tom Martin's physician for close to twenty years. Though Kat worked for AMP in the new clinic right in Justice, the people of Justice had grown used to driving for their medical care and it was going to take some time for them to feel comfortable turning their health over to a new doctor. Even if she was a hometown girl.

It was happening slowly. They were testing her out with sore throats and sprained ankles and the like now. But she was winning them over, and she and AMP were confident that eventually they would trust her with everything.

But Brickham was the guy she had to impress. She'd done her residency with AMP and had experience in all of the other AMP clinics in the area, but the clinic in Justice had been finished earlier this year and she was the primary physician there now. The AMP partners had been thrilled to have a hometown girl so obviously excited and capable of taking on the Justice clinic. But she knew Brickham had some qualms. He'd arranged for there to always be another physician with her for the first few months to ease the transition for everyone. She'd only been left completely on her own for about three months now.

Kat knew he liked her, and her transcripts and resume spoke for themselves. But Dr. Brickham had cared for the people in this area for a long time. His reluctance wasn't so much about her and her skills as about his patients. He cared about them and letting someone else take over wasn't easy for him either. Still, the area needed another physician. It was a great business move and Kat was unquestionably the right choice.

But he was going to be pissed now.

Tom Martin and his wife Julie had only switched their care from Brickham's office in Kingston to Justice two months ago. She'd only seen Tom one other time—for a sinus infection—and had yet to treat Julie.

Nancy's phone chimed with another text and Kat held her breath.

"Luke's looking for you," Nancy said.

Luke.

The man she'd *finally* kissed. The man who said he wanted sex. And more.

Dammit.

She couldn't let him see her shook up like this. Then he'd want to know why and...she just couldn't tell him. For one thing, she really couldn't tell him. Tom's condition was definitely not something she could speak to anyone about other than his family and the other health-care providers involved in his case.

But more, she just couldn't tell Luke—or anyone—that she might have screwed up like this. Not until she knew more. If then.

The idea of Luke Hamilton thinking less of her made her want to throw up.

Kat pushed up out of the chair. "I'm going over there."

"Over where?" Nancy asked, looking concerned.

"To Alliance, to the hospital. I want to see what's going on."

"I don't think that's a good idea." Nancy shook her head.

"There's nothing you can do right now and it's just going to upset you."

"I'm already upset."

"You have other patients, Kat. Tomorrow. Bright and early."

Oh, yeah. Patients. Who hopefully weren't having a stroke.

Her heart thundered in her ears and she had to force herself to swallow. What if she missed something else? What would happen when people found out that she'd missed this in Tom? What if...

"Nancy?"

"Yeah?"

"I'm freaking out a little here."

Nancy grasped her upper arms in gentle but firm hands. "Listen to me. I know this is making you crazy, but rushing over there isn't going to solve a damned thing. He's in the right hands there and you need to be here to see your other patients. I hate to point this out but..."

She really did look worried, which further freaked Kat out. She never saw Nancy worried. Nancy had been a nurse for twenty-two years. She'd seen it all. She was a wonderful, steady presence in the clinic for both the patients and for Kat.

"Point it out anyway," Kat said, bracing herself.

Nancy took a deep breath, then said gently, "Everyone's going to know about Tom soon enough."

If they didn't already. Justice was a small town with a grapevine that spread news faster than Twitter. Kat had to breathe deep again.

Nancy went on. "If you suddenly cancel everyone and go flying over there, *they* are all going to freak out. What everyone needs to know is that yes, sometimes bad things happen, but that's why we have our ambulance and paramedics and that you trust the ER in Alliance, and the doctors there to take care of things. You have to send the message that it doesn't matter who's on call, that any of the doctors who might end up caring for us will do a great job."

Kat nodded. That made sense. "I still want to go."

"They're not going to let you do the CT scan or read it. Dr. Brickham is there, the other partners are five minutes way. You're an hour away. And there are people here who need you."

Okay. That was all true.

"Then I'm going home." She just couldn't stay here. The party room wasn't just full of Luke's family and friends. Her family and friends were in there too. Yes, they loved her. Yes, they'd support her. Yes, they trusted her.

But she really didn't want any of them to know about this.

And she knew she couldn't hold it together and pretend nothing was wrong. Not with her mom and dad. Or Sabrina and Marc. Or Luke.

"Good idea. Drink some wine and go to bed," Nancy ordered. "Do not let yourself sit up all night stewing about this. I'll see you in the morning."

Kat glanced at the grandfather clock behind the hostess stand. It was almost one thirty in the morning. She'd be at the clinic in six hours.

A lot could happen in six hours.

Hell, her whole world had been turned upside down in one-sixth of that time tonight. For better and for worse.

Chapter Two

Luke entered the kitchen of his restaurant and immediately groaned. "Are we going to have to come up with a signal like the tie on the doorknob in college?"

Marc pulled back from Sabrina—slowly. He grinned over her head at Luke. "Maybe you should just stop coming into the kitchen. That's about the only place this stuff happens."

Luke heard Sabrina giggle from where her face was pressed into her husband's chest.

He rolled his eyes but grinned too. Maybe he'd spent years believing he was in love with Sabrina, but seeing her with Marc made him wonder how the hell he'd ever thought that. They were so obviously perfect together that it made his chest hurt. Not because he was jealous or wanted her, but because he wanted...*that*. What they had.

And now it was going to happen.

If he could just find the woman of his dreams.

She was around here somewhere. He'd last seen her talking to Nancy.

He had the life he wanted—pretty much. He'd always planned to own a business that was popular and important to his hometown—The Camelot was definitely both of those things. He'd wanted to be close to his family and friends—he lived four blocks from his parents and his best friend was his business partner and married to another of his best friends. He'd wanted to make a difference and impact on the community—not only did he buy and hire locally for the restaurant, but he also volunteered and donated whenever he could to projects and committees.

But there was something obviously missing. He wanted a

wife and family. He wanted someone to share his dreams with—cheesy as that sounded. He wanted someone who would volunteer with him, who would understand his need to serve this community, who would work and live here because she loved it as much as he did.

He also wanted kids. He wanted to play in the park, coach baseball, go on Boy Scout camping trips. He wanted it all.

And damned if he wasn't watching his best friend do and have all of that with the woman Luke had envisioned himself with for years.

He didn't want Sabrina. But he wanted the life she was giving Marc.

When she'd come home broke, pregnant, finally determined to settle down, he'd been sure it was supposed to be with him.

He'd been wrong.

Marc whispered something in her ear and she hugged him in response.

He'd been really wrong.

He cleared his throat. "Josie told me you wanted to talk to me," he said to Marc, who hadn't quite pulled his hands from his wife's derriere yet.

"Yeah, we have a favor to ask you," Marc said.

Sabrina turned, with her arm around Marc's waist. She was obviously pregnant now. Twenty-five weeks to be exact. She was definitely showing, but it seemed that each week that passed made her smile more and talk more about the baby. It was real to all of them now and Luke thought she was actually settling into this beginning stage of motherhood well.

"What kind of favor?" Luke grabbed an olive from the bowl on the counter and popped it in his mouth.

"We want you to drive the RV down to Nashville for us."

Luke paused midchew and frowned. "What the hell for?" The RV was a monster. And Nashville was something like eighteen hours away.

"We just found out that the band and I were selected to

play in a huge outdoor country music festival," Sabrina said with a huge grin. "But Marc doesn't think I should drive that far. We were hoping to fly and then have you bring the RV for us."

"We'll put you in the hotel during the festival," Marc added. "A suite even."

"If you're staying in a hotel, why do you need the RV?" Luke asked, reaching for another olive.

"I'll sleep a lot better in the RV," Sabrina said. "I'm used to that bed."

"And she'll need a place to relax when they're not performing," Marc added. "She'll also eat better if we can cook our own stuff."

Luke looked at his friends. They were serious. And Sabrina had that look on her face—the hopeful, you're-the-best, I-can-always-count-on-you look that he'd been a sucker for as long as he could remember.

He sighed. "And you used to think that *I* did ridiculous things for her," he said to Marc. It was good that they were at a place in their relationship where they could talk honestly—and with humor—about his and Sabrina's past.

"Well, now I understand why," Marc said unapologetically with a little shrug. "She's pretty sweet and downright charming."

"And she's willing to sleep with you."

"There is that," Marc agreed with a cocky grin.

"Not to mention that she's spoiled rotten," Luke muttered.

"And really grateful," Sabrina said, batting her eyes.

"Uh-huh."

"So you'll do it?" Marc asked.

"Who will run the restaurant while we're all partying with Brad Paisley and Miranda Lambert?"

Sabrina's eyes widened. "How do you know who Brad Paisley and Miranda Lambert are?"

"You played some of their stuff the other night. I got on

YouTube. I like you better than Brad but Miranda better than you."

You referred to Sabrina and The Locals, the band she sang with regularly at The Camelot and various area events.

She was evidently not offended that he preferred Miranda Lambert's "Only Prettier" to her own.

"I'm impressed," she said. "Honestly. But I'm sorry to tell you that Brad and Miranda won't be there. This is more of an amateur festival."

Like it mattered. If there was a chance to be on stage in front of an audience, Sabrina would eat it up. And if Sabrina was into it, Marc was into it.

And Luke suddenly had a really great idea.

Luke ate another olive. "Do you think it's interesting or pitiful that I can't say no to you even when you're married to another man?"

Her face lit up. "You're the best, Luke." She yipped as Marc pinched her butt. "Second best," she amended.

Luke shook his head and smiled. Actually, this was the best birthday present Sabrina had ever given him.

"When do we leave?"

"We?" Sabrina asked.

"Me and Kat."

It was perfect.

They'd be sleeping, showering, dressing—and undressing—in that RV together. There would be no interruptions, no other responsibilities, no distractions. They'd be alone, twenty-four hours a day for at least four days in a very small space, far from home. Oh, yeah, this was perfect.

The moment Kat had climbed up on his lap and kissed him like she'd never get enough, she had accepted her fate.

He was going to fast-track this relationship, and this trip to Nashville together was the ideal way to do it.

"You and Kat?" Sabrina asked.

"Yeah."

He wondered how Sabrina would react. She was madly in love with her husband, but there had never been another female more important than her in Luke's life. This might be a little difficult for her.

"*Finally,*" Sabrina breathed. She rolled her eyes. "I cannot believe it's taken you this long."

Or maybe she'd be fine with it.

"You knew how I felt about Kat?" he asked.

"No one knows you better than Marc and I do," Sabrina told him. "And even if we hadn't known for sure, we know you're right for each other. She's got everything you want and vice versa."

It was true.

"And you've been moping around since the wedding," Marc said. "You hoped something would happen with her that night, didn't you?"

He shrugged. "You know Kat. I couldn't make the first move. But as best man and maid of honor I figured we'd be together a lot, it would be romantic...there would be free liquor."

Marc grinned. "You don't need to liquor her up. She has feelings for you, buddy. She brought Dan to the wedding because she didn't know how *you* felt."

He hoped so. But it didn't matter anymore. Her destiny had been decided as soon as she'd locked his office door. "She knows now. And I'll make sure to reinforce it on this trip. Repeatedly." He watched Sabrina's eyes widen. "I'm not talking about sex. Well, not just about sex."

"Still, I'm thinking you might want to take the scenic route," Marc said with a grin.

Marc knew all about road trips—and what they could lead to.

In an attempt to keep Sabrina from breaking Luke's heart—again—Marc had run interference by driving to pick her up when her car had broken down in Wyoming on her way home to Justice. Luke didn't know—or really want to know—the details of the trip. But Marc's comment made him pretty sure that Marc had started falling for her even then.

"When do you need the RV down there?" he asked.

"Friday," Marc said. "We'll fly in that morning."

It was Sunday now—well, Monday morning.

"We'll be there." He started for the door.

"You going home?" Marc asked.

"To Kat's." He wanted to see her. Everything had changed so quickly and so dramatically tonight. Things were finally coming together and he didn't want to waste a minute.

"She got a call from work," Sabrina said. "I asked Nancy where she was when I couldn't find her."

He blew out a frustrated breath. He couldn't be with her now then. It looked like he was going to get some sleep after all.

But this was the last night he was going to be well rested for a while.

Some days a girl just needed kick-ass boots.

And Kat had a closet full of them. She loved boots. They made her feel tough, confident—and taller, which never hurt.

But she'd opted for ankle-high boots with only a one-inch heel that morning. They were cute, but didn't make her feel very kick-ass. And it was becoming increasingly obvious that she needed at least three-inch heels and knee-high—no, make that, thigh-high—boots today.

Because the day was starting to kick *her* ass.

"Dammit!" She started to slam the cordless phone down on the countertop but Nancy's hand shot out and cushioned the blow before Kat could break the receiver.

"I take it they won't tell you anything either?" Nancy asked dryly.

Nancy had already called the Emergency Department in Alliance, Nebraska, twice, but the staff wouldn't tell her anything about Tom Martin. All they knew from Jeff was that Tom had been admitted to the hospital after his tests in the ER. Now they had no one who would tell them anything.

"No," Kat grumbled. "I'm his damned doctor!"

"Except that Brickham is there."

Yeah, Dr. Brickham was probably still there. Or had at least left instructions that he be the one they called with updates and news.

That definitely didn't make Kat feel better. She slumped into the chair behind the receptionist's desk, vacant because they'd sent Mandy on a coffee run to get her out of the clinic. Kat just couldn't listen to her going on about her cat's kittens being sick today. Just like she'd been tempted to tell Steve, the guy who delivered the water for their watercooler, that she really didn't care about his son's baseball game.

She wasn't this bitchy usually. It was a bad day, and she knew that her agitation came not from the ER staff's tight lips but from the fact that any minute Dr. Brickham was going to call and yell at her. And that eventually people in Justice were going to hear not only that Tom was in the hospital but that he'd been in to see her before that. And all of that freaked her out.

"Dr. Dayton?"

She looked up to find Robbie Paxton holding a huge bouquet of flowers.

She knew instantly they were from Luke. He'd called her cell three times and the clinic twice, but she'd been in with patients—she was spending extra time with everyone today—and she hadn't wanted to talk to him anyway. She couldn't afford to get distracted from her work.

"Hi, Robbie."

"These are for you."

"Thanks. You can put them on the desk there." She wasn't sure she had the energy to even get out of the chair. This whole Tom situation was sucking the life out of her.

"Well, I'm supposed to wait for your answer."

Ah. Well, whatever it was she'd probably say no. It was all too much. Between what had happened with them last night and now this mess—she could only concentrate on one earth-shattering situation at a time and her conscience demanded she focus on the patient who had trusted her with his care rather than on the guy who wanted in her pants.

"Answer to what?" she asked.

"The question on the card." Robbie handed it to her.

Luke had written on the tiny card himself. At the sight of his handwriting, her heart flipped. How stupid was that?

Say I'm going to see you tonight.

She smiled, then sighed, turned the card over and wrote *hope so* before handing it back to Robbie.

The Camelot was her favorite place to unwind. And she really did stop every night. It wasn't just about feeding herself—though it was pretty much the only real meal she ate each day—it was also about the atmosphere. Her friends and family went there, the music was great, the food amazing. Ninety-eight percent of the town ate there on a weekly basis and a good percent showed up more than once a week, even if it was just for drinks or dessert.

Kat didn't stop there every night just because the shrimp salad and chocolate caramel cheesecake were the best in the state.

She stopped because Luke was there.

She'd long ago acknowledged that she was pathetic where Luke was concerned, but she figured there were worse addictions.

And how could she really help it?

Her heart raced when she saw him. She stopped breathing when he smiled directly at her. She tingled when he put his hand on her back or arm—or anywhere. His wide shoulders, dark hair, blue eyes, big hands...he physically appealed to her on every level.

But what really got her was who he *was*.

Luke was a good guy. The best she knew. Dependable, honest, loyal. He was the first to pick up a hammer if someone needed help building or repairing something. He was the first to pick up a spatula to serve pancakes at the church breakfast. He was the first one with an idea or suggestion or donation when something needed done.

Everyone loved him.

He was easy to love. He did the right thing for the right reasons, always did what he said he would do, and always kept his sense of humor.

And he made her feel calm. Which sounded pretty stupid. But it had always been true and he didn't even have to try. Just being around him made her feel good.

Her work life was dramatic. Illness, injury, trauma, emotions. That's what she did every day. Sure, some days were more hectic than others, but the fact that she never knew what was going to come in, had to be ready to go all the time, had to give one hundred and ten percent whether she felt energetic or happy or well rested—or not—made it tough to be laid back. When she was the patient she didn't want her providers to be laid back. She wanted them intense, focused, dedicated. And she gave that to every person who trusted her to take care of them. At least she tried to. Her head ached thinking that she might not have given that to Tom.

But that was how it had become a routine to see Luke every day. Being around him helped bring her down from the tension of the day. And she could really use that today.

Along with her kick-ass boots.

"When's my next appointment?" she asked Nancy.

"Twenty minutes. Pull yourself together."

"Right. I'll be back in fifteen." Kat made a beeline for the front of the clinic. She needed all the help, all the confidence, she could find for this day.

"Where are you going?" Nancy called after her.

"I need to change my boots."

The Camelot was the only place she wanted to be.

She'd waited all day for a call from Dr. Brickham. Sure, he'd be upset with her, but he might at least tell her what was going on. The not knowing was going to kill her. But he'd never called and now she was wound tighter than before and there was only a tiny chance *anything* could settle her down at this point anyway. The Camelot was her best bet.

Kat pulled into the parking lot and stopped the car. Then took a deep breath.

It wasn't The Camelot she needed. She needed Luke. Even without the kiss last night, she would have needed to see him. He made her feel good, unlike anyone else could. He made her laugh, he made her feel confident and intelligent and capable. And, after last night, he made her feel sexy and wanted.

Her ego needed some of all of that today.

She knew that most people saw her as a tough, confident, no-bullshit kind of woman. And that was absolutely the image she worked to project. Most of the time it was easy and most of the time it made her feel that way. But there were days like this, when even the boots, the makeup, the piercings and body paint didn't make her *feel* tough.

It had always fascinated her how outward appearance colored the way people perceived things. She'd chosen her battle armor back in junior high. She changed the color of her hair and the body jewelry and paint she used, but her general look was the same—*don't mess with me.*

It had worked like a dream in junior high and high school to keep the mean girls away and the cocky boys at arm's length. A guy had to really want to get close to make a move. She admired those that tried.

The look had followed her to college and even med school. She was very comfortable with it by then and liked seeing how people responded to her. Some avoided her, feeling intimidated, some labeled her a rebel, some a bad-ass slut. Some found her intriguing, some figured she was just trying to be odd, still others assumed she was disturbed and felt sorry for her.

And then there were the ones who prayed for her. She'd never confirmed whether it was the black clothing, the piercings, or what, but something had her permanently on the prayer list for the ladies at the nondenominational church.

But who couldn't use a few additional prayers?

She was more than a little fascinated by the whole thing. She'd grown up in small-town Nebraska, so she knew she was an anomaly. After all, it was completely on purpose.

No one knew that behind closed doors she preferred baggy sweats, no makeup and that nothing was pierced or painted anywhere others couldn't see it.

It was armor, a costume, a Spiderman suit for the Peter Parker that lurked inside her—awkward, unsure, and breakable.

She took a deep breath. Then another. She wanted to go inside and see Luke, but there were a lot of other people in there too. Many of whom had surely heard about Tom by now. Not the details, of course, but that he was in the hospital for sure.

She shut her car off and headed up The Camelot's front sidewalk. She might regret it later, but she wanted to see Luke more than she wanted to avoid the questions.

It was almost as if he'd been waiting for her. Luke was beside her two seconds after she stepped through the doors.

"If this is your way of saying you're sorry for not calling me back all day, I approve," he said, taking her elbow and starting for his office.

She'd gone home to change before coming in. She'd chosen her outfit with Luke in mind. Even if she wasn't feeling like the world's greatest doctor at the moment, she knew one thing that always made her feel confident—making men crazy.

The skirt was black leather and hugged her waist, hips and thighs where it stopped two inches above her knees. The front had crisscrossed mini silver chains hanging from it and the back dipped into a deep *v* ending just short of being scandalous and had corset lacings that crossed over her lower back, showing more than a hint of bare skin between the laces.

Her top was basically a jacket, with only one button fastened—the one just below her breasts. It kept the lapels over her breasts but showed plenty of cleavage and gapped below, showing off her stomach and the bright red jewel in her belly button. And, of course, she wore knee-high black leather boots.

"Maybe this isn't for you."

He scowled at her. "It is now."

She smiled. "Now what?"

"Now that I've seen you."

"You're staking a claim?" Her heart pounded at that. She wanted him and wanted to be his but there was nothing wrong with teasing him a little.

"Definitely."

"Whether I like it or not?" As if there was anything about that she wouldn't like.

They stepped into his office and he immediately moved in close, pressing her back against the wall. "You'll like it."

She did have to take a deep breath but she still asked, "Even if I like the actual claim staking, I don't get a vote about it happening in the first place?"

"Look me in the eye and tell me you didn't wear this for me." He put a hand on her hip and slid it up and down over the soft leather.

She met his gaze and felt swirling, take-me-now heat. "I wore it for you."

He gave her a cocky half smile. "I appreciate it very much."

"I'm hoping it makes you more apt to say yes to my request."

He moved in closer. "Yes. Whatever it is, yes."

She leaned into him. "Strip off my clothes, lay me back on your desk and fu—"

"Katarina Dayton," he interrupted, his voice sounding like he'd swallowed sand. "Are you testing me?"

She didn't think so. She just really wanted to have sex with him.

Everything she wanted from Luke seemed within her grasp and she was afraid it was going to start unraveling any minute.

So, she was going to take what she could get from him for as long as she could get it.

"I've had a bad day at work and could really use some distraction and release and getting what I want," Kat said, putting her hand over his heart. "I've been thinking about you all day and there is only one thing I'm sure of at this point—I want you."

His heart was beating fast and his pupils dilated but he pulled in a breath and said, "I want more than that, Kat, and I'm going to prove it."

Dammit.

She wasn't surprised that he was jumping in with both feet now that he knew their attraction was mutual. Now he'd want to focus on what had happened, what was going to happen next, make a plan, and go full steam ahead. That was Luke.

It happened with the Camelot—the restaurant was built in six months. It happened when the church needed a new roof—Luke got a committee together and they got the thing done in two days. It happened when a family in town found out their little boy had leukemia—Luke talked to the other businesses in town and they raised twenty thousand dollars in one weekend. It happened with Sabrina too. When Sabrina came home this last time penniless and pregnant, he decided to marry her within two hours of finding out. Luke was known for quickly analyzing a situation, making a plan and going for it.

The problem was, Kat wasn't sure she could just go for a whole big relationship right now. "Lucas Hamilton, are you telling me that you don't want to have sex with me right now?" she asked, pressing against him and running her hand up his chest. She could talk him into this, she was sure.

He cleared his throat. "Somehow I don't think there's a correct answer to that question."

Her eyes widened. "You really do think I'm trying to trick you?"

"I think you really want me to say yes." His fingers slid to the bare skin on her back just above the waistband of her skirt. He stroked back and forth along the strip of skin. "I think that your nipples are hard right now and your panties are wet and you're imagining what it will feel like the first time I thrust into you."

Holy... She took a shaky breath and wet her lips. This was definitely different. She and Luke flirted but they'd never been blatantly sexual with one another.

She liked it. A lot.

"But I think you also really want me to say no," he went on. "You want to know that even though I'm hard enough to drive nails right now and want so badly to make you come hard, fast and loud, I can still say no because I want even more."

She was barely breathing, staring up at him. *Hard enough to drive nails. Come hard, fast and loud.* Oh, yeah. *This* she could handle. "I, um... No, I really do want—"

"I also think wearing this—" again he ran his hand up and down over the soft leather at her hip, "—and testing me is kind of like a matador waving a red cape in front of a bull. The matador not only knows the bull's coming—he *wants* the bull to come." He gave her a little grin and dropped his voice. "And I do plan on coming."

"Wow," she breathed. If she'd wanted him before, hearing him talk like this and look at her like that made her certain she'd do anything he asked. "So let's go. Your house? Or your desk? It's closer."

"Not yet."

She stared at him. "Seriously?"

"Seriously."

This was really typical of Luke. Most guys would take her

signal and ask her to dinner. Luke would take it and jump to something much bigger, something like...

"Let's go away for a few days."

Something like that.

"Dammit," she groaned. She tipped her head back, thunked it against the wall and closed her eyes. "Dammit."

"Kat—"

Her eyes opened. "Sex I can do. But it's not a good time for a trip."

"It's perfect. We're perfect. We don't need to do all the normal dating stuff. We know each other, we know where this is going to lead. There's no reason not to do this right now."

And there he was jumping in with both feet again.

Words like *perfect* and *right now* were exactly what she was worried about. And his assumption that they knew each other well enough to fast-forward on the dating stuff.

There were things about her he needed to know—other than the obvious I-almost-killed-a-man thing—that she wanted to show him slowly. A little at a time. So as not to spook him.

She *definitely* wanted the normal dating stuff. Well, and the hot sex.

But of course he saw no reason for them to take things slow. Of course, he thought she was the perfect woman for him. She had, after all, been working at it for years.

Luke was a pretty easy guy to understand. The things that were important to him were obvious. He loved this town and planned to live here, work here, play here until he was buried here. She liked Justice too. So, she hadn't just moved home to live, hadn't just pushed to open the clinic in Justice, she'd also volunteered and sat on committees and socialized. She was almost as much a part of this community as Luke was, and she knew that was a major draw for him.

Yes, they were friends, enjoyed each other, admired each other and were, obviously, attracted to each other. But she also had to want and to fit into the life Luke wanted.

She'd done a great job being that woman. But she'd had to bite her tongue at times, put on her poker face, not go with her gut every time. Hell, he hadn't even seen her without makeup in thirteen years.

He didn't know that the new minister drove her absolutely crazy and she had decided she was not serving on another church committee. He didn't know that she could be a real bitch when she wanted to be. And a bully. And moody. And that she could hold a grudge. And that she hated celebrating New Year's Eve at The Camelot. She would have much preferred to ring in the New Year quietly with the people she loved instead of the whole frickin' town.

But she never showed him those sides of her. She didn't want him to think she was anything but perfect.

Now the whole perfect thing could really bite her in the ass.

"I just—" Her question was interrupted by her phone. She hadn't let it out of her hand since leaving the clinic. Her heart tripped and she looked at the display. It was the hospital. Finally. "Sorry, I have to take this."

She slid out of his hold and stepped into the hallway outside of his office. "Dr. Dayton," she finally answered.

"Kat, it's Britney." Britney was a nurse in the ICU in Alliance.

"Hey, Brit. Are you calling about Tom?" She glanced behind her. Luke was still inside his office and couldn't hear her conversation.

"Yes, sort of. Dr., um, Brickham asked me to get ahold of you."

"Oh." That didn't sound good. "Should I call him?"

"He's actually, um, right here." Britney sounded nervous and that did nothing for Kat's own nerves. "He wants to talk to you."

"Great," Kat said with fake cheerfulness.

"This is a damned mess, Kat," Henry Brickham said a moment later without preamble.

Frick. She went straight for the info she really wanted. "I understand Tom underwent a CT scan—"

"Massive ischemic stroke," he said, confirming Kat's fears. "And worse. There was a previous minor stroke confirmed on CT. The chart says that he came to you with arm weakness."

Kat's heart started to pound and she struggled to at least sound calm. "That's right. Arm weakness and headache after working in the yard."

"The yard work started the symptoms?"

"He wasn't sure but that was all he could contribute—"

"No specific incident? No pain?"

"No. He couldn't recall anything, but he's an active guy. He could have—"

"Had a stroke," Brickham said.

Kat closed her eyes and rubbed the middle of her forehead. Yeah, it could have been a stroke. Or not. Fuck. This was bad.

"He could have hurt his arm doing yard work."

"But he didn't. He had a small stroke, then a larger one. Had you recognized what was happening, we could have prevented the stroke that now has him hospitalized."

Which was exactly what she had been afraid of. Her heart pounded hard enough that the pressure felt like it was filling her head too.

"His only risk factor is high blood pressure which has been controlled with medication for over a year."

"Tell that to his brain," Brickham said bluntly.

"I'm going to come over right now. I'll—"

"No." Dr. Brickham's tone was firm. "The family has asked that I stay on as the attending and I agreed. Right now we're trying to get him stabilized and they need someone they know and are completely comfortable with."

She'd only been Tom's doctor for two months. She'd only seen him twice. What Brickham said made sense. But it still hurt.

"There may be other injuries from the fall when he lost

consciousness. We need more tests. We also need to be sure that everyone there—all his friends and family—know that everything is being handled here and that there's no need for concern over the care that Tom is receiving."

She understood where Brickham was coming from. The hospital in Alliance was small and like all small hospitals they had to contend with the idea that bigger was better when it came to health care. Serious conditions went to Denver, but it was important for the communities that AMP served to trust that the Alliance hospital could care for ninety-plus percent of what came to them and would promptly send on what they couldn't handle.

"I'll be sure to—"

"So Dr. Davidson will be covering patients in Justice for the next two weeks while you—and we—regroup."

That sucked the air out of her lungs and a cold lump settled in her stomach. "Dr. Davidson is going to see patients here with me?" she asked, frowning at the pattern in the carpet. She didn't need a babysitter.

"Dr. Davidson will be covering your time off."

"My time off?" she repeated feeling the cold start to seep from her gut throughout her body.

"Tom is well-known and liked in town. There will be a lot of questions, speculation even. Having an objective physician in there to address those questions and concerns will be better. I'm afraid you're too green, and too close to the community and the situation, to be impartial and handle this appropriately. We have to avoid incriminating...anyone."

Kat was speechless. Impartial? Of course she couldn't be impartial. He was convinced there would be speculation. He had no confidence in her ability to handle the situation. *She* would be the one incriminated. What a horrible word.

"What do I tell everyone about my sudden time off?" she asked hoarsely.

"We'll tell them it was a planned vacation. Everything will be fully covered so it shouldn't affect anyone negatively."

No one besides her anyway, she thought bitterly.

"But if I run into someone who asks—"

"I think you should consider getting out of town for the first few days."

"Won't it look *more* suspicious that Tom has a problem and then I just suddenly take off?" she asked, her annoyance slipping into her tone.

"Again," Brickham said impatiently. "We'll tell them it was planned time off. It won't look bad if you were already planning the time off before this happened. Tom is out of your hands at this point anyway. And no one's said anything about a lawsuit or anything at this point."

A *lawsuit*? Kat worked on not hyperventilating.

Her boss was basically ordering her out of town because she'd fucked up. This was bad. And it might get worse.

She took a deep breath. "Fine."

"Good," Brickham said.

"Will you keep me informed on Tom's status though?" she asked, but Brickham had already handed the phone back to Britney.

"I'll text or call you," Britney promised.

"Thanks." Kat disconnected, a jumble of emotions knotted in her chest.

"Kat?"

Luke.

Something like panic shot through her. She didn't want him to know. It wasn't completely rational but she knew it without a doubt—she did not want Luke to know that she'd screwed up. And that she was essentially being disciplined for it. And again, it might get worse.

It had been a mistake. An honest one. But she didn't want Luke to know even that.

She turned with a bright, fake smile. "Sorry about that."

Luke came toward her. "Everything okay?"

She breathed deep, trying to force air past the ball of regret that threatened to choke her. "Sure."

"Really?" He stopped and looked down at her, clearly not believing her.

"Yeah." And suddenly the only possible solution struck. The news about Tom was going to start spreading any minute now. "So, what were you saying about going out of town?"

"Nashville."

Kat blinked at him. "Nashville?"

"Let's drive Marc and Sabrina's RV to Nashville."

She looked like she was waiting for the punch line. When he just grinned she said, "Why would we do that?"

"Uninterrupted time alone."

She tipped her head to the side. "Naked uninterrupted time alone?"

He felt his grin grow. "There will definitely be naked time."

"Then why can't we start now?"

Heat seemed to zing between them and Luke thought maybe they should get some practice naked time in before they left. He reached for her, a hand on each hip, and drew her closer. "I love that you want this as much as I do."

"I do. Definitely. Just not sure I'm RV material."

She might be right. It was very likely she had no appropriate camping clothes. Kat looked like she always looked—sexy, confident, touchable—if you were willing to lose a finger or two. Her mother was Italian and Kat had inherited her silky, dark hair—that she routinely colored all or part of—dark eyes, olive skin, make-a-man-pant curves and make-a-man-beg lips. In addition, she wore clothes that made people take notice and had an attitude that made a guy have to *really* want to be with her to even think about it.

Luke *really* wanted it.

He wanted to know what it was like to run his fingers through her hair when it was wet from the shower. He wanted to know how she kissed when she was just waking up in the morning. He wanted to hear her sighs, her moans, her giggles, and her whispers—in bed and out.

"Sabrina and the band made it into an amateur music festival. They're flying down and want the RV to stay in while they're there. They asked if we'd drive it down. I thought it would be a perfect way for us to take this relationship to the next level."

"By essentially living together for a week?" she asked.

It was four days down and back, then at least a couple of days in Nashville. Luke grinned. "With our full focus on us." They both had jobs that regularly interfered with...everything. Kat was on call for her patients in Justice twenty-four seven. Luke's job wasn't life and death, but The Camelot—the building, the staff, the clientele—needed a lot of attention. Getting away from all of that seemed the best way to really get Kat where he wanted her.

They didn't need to date. They didn't need to eat a bunch of dinners or go to the movies or meet each other's friends and family to know they were compatible.

There was no woman he'd be more compatible with than Kat.

He was already living the life Kat wanted, in the place where she wanted to be. He was already the guy she wanted. There would be no beating his head against the wall, trying over and over to guess what she wanted and needed, bending over backwards constantly...

He stopped those thoughts as he felt the tension building in his shoulders. That was the past. This was now. This was Kat and it was—perfect.

She was chewing her bottom lip. "That's a really small space for an extended period of time."

"And pj's are optional," he added.

That got a little smile. Then she sighed. "On a trip like that we're going to get to know each other really well."

"We already know each other really well."

"But I mean *really* well." She didn't look especially thrilled by that.

"Don't worry if you snore or something," he teased. "As long as you sleep naked, I'll forgive anything."

That did not get a smile. "Yeah, snoring," she said with an eye roll. "Look, I've got the time and energy for sex. Not sure about the whole relationship thing. How about we go to Omaha for the weekend or something? I promise lots of naked uninterrupted time there."

The constant talk about naked time was making it hard to ignore that she'd asked him to lay her back on his desk. Which was about six steps away.

He frowned. "Well, that's the deal, dammit. Nashville. RV. Spending time together. A relationship. Not just a weekend of sex."

Her eyebrows went up. "You sound really sure about that."

"I am."

"Okay," she said with a little shrug. "I guess there's nothing I can do to change your mind." She patted his cheek then turned and headed into the restaurant.

Shaking his head, he went ahead and appreciated the view from behind as she walked away from him.

Great. He'd been waiting to see her, to get her enthusiastic reaction to the trip together and she showed up wanting nothing more than a quickie on his desk.

He wasn't sure he could last another day without knowing that they were moving forward. It sounded ridiculous, but it had already been iffy. Something was clearly happening between them, but she said she could only do sex. Well, sex wasn't what he was missing in his life. He wanted more. A lot more. More as in babies and anniversaries and in-sickness-and-in-health.

And she was the one he wanted it with.

He wasn't the most patient guy when it came to getting what he wanted. Something had to give. Soon.

He got busy making the rounds, greeting friends and guests, chatting about the upcoming town festival and making sure everyone was happy and taken care of. But his attention was never far from Kat. It was almost like he couldn't help looking over periodically to see where she was, who she was with and what she was doing.

He watched her move, watched her laugh, watched her cross her legs on the barstool, then watched her slide into a booth across from Sabrina, her skirt pulling up on her thigh as she moved across the seat. Then she waved at someone across the restaurant and that made his heart beat as fast as the tight skirt.

Everyone in the restaurant welcomed conversation with her. She had grown up here and, in spite of her different way of dressing and doing her hair and makeup, everyone loved her. She was their doctor and a hometown girl. The fact that she fit here, that she was comfortable, accepted, was just one of the many reasons that Luke knew she was the one for him. Whoever he shared his life with would share all of this too—his work, his place in the community, The Camelot.

The Camelot was so much more than work or a paycheck to him. He'd known in high school that he wanted to have a business in Justice, but he'd wanted it to be big, important, something everyone wanted and needed. He and Marc did more than feed people, they gave them a place where they felt comforted, cared for—a place where they all belonged.

His phone vibrated in his pocket and he pulled it out, still watching Kat as she texted someone. He glanced down at his phone, prepared to ignore what it was.

Oh. Duh.

By the way, my panties aren't wet.

Like hell they weren't. He frowned and hit reply, but before he could type a letter another message came in.

I'm not wearing any panties.

He swallowed hard and typed, *Like waving a red cape in front of a bull.*

He saw her smile and then her fingers move.

Ole.

Luke stared at the word. Suddenly a weekend of just sex didn't sound so bad after all.

He was really going to have to focus. He wanted her on this trip with him, not just in his bed. And when they got back from Nashville there would be no doubt in anyone's mind—even hers—that they were a couple. In every way. For good.

Chapter Three

"Nashville? Really?" Kat asked Sabrina.

Her friend smiled. "Sounds fun, right?"

"No offense, but I can come up with about fifty scenarios that sound more fun than an amateur country music festival. And they all involve whipped cream."

Yeah, as if the country music was really her biggest objection.

"There's a fridge in the RV that will easily hold a dozen cans of whipped cream," Sabrina said, with a grin. "You need to concentrate on the fact that you'll have Luke all to yourself for all that time. No distractions."

Yeah. No distractions from things like work...or the fact that it took her a solid hour to look good in the morning.

"It's just not good timing," Kat hedged, running her finger around the edge of her wineglass. "Work is crazy."

Yes, things with work were bad. But even without that, this trip wouldn't be her fantasy. An airplane, a hotel suite, a beach...those were things she would go for. An RV and a weeklong trip to Nashville? Not so much. Like she'd said to Luke, the RV was small. Really small. And it would involve being together for more consecutive hours than she'd ever spent with a man. No way to spread out, find some quiet time...hide.

He had no idea how much time and space she took up in the bathroom. Or that she couldn't sleep at night unless she read for at least a half hour and slept on the right side of the bed. And it would be six days minimum, just the two of them. Could she go six days without Hostess cupcakes or wearing sweatpants or checking Twitter? She wasn't sure she was ready for morning breath and sharing a bathroom with Luke. And what would they do the whole time? Talk? There were a lot of deep dark secrets that could be spilled in that much alone time. Like the fact that she might have missed a life-threatening condition in a patient.

"You never take time off," Sabrina said. "There's no way they can be upset that you're taking a few days."

"It's not really that." She took a deep breath and looked up at the only woman she'd ever been close to, besides her sister. "If you won the lottery, but you cheated, would you keep the money?"

Sabrina looked like she wanted to ask what Kat was really talking about, but instead she said, "Well, I'd have to *really* want it, need it, be *desperate* for it even, to cheat in the first place."

Kat swallowed a mouthful of wine. Yeah, so would she. "Okay, so you wanted it so bad that you cheated. And you won. Do you keep your winnings?"

"Maybe," Sabrina said.

"Yeah?" This could be good. She needed an excuse—no, make that an *example*. "When would you keep it?"

Sabrina took a bite of cheesecake, watching Kat as she chewed. Then she said, "I guess it would depend if I was still desperate to have it. Because I might have started cheating a long time before I actually got what I wanted."

Kat's chest tightened. Desperate was such a...desperate word. But accurate in so many ways.

"And," Sabrina went on, scooping up another bite of cheesecake, "if I thought I would always be desperate for it."

Kat thought about that. Did she want Luke as much now as she had when she'd first started analyzing what he wanted in a woman? Would she always want him? Then she sighed. Yes and yes. If anything, Luke had gotten better with age.

Did that mean she could keep him even if she wasn't sure *she* was exactly what *he* wanted?

"Bree, I—"

"Just go on the trip with Luke. Quit thinking about it so hard."

Kat stared at her friend. Sabrina's grin told her that the other woman had been paying more attention than she'd realized.

"I want to *date* him," she said. "Not live with him."

"Why not? Makes constant sex easier if you're together constantly." Sabrina took another bite.

"Sex is great." At least she was sure it would be great. Or even better than great. "But I just think it might be a mistake to jump from mild flirtation to showing each other our holey underwear."

"So be sure to shop for new panties before you go," Sabrina said.

"It was a metaphor."

Sabrina stuck her tongue out at her. "No kidding."

"We should take this slower. Don't you think?"

"What are you afraid of?" Sabrina asked, finally putting her fork down and leaning onto the tabletop. "Luke thinks you're amazing. Even with holey panties."

Kat sighed. "I'm not amazing twenty-four seven."

"No one is," Sabrina said.

"Does Luke know that?"

Sabrina took a moment to think about that. "Okay, it might be a surprise to Luke."

"Exactly!" Kat slumped back in the booth. "He's got this whole thing with me built up in his mind. Just like he did with you. And when he realized he was wrong about you he was *crushed*."

Sabrina frowned at her. She hated reminders of how things had been between her and Luke at that point in their history. "Luke's grown up, Kat. I'm sure he doesn't expect that you're perfect."

Kat raised an eyebrow, just watching her friend.

Finally, Sabrina sighed. "Okay, maybe he does."

"It's too soon for him to find out differently."

"So he finds out that you suck at world history, you can eat your own body weight in Doritos and you only scrub your bathtub once a month."

"I'm the only one who uses my bathtub," Kat grumbled. "Once a month is fine."

Sabrina laughed. "I'm sure he'll see your side of it. Or you could, you know, start scrubbing it more often."

Kat rolled her eyes.

"The point is," Sabrina said, "none of this is insurmountable."

No. It didn't seem to be. Because Sabrina didn't even know what all Kat had been faking.

Sabrina thought Kat had raised all the money they'd needed for the new soccer uniforms, when actually she had dipped into her own savings to make the goal because she was sick of fund-raising. Sabrina didn't know that Kat had agreed to sit on the carnival committee only to avoid getting involved with upgrading the church's kitchen. Sabrina didn't even know that Kat hated thongs. Liking thongs was part of her sexy bad-girl image.

And Sabrina didn't know about her screwup with Tom, either. Yet.

Kat's phone beeped with a voice-mail message. Speaking of her bigger problem... "Sorry, I should probably take this."

"Sure." Sabrina pushed her plate away and then slid to the edge of the booth. "I have to get back onstage soon anyway."

"Thanks for listening," Kat said.

"Well, God knows I owe you some listening. I was a mess with everything with Marc and the baby." She got to her feet a little more awkwardly than she used to.

"When you first came home maybe," Kat said. "But you've got your stuff together now."

"Well, not all by myself," Sabrina said, putting a hand on her stomach. "It's pretty damned tough to have it all together without help."

Yeah, she might have something there. Kat thought about that as Sabrina headed over to kiss her husband before taking her place back onstage. At least Kat could talk to Nancy about what was going on with work. But not about how it affected her situation with Luke. She could talk to Sabrina and Marc about Luke. But not about what was going on with Tom. For one, she couldn't discuss her patients with anyone besides other caregivers. For another, she didn't really want Sabrina and Marc to know she'd screwed up.

Or anyone else for that matter.

She'd kind of gotten used to being respected and trusted.

The missed call on her phone was from the hospital so she dialed her voice mail with trepidation. She listened to the message from Britney with growing frustration and alarm. The results of further testing showed Tom had suffered a hip fracture and a skull fracture when he'd lost consciousness and fallen to his kitchen floor.

The skull fracture was of concern not so much because of the fracture itself—little was done with a crack in the skull—but because there could be a brain injury under the crack. Though CT scan could show an injury, it would be difficult to assess the effects—just like with the stroke—while Tom was still unconscious. They would stop any bleeding, deal with any swelling and so on, but they wouldn't know if Tom's motor skills or memory or problem-solving skills were affected. Or to what extent.

Feeling frustrated, guilty and helpless, Kat had decided that the only thing powerful enough to take her mind off things was Luke. Specifically, Luke naked and doing delicious, dirty things to her. She wasn't convinced the trip was a good idea, but she was quite certain sex with Luke was.

It was also the best way to avoid conversations with any of the other restaurant patrons. Conversations that might lead to questions about Tom. She could, of course, fall back on HIPAA to avoid truly discussing anything, but bursting into tears might be a giveaway that things were not all fine and dandy.

And she had to pull out all the stops in seducing Luke this time. Once he found out that she was far from the perfect woman he thought she was, she might not have another chance.

Luke was in his office when she finally found him. She was restless, wound up, tense. Worry about Tom was eating at her, worry about her boss distrusting her was wearing her down and the fact that she could do nothing about either thing at the moment, that she just had to wait, was making her nuts. Then there was Luke and all this sudden emotion. She felt like her mind was bouncing from one impossible situation to the other and it was making her dizzy.

The difference was she could do *something* about the Luke situation.

He was part of her tension so he could, by God, help her get rid of some of it.

"I was wondering if you know where the handcuffs are."

He looked up to where she was standing with her shoulder propped against his open office door. Only one corner of his mouth curled up but even across the room she could see the heat in his eyes. "Is it someone else's birthday?"

"Don't know...or care. Those cuffs are only for you and me." She pushed away from the door and moved into the office.

"I knew it was going to happen one way or the other." He pushed his chair back and stood, coming around the desk to meet her in the middle of the room.

Damn right it was going to happen. She was glad he was giving in so easily.

"It was inevitable," she agreed. Her voice was a little husky already, but hey, she'd had feelings for this guy for *years*. She wanted him, he wanted her and the idea of being with him was the best thing she'd thought about in a really long time.

"Inevitable. I like that word." He reached for her arm and drew her up against him. "And the sooner we get started the better."

"Yeah, I'm thinking right now." She grinned at him. "Like *right now.*" They didn't need to drive to one of their houses. His desk was sturdy. And here.

She started to nudge him backwards toward that sturdy desk, but his hands went to her shoulders and stopped her.

"You want to leave right now? Tonight?"

"Yes, I want... No, we don't have to—" She looked up at him in confusion. Something didn't sound quite right. "Leave? You mean go to your house? And of course I mean tonight."

"To go to Nashville."

She blinked up at him. Then started shaking her head. "No. No Nashville. No *RV.*" No small spaces where she couldn't get away from him, where she might be tempted to tell him...everything.

"I want you all to myself," he said huskily, drawing his thumb along her bottom lip and making ribbons of heat swirl through her. Then he grinned. "And I want to be all you have to think about, see and...do for a few days."

She took a step back from him. A big step. "Whoa. This all sounds... You want to..." Too many thoughts were tumbling through her mind. "I get it. You're trying to cram months of dating into a few days on a road trip. What are we going to do first when we get back—order the wedding cake or pick out the china pattern we want?" She turned and stomped toward the door. Of course this couldn't just be sex. Of course he couldn't just focus on the no-panties thing. This was Luke. He always had a plan and he knew nothing about not getting his way.

He sighed. "Don't be ridiculous. Marc will make the cake, so obviously we'll pick china out first."

She swung back to face him, prepared to tell him what he could do with the cake, but the heat in his eyes stopped her words. He reached up and unknotted his tie as he started forward. "Turn around."

Something in his tone, or in his eyes, or both made her heart kick against her chest. The air heated as he approached and she felt her breathing quicken.

He slid his tie free from his collar and unbuttoned the top button of his shirt.

Okay, clothing being removed was good.

"Turn around?" she repeated even as she turned. Hey, this was Luke Hamilton and he was taking stuff off. She was very okay with that.

"Now just hold still."

No problem. As long as he shut up about Nashville—and well, maybe everything. He needed to use his mouth in other ways.

"Close your eyes," he said, his lips against her ear.

She did, shivering a little though she was feeling anything but cold.

Then she felt the brush of silk against her cheek and felt him slide what she assumed to be his tie over her eyes. She was sure of it as she felt the gentle tug of him tying the ends behind her head.

"Uh, Luke?"

"Yeah?"

"Did you just blindfold me?"

"Yeah."

"You're actually *blindfolding* me?"

"Yep."

Her heart sped up. Okay, now they were moving in the direction she wanted.

"It's very likely I'll peek," she told him.

"I'm sure you're right."

Then he leaned in.

Kat felt her breath catch and she felt herself drift closer to him, seeking his heat.

"This will fix that."

But she didn't ask what he was talking about because his lips met the back of her neck. Tingles spread quickly. She found herself wanting more, tipping her head forward to be sure he knew she was *fine* with this. His response was to slide his hands down her arms bringing her hands behind her back. Then his tongue licked a spot behind her ear and she lost track of anything else.

A moment later, she felt the cold metal of the handcuffs click around her wrists.

She couldn't have really explained to anyone how it happened. It was fast and smooth.

She tugged on her wrists. "What are you doing?"

"Handcuffing you."

"What is going on?" she demanded, trying to sound annoyed.

She didn't think she pulled it off. She sounded breathless and turned on. Which made sense since that was exactly what she was.

Suddenly she felt him move in front of her and the next thing she knew her world tipped—literally—and she was being carried over his shoulder like a sack of potatoes.

"Whatever I want," he said putting a big palm on her right butt cheek.

Yeah, she couldn't argue with that assessment of the situation.

Oh, sure, she could scream, kick, run, try to get away. But then she might actually *get away* which, she was honest enough to admit, was the last thing she really wanted.

Twenty minutes later she'd changed her mind.

She was handcuffed to a chair in the kitchen area of Sabrina and Marc's RV.

Luke sat in the driver's seat. Driving. Away from Justice.

She'd tried everything to get him to free her. She'd even offered him a blow job.

He'd turned the radio up at that point and hadn't turned it down since.

She saw the sign for Martinsburg—he'd removed the blindfold as soon as she was secured to the chair—so she knew they were headed east.

Finally she sighed. Whatever he had planned, he was winning so far. The farther they got from Justice the lower her chances were of hitchhiking back or calling for a ride.

"Are you going to tell me where we're going at least?" she yelled over Green Day's latest hit.

He leaned forward and lowered the volume. "Nashville." Apparently he could hear better than he'd let on.

Then she focused on what he'd said. Nashville? Well, of course they were going to Nashville.

Son of a bitch. She tugged on the bindings at her wrists. He was *kidnapping* her to Nashville.

"You don't think that Marc will notice when the RV is gone?"

"Marc helped me pack all the supplies."

Dammit. Then a thought occurred to her. "What about clothes? I don't have anything packed."

He glanced in the rearview mirror with a grin. "I hope you're not thinking that will convince me this is a bad idea."

She rolled her eyes. Okay, being naked with Luke for several days straight was not much of a deterrent for her either.

"But Sabrina packed your bag," he added.

"She did? She knew about this? That you were *kidnapping* me?"

"Well—" He shrugged. "Yeah. And I told Diane you were taking a few days off, so it's all covered."

"Diane?" Kat repeated. "As in the office manager for AMP?"

"Yep. She said it was all fine, that Dr. Davidson could cover you." Sure he could. Since he was going to be anyway. She supposed she should be grateful that Diane hadn't spilled that little detail.

Until this moment Kat hadn't even thought of work since stepping into Luke's office. Which just went to show how crazy all of this was. She *always* thought about work, even when none of her patients were in the ICU with a massive stroke. She was a small-town doctor. It was pretty much a twenty-four seven gig. She'd run into patients at the grocery store and post office and they'd "just take a minute" to ask her a medical question. She had been having dinner at The Camelot one night and a patient had asked her to talk to the pharmacist—who was sitting three tables away—about refilling the woman's prescription.

"She was having dinner and I asked for help getting you a few days off for a surprise trip out of town."

The time off was supposed to seem as if it had been planned before Tom's stroke. She wondered how many people had been sitting with Diane and how many in the close proximity had heard the conversation. She breathed in and out trying not to yell. "I certainly hope everyone knows that I'm not there to treat their medical issues because I'm off having sex with you—handcuffed and blindfolded."

Luke chuckled.

Chuckled.

"I didn't say it quite that way."

Kat tugged on her wrists but they held tight. "I am not driving Sabrina and Marc's RV to Nashville with you."

"They need the RV and you know that Sabrina can't ride eighteen hours," he said.

"I don't do RVs."

He chuckled at that. "This is a hotel on wheels."

It was true that Marc had spared no expense. He'd purchased the RV as proof to Sabrina that he would go wherever she went, whenever she went, because he was in love with her.

It had cost more than their wedding.

And of course Luke was willing to drive the damned thing eighteen hours one way so that Sabrina would be comfortable but still be able to perform.

Luke had no ridiculous-meter when it came to Sabrina.

"She should be close to home at this point," Kat said with a scowl.

"Not if her doctor's there with her."

And of course he wouldn't hesitate to drag her down there too if it was good for Sabrina. "Why can't they just stay in a hotel down there? Why do they need the RV?"

"She sleeps better in the RV than in hotels. She's used to this bed and she likes having all her stuff with her. Plus, the festival is four days long but they only perform a couple times a day. She needs a place where she can go lie down and relax during their off time. Not to mention that she'll eat better if she can cook in the RV. Right?"

"You can take it down there yourself, can't you?" she snapped.

"Marc really wants you to come so you can check on her, make sure things are okay."

Marc.

He was perhaps the only sane person among them. He was Sabrina's soul mate, knew she wasn't perfect and loved her anyway. He was also a great friend to Kat.

And he thought she should give Luke a chance.

"Total crap," Kat muttered. Marc and Sabrina hadn't said a word about Kat's being there to check on things. In fact, they hadn't mentioned the trip at all. Probably because they knew she would have advised against it.

Still, Sabrina and the baby were healthy and these music festivals made Sabrina incredibly happy—those things were all that mattered to Marc. They would have gone whether Kat gave her blessing or not.

She shook her head. This was out of hand.

"Are you going to keep me handcuffed the entire time?" An hour ago she would have thought that sounded kind of hot. Now she was pretty sure she'd gotten herself into more than she'd bargained for.

"I'm thinking I should keep you back there until we're more than an hour from Justice. That's probably far enough that you won't consider hitchhiking or calling for a ride."

Exactly what she'd been thinking.

Calling for a ride didn't seem to be an option. Apparently Sabrina and Marc were off the list of people she could count on. She'd never tell her parents about this. Obviously Diane thought it was all fine.

Who else could she call? That was easy—no one.

Not that she didn't know people who'd come get her if she was in trouble. But no one would believe she was in trouble with Luke.

She supposed she could call her sister. But Isabelle was in Omaha. Which was another four and a half hours east. Not really on Isabelle's way to come get Kat and take her back to Justice. But even though it was ridiculous and Kat would never ask her to do it, Isa would come if Kat called. She was the one person in the world that would do absolutely anything for Kat.

Well, other than Luke himself.

A hot flash shot through her at that realization. It was a bit out of the blue, but it was nonetheless completely true. Luke would do anything for her. He would drive four and a half, or more, hours to pick her up if she needed him.

And she really liked knowing that.

"My hands are going to sleep," she lied. She was feeling very vulnerable and out of control here—two things she detested.

"Good thing it's only another twenty miles or so to the point of no return," he said.

The point of no return.

That was exactly where she was afraid she was headed. RV or not.

Luke was surprised by how quiet Kat was. It should

probably make him nervous, but the whole thing had been going so smoothly that he couldn't help but feel smug. She'd tried negotiating—the blow job offer had taken some willpower on his part to decline—but they both knew that she could have really fought him if she didn't want to go. She hadn't even struggled against the handcuffs that much.

He liked that.

It showed a level of trust. And had fueled a few new fantasies for him.

"Do you know anyone in Marshall?" he asked her, looking into the rearview mirror. She looked so sexy bound to the chair that he had to pull his eyes back to the road to avoid the ditch.

"No, why?"

"Good. That's where we'll stop then."

She rolled her eyes. He wondered if she really would call anyone to come get her if she had the chance. Maybe. Kat wasn't the type of woman to take too kindly to not being in control.

It was better to just not give her the chance to change his plans. This trip was a brilliant idea. If he did say so himself.

Five minutes later he pulled into the parking lot of a café off the highway. It was a typical small-town diner with good food and outdated décor. In spite of the fact that he took great pride in making his own restaurant shine with the most modern interior and exterior design, immaculate cleaning staff and updated everything, Luke appreciated places like this. Their focus was food and community. That was at the heart of his restaurant as well.

He climbed into the back of the RV. "Here's how this is going to go," he said, hands on his hips. "I'm going to unlock you, then we're going to go in, get a table and have coffee together. There will be no cell phone allowed, no pay phone usage, no flirting with any truckers headed west. We're leaving here together, in this RV. Or I'll keep you out here and bring you a to-go cup when I'm finished."

She raised an eyebrow. "You know that I'm not going to

Nashville with you."

"I don't know that at all."

"This is very overbearing of you," she said.

It was overbearing and not like him. Luke didn't generally operate this way. He would never think of kidnapping someone else and forcing them into taking a road trip with him. He would never dream of interfering with someone's work schedule like this.

But this was Kat. Dealing with such a unique woman required a unique approach and mindset.

"Good thing that overbearing men turn you on," he told her.

Overbearing men drove Kat crazy.

"Sure. I was just thinking about how hot I am for you right now," she said sarcastically.

But her gaze dropped to his mouth and Luke felt awareness and heat charge through him. Her cheeks flushed pink and she licked her lips. He held back a groan. She certainly seemed hot for him right now. She was breathing hard now, just like when he'd initially blindfolded her.

Maybe Kat Dayton didn't mind having a man who was willing to take charge once in a while.

"Are you going to be good in the diner?" he asked, his voice husky.

She sighed. "Yeah." She seemed disappointed to have to admit that.

Luke smiled and unlocked the handcuffs. "The trip could be fun, you know."

She looked away and got to her feet. "We'll see, I guess."

Kat ducked into the RV's small bathroom with the bag Sabrina had packed her and changed into something a bit more modest.

It didn't do a thing to keep Luke from reacting though. She wore a flared skirt that hit just above her knees, a fitted cotton T-shirt and calf-high leather boots. All in black.

And she still turned heads when they entered the diner.

They were seated in a booth by the front windows and had both ordered coffee and pie when Kat leaned back in her seat and crossed her arms.

"Okay, what exactly do you think is going to happen on this trip?"

He put his elbows on the table and leaned in. "We're going to make memories to tell our grandkids about."

He watched her pull in a quick breath. "True or false," she said. "You think we're going to have a lot of hot, the-neighbors-can't-hear-us-so-let's-get-loud road-trip sex?"

"You seem really focused on having sex with me lately," he said with a grin. Not that he was objecting.

She nodded. "I am."

He also didn't object a bit to her blunt honesty. "Yes, we're going to have a lot of sex."

She took a deep breath. "And true or false, you think I'm going to tell you all my deep, dark secrets?"

"And your shallow, light ones," he tossed back. He wanted to know everything about her. He wasn't crazy enough to think that knowing her all these years meant he knew every tiny detail about what made her tick. He knew enough, but yeah, he wanted to know it all.

"And true or false," she continued. "You think this trip is going to end with us madly in love with one another?"

"False."

She raised an eyebrow. "False?"

"We're already there. You're not admitting it, but that doesn't make it untrue."

Kat sighed. "You're nuts."

But she didn't deny being in love with him.

Luke would take what he could get. For now.

She pushed her hand through her pink-streaked hair that she'd crimped into tight waves around her face today. It drove him a little crazy that he never knew what to expect. Sometimes her hair was dark, sometimes light, sometimes crazy colors. She wore it in spikes, curly, straight, wavy Sometimes she even put extensions in, making it longer.

He liked things predictable, truly hated change. But underneath, Kat was always the same—dependable, loyal, sexy and smart. So he could live with a little hair dye.

This close he could see the deep brown of her eyes behind the thick eyeliner and dark shadow. She'd transformed her appearance over the summer between eighth and ninth grade and he hadn't seen her without makeup and hair dye since. He *wanted* to see her without makeup and hair dye. He wasn't sure why. She turned him on just walking into a room no matter what she wore, but he wanted to see her underneath the stuff. Or maybe it was that he wanted her to *let* him see underneath.

Kat cleared her throat. "And are you going to tell me all your deep, dark secrets too?"

"I'll tell you whatever you want to know."

She got a contemplative look in her eye, then slowly leaned in too. "Well since you're the one who wants to speed everything along, I'm going to jump to a question that I would usually wait several dates to ask."

"Bring it on."

"Is it possible that there will be a time when we're sitting on the couch kissing and suddenly Sabrina calls needing a ride home from somewhere and you jump up to go get her?"

The kiss. That night in college. They'd never talked about it, and they'd never repeated it—until now.

He remembered it clearly though. He and Kat had been in his dorm room while Marc was on a date and Sabrina was at a dance. Dorm rooms were small and the only place to really sit comfortably had been on the bed. Together. They'd been watching a movie and he'd looked over to ask her something and suddenly he had to kiss her. He remembered that distinctly. The need had swept through him and he couldn't resist. So he'd kissed her. It had gotten really hot, really fast. Their mouths had been hungry, their hands bold. There had even been some bare skin. They both knew they were on their way to much, much more than a stolen kiss. And they were both completely okay with that. It was going to change everything between them and they'd gone full speed ahead.

Then Sabrina had called. She'd needed a ride home.

He'd been torn. He wanted to be with Kat, but there was no way he could leave a friend stranded.

And now it was coming back to bite him in the ass.

"Your friends are important to you and I'm sure you appreciate the fact that they're important to me. In fact, I would hope you would *expect* me to help a friend out, no matter when they need me or what I'm doing." He tried to gauge her reaction but she was just watching him. "That's just one more reason you're the perfect woman. All of my friends are your friends. You would do that same thing if Marc called and needed your help."

"Well, don't forget to add that to your list of criteria," she said dryly. "Someone who will put up with the short leash Sabrina has on you."

That wasn't fair. Now. "Marc is the only one on any leash," he said. "She's his handful now."

"And yet, here we are driving that thing—" she gestured out the window at the RV, "—to *Nashville* so she can sleep a little more comfortably and eat more fruit."

"You don't care if she's eating well?"

"I'm guessing they have apples in Tennessee." Kat leaned closer, pinning him with that look that made her patients confess all their sins. "Want to know something else? This is going to shock you, but I don't give a bat's behind what Sabrina eats while she's in Nashville. *My* whole world doesn't revolve around her."

Right. Neither did his. Now.

"Okay, you want to know how I feel about Sabrina," he said. "Here it is." He pushed his cup to the side and met her stare. "I fell in love with giving her the stability she needed when she was a kid. She didn't have anyone else and I got to be the most important person for her. I liked that. It made me feel good. As we grew up, I think it was natural to envision us together. She was always there and I figured she always would be."

He took a deep breath. Even though Kat was the perfect person to confess the rest to, his ego wasn't large enough for the truth to not sting a little.

"When she went to Seattle it was a great excuse. We weren't together because she was too far away, wanted other things. But when she came home I had to face something—it wasn't Justice, or marriage and family, or any of that she didn't want. She's got all of that with Marc. I realized that she didn't want *me*."

Kat's gaze wavered. "She—they—"

"But," he continued, not letting her interrupt. "I also realized that once she was settled, happy, taken care of, I felt...done. It was like I'd been waiting to be sure she didn't need me to really move on. With Marc, I know she doesn't need me anymore."

Kat was staring at him, her expression unreadable.

"You okay?" he finally asked.

She took a deep breath. "She was never right for you."

He knew that. He really did. "You are."

Kat swallowed hard. "That certainly seems to be the case," she agreed.

Thank God. He smiled. "Absolutely."

"Because I fit, what, nine of your top ten?" she went on.

"My top ten?" he asked.

"The top ten things you look for in a woman." She took a bite of pie while watching him. She chewed and swallowed. "I bet I can get six of your top ten without even thinking too hard."

"Do you have a top ten?" he asked, distracted by the thought.

"Of course."

"What's on it?"

"Why?" She looked at him closely. "You worried?"

"Maybe. You're not like other women." God, that was the truth.

"That's the second time you've said that to me in two days. But thank you. Again."

He chuckled. "It *is* a compliment." He loved that she was different and celebrated it. But he was very interested in this list of hers. He thought he was perfect for her—but what if she thought the perfect man could quote Shakespeare or juggle or speak French? He'd work on changing her mind, of course, but he'd like to know what he was working with—or against.

"Why are you worried about my list? You're so convinced we're perfect for each other." She was watching him closely in spite of the light tone of voice.

"It takes more than charm to get your attention." Luke had plenty of charm. That wasn't the problem.

She chuckled. "True. If charm was all I needed, Chad Watson and I would be happily hitched right now."

"Chad Watson is a dumb-ass." She'd gone to their senior prom with Chad.

"A charming dumb-ass, but yeah, I knew within two dates that I couldn't stand him."

He smiled. "Okay, charm is important but we've got nine more to go. Spill."

"Some are about sex."

He coughed on a bite of apple pie. After he took a sip of coffee he said honestly, "Some of them better be about sex." If she didn't think sex was important enough to put on her top ten, he had some work to do.

"You have to promise not to think I'm a slut," she said.

"Of course. Great sex is every person's God-given right."

"Alleluia, brother."

He grinned at her. "I love that you love sex and aren't shy about it."

"Yeah, I'll bet you do."

"What do you mean?"

"Women who are uptight about sex can't give good blow jobs. Physically impossible. So, I'm sure you're glad I'm not uptight."

Luke cleared his throat and shifted in his seat. Damn. That was the second time tonight she'd mentioned a blow job. He was going to need to dump his ice water in his lap if this kept up. "We're not talking about *my* top ten."

She raised her eyebrows. "Blow jobs are in your top ten?"

"Um, yeah. Absolutely."

She grinned then grabbed her napkin and wiped her hands, pushing her plate to the side. "Okay, in no particular order they are kind, generous, funny, intelligent, charming, able and willing to perform oral sex, likes to talk during sex, is okay with me having and using my vibrator—even without him once in a while—not hung up on lingerie—I don't like most of it personally—and reads some kind of fiction on a regular basis."

He processed her list slowly, savoring it, memorizing it. This was good information. It made him want to strip her down and show her how willing he was to fulfill number six right here on the table.

"It's official," he said, wadding up his napkin. "I'm the perfect man for you."

The waitress refilled their glasses and Luke downed half his water.

"Okay, now you," Kat said.

"My top ten?"

"I know you have one."

"I don't," he answered. It wasn't actually written down anyway. He knew what the perfect woman looked like. He was looking at her right now. He didn't need a list.

"You're a perpetual planner and list maker," she pointed out.

That was true. He was organized to a fault.

"There are more than ten things that are important to me,"

he said. And she had them all.

She rolled her eyes. "We're talking about the most important ten."

"And you think you can get six?" He pushed his coffee cup to the side and leaned his elbows on the table. "Go for it." This would be interesting. How well did Kat know him?

Chapter Four

This would be a piece of cake. She could get all ten without breaking a sweat. This was a subject she'd been studying for years.

"One, she has to be from Justice."

He made a sound like a game show buzzer.

"Yes it is," she insisted.

"It's close," he agreed. "But number one is she has to love Justice as much as I do and number two is that she has to want to make our life there. Being from Justice just makes those two things more probable. Not that it matters." He winked at her.

She chose to ignore that. "Those really are number one and two on the list, huh? In order?"

"Yep." He lifted his cup and sipped, watching her the whole time. "Think you can get the rest?"

"Maybe not in order."

"Let's hear them."

"Well, we know blow jobs are on there."

"Definitely." He gave her a wicked half smile and a wink.

She took a deep breath, trying to slow her pulse. "Okay, let's see. She has to believe in giving to charity, has to like to socialize, and has to have a career that she can pursue in Justice."

It was important to Luke to contribute directly to the community with his work and she was sure he felt the same way about his would-be wife.

If it weren't for the satellite medical clinic in Justice, she wouldn't fit that criterion herself.

Frick.

She shouldn't be having this conversation with him. Why confirm all the ways she seemed right when it would make it that much worse when—no, *if*—he found out some of it wasn't true.

But she couldn't resist.

The idea of being Luke's perfect woman and having him know it, even if it was temporary, was too tempting.

"She has to fit into your family, get along with your friends, love The Camelot and she has to want kids," she said.

"Hey, only one of mine was about sex. You got four."

"It's your list, not mine."

"Liking lots of foreplay, having a vibrator—that I get to watch her use at least some of the time—and being good at dirty talk should all be on there too."

"Top ten," she reminded him, feeling her body get a little warmer with his words.

"Well then let's move the family and friends down the list. Because honestly, vibrators and dirty talk would outrank those people any day."

He grinned and she really wanted to grin back, but with his words the truth suddenly smacked her in the face and left her eyes stinging a bit.

He would never move family or friends down the list. But it was a moot point.

He'd never *have* to rearrange or change his list at all. Blow jobs and best friends would be equally appreciated by the right woman. Like Kat. Which was obviously the whole point.

She knew she fit every criterion—she'd made sure of it.

Her crush went back years. When you were crushing on a guy you didn't let him see your flaws, your mistakes, your bad hair days, your bad *anything*. You tried to be what he wanted and you made sure he knew it.

But—and here was the realization that had her pie sitting like a rock in her stomach—a real relationship was about thinking someone was perfect even with the flaws, mistakes and bad hair days. It was about being yourself and being loved for it.

Dammit.

She had really screwed this up.

How would he react when he found out she wasn't perfect for him? And how would her heart react?

She'd started the stupid top ten list conversation as a flirtation, just for fun, but now she was restless.

Because he should want her—or *whoever* he was with—whether his family and friends loved her or not. Whether she wanted to live and die in Justice. Whether she worked out of town or hated bake sales or had no desire to watch the high school basketball team play.

Whether she fit all his criteria or not.

Whether she was perfect or not.

"Well, that's quite a list," she finally said, grateful that her voice sounded normal.

"Proof that I know what I'm talking about, right?" he said with a cocky grin. "Not only do you fit all those requirements, but you can list them in twenty seconds or less."

She gave a humorless laugh. "*Requirements* is an interesting word." That made her stomach hurt.

"Well, I have requirements that need to be met when I buy a car or hire a waitress or choose a vacation. I think the person you're going to spend your life with should be as careful a decision, don't you?"

Oh, yeah, this just kept getting better and better. "Did you really just compare a romantic relationship to buying a car?" she asked.

"That's my new approach."

"To make unflattering comparisons between something emotional like love and something practical like hiring an employee?"

He shifted on the seat of the booth and then drank from his

now-empty coffee cup.

She watched him acting very uncomfortable for a moment. Then a thought hit her and she sat up straighter. "Is this about Sabrina?"

He sighed. "Yes," he admitted.

Well, of course.

"What about her? Exactly?" she asked.

"I made mistakes."

"Uh-huh." She personally thought both he and Sabrina had made a number of them.

"I reacted on emotion, got caught up in how I felt, without thinking, without being concerned about compatibility and...requirements."

She blinked at him. He wasn't kidding.

Awesome.

Yeah, he'd definitely been caught up in Sabrina. Kat felt a surge of jealousy at the thought. She wanted him caught up in *her*. But he clearly thought that was a mistake. Which meant he wasn't overcome by his emotions for *her*...and he obviously didn't intend to be.

"So this time you're being more logical and less emotional about it all," she said in a very logical and nonemotional way.

"Right."

She stared at him, her heart heavy in her chest. "Because you wouldn't want a relationship to be *emotional*."

He sighed. "What I want is a relationship that will *work*. It can't be *only* emotional."

Shit. He just had to be...well, honest. This was honestly how Luke felt.

Things with Sabrina had been complicated and messy and, yes, emotional. Illogical, painful even, but emotional enough that he did it anyway.

He'd been there for Sabrina no matter what she did wrong, no matter what she said, even after she broke his heart and left. Not because it made sense, but because of how he *felt* about her.

Kat wanted that.

She didn't want to have to be perfect for him. She wanted him crazy about her anyway.

She deserved that. She deserved someone who would be so stupid in love that he wouldn't be able to think rationally, so preoccupied with thoughts of her he couldn't make a grocery list, not to mention a list of qualifications in a potential mate, someone who would be unable to be *without* her rather than someone who needed a checklist to know he wanted to be with her.

Especially a checklist that might show how *not* right for him she really was.

She wiped her mouth with her napkin, laid a ten dollar bill on the table and slid out of the booth. "I'm going back to the RV."

But only because it really was too far to walk, she didn't have anyone to call and she hadn't seen anyone she was willing to hitchhike with.

Well, dammit.

That was all Luke could really come up with as he paid the bill and headed for the RV.

Something had gone wrong in the diner, and he had come to the startling revelation that he was in new territory.

He simply wasn't used to the woman he was interested in thinking he was an ass.

Which Kat quite clearly did at the moment.

On the heels of that realization, he also understood that he tended to gravitate to women who thought he was amazing.

That sounded stupid, of course. Most, if not all, people tended to date other people who thought they were great. But it was more than that for Luke. He didn't take chances. On anything, really—a fact that drove Marc nuts—but especially on women. He made sure that the woman would definitely say yes before he asked her—anything. Of course it came from his history with Sabrina, but regardless of that, he was used to women agreeing with him on where they were going, what they were doing and how the night was going to end.

He didn't sleep with all of them.

But if he wanted to, they didn't turn him down—because he made sure they wanted it, *him*, before ever even insinuating anything.

Now there was Kat Dayton. Who thought he was an ass and wasn't shy about telling him. But he really wanted her anyway.

He approached the RV with the knowledge that they were about to spend the night together and for the first time—with a woman other than Sabrina—he didn't know what was going to happen.

Well, *dammit*.

She was sitting at the table in the kitchen area, her feet up on the bench across from her, a bottle of tequila in one hand and a shot glass in the other.

"What are you doing?" he asked carefully.

"Drinking tequila." She took a shot.

He propped his shoulder against the doorjamb. "Where'd you get that?"

She pointed with the bottle. "That cupboard. There's also Kahlua. My second favorite."

She hadn't even known they were taking this trip so she hadn't packed those herself. "Is it just a coincidence that your favorite liquors are here?"

"I'm thinking Marc is an even better friend than I realized."

"He stocked your favorite liquors for you?"

"He's the best."

"Why would he think you'd need liquor?"

"Because he knows *you*."

Luke couldn't help his smile. "And he knew you'd need to

drink to be around me?"

Kat shrugged. "He wasn't wrong, was he?"

"So the tequila is making you—happier with me?"

"Not so far." Then she took another shot.

"There's only one bed."

"So?"

If she thought this was the way to keep him from seducing her, well...it might work. He wanted her fully aware and with him every step when they made love.

But it was a *when*, not an *if*. She couldn't rely on tequila for the entire trip.

"We'll have to sleep in there together, you know."

"Hmm."

"Maybe you should put the tequila down."

"You afraid I'm going to throw up on you?"

He was afraid that he was going to explode if he had to sleep next to her all night without touching her. Though the throwing up seemed more likely than the touching at the moment. "Maybe."

"Yeah, well this whole trip was your idea. If you get puked on you have no one to blame but yourself." She took another shot, then swallowed hard and coughed.

"Just so we're on the same page—you're mad at me because...?" He trailed off hoping she'd fill in the blank because he really didn't know.

"I'm mad at myself."

Okay. Now he was really confused. "Why are you mad at yourself?"

"I just won the lottery, but I cheated," she said, watching him intently. "Now I'm trying to decide if I can fully enjoy the winnings knowing that I didn't get them honestly."

He had no idea what she was talking about.

"Kat, I—"

"Could you?" she asked. "Could you enjoy having

everything you ever wanted if you'd gotten it dishonestly?"

"I would..." It was a good question. One he had to think about. He leaned back against the counter. "Maybe for a while. But I think the truth would get to me eventually."

She tipped back another shot. "What if it was the only way to ever have what you wanted? There was no way in hell it would have happened otherwise?"

He felt like there was something really important right in front of him but he couldn't grasp it. "I guess I'd have to think that maybe I just shouldn't have it then."

She took a deep breath, then let it out in a *whoosh*. She nodded, poured another shot and drank. "I guess then you'd want to really live it up and enjoy it before your morals got to you, huh?"

He shrugged. "As long as you don't think you'd feel guilty about the stuff you did or bought or whatever before your conscience kicked in."

She seemed to be thinking about that, turning the tequila bottle in her hand, sloshing the liquid against the sides. "I'm thinking that even if I felt guilty later it might be worth it."

"I'd be sure I made it something big then."

She looked him up and down and he shifted as his body responded to her perusal.

His brain might be struggling to figure out what was going on under the surface here, but his body didn't care.

"I think you've got something there," she said.

He wanted to get deeper into this—whatever the hell it was. "Tell me more about this lottery."

She shook her head. "Can't." Then she took another shot.

"Why?"

"Because there are things about me you don't know." She frowned, as if she hadn't meant to say that.

Now this was getting interesting. He moved to the table and slid into the chair across from her. "There are things about you that I know that you don't know I know."

She frowned harder as she tried to follow that with tequila in her bloodstream. "You do?"

"You always pay for the appetizers and dessert when you have dinner with friends."

Kat narrowed her eyes at him. "So?"

"You get the ones they want even though you don't like them. And I think that's sexy."

"You find chicken wings and mozzarella sticks sexy?" she asked.

"You like mozzarella sticks. You order the chicken wings and chips and hot salsa because everyone else likes them, but you don't like things that spicy."

She was staring at him. "How do you know that?"

"I've been paying attention." He liked surprising her. He gave her a slow smile.

She narrowed her eyes. "What are you doing?"

"Showing you what I do know about you." He had never been oblivious to her. She'd always been this hot, funny, sweet woman he took for granted. He was done with that. Right now. "I know I don't know everything there is to know about what makes you tick, but I want to. Starting on this trip."

She just watched him.

"What's the best vacation you've ever been on?"

She blinked at him. "I think we should just have sex."

Okay, well he wasn't necessarily against that idea, but she was a little tipsy. "Why is that?"

"It's easier than the talking. And I'm sure it will go well. The talking is a real crapshoot at this point."

He smiled and, for the moment anyway, ignored her suggestion. "How do you feel about your mom?"

"My mom's great. Let's have sex."

"What do you do to relax?"

She sighed. "Can we at least play strip-get-to-know-you-better? It's much more efficient since we're both going to end up naked tonight anyway."

"How would that go exactly?" Though any mention of her stripping made everything in him pulse with need.

"Every time one of us answers a question, the other one has to take something off."

He grinned. "That's a hell of an idea."

"I know." She finally gave him a grin too. A goofy, little-bit-drunk grin. "I'm going to do something big before my conscience sobers up."

Something niggled at *his* conscience with that. "Do I need to know what you're talking about before we do this?"

She shook her head. "Absolutely not."

He hesitated. "What's the capital of Croatia?"

She stared at him. "Croatia?"

"It's one of the countries that used to be Yugoslavia."

"Okay. But I have no idea what its capital is."

"Because you're drunk?"

"Because I've never known the capital of Croatia."

She didn't seem drunk, capital of Croatia or not. "Okay, let's do this."

"Take your shirt off."

Luke cocked an eyebrow. "Sorry?"

"I want you to take your shirt off."

"I want you to take your shirt off too."

"But I didn't ask you a question," she said.

Fine. He'd play. He watched her as he unbuttoned his shirt and shrugged out of it.

She frowned when she saw the white T-shirt he wore underneath his dress shirt, and Luke barely bit back a grin.

He also took the shot of tequila she poured. Shuddering as he swallowed. He regarded her carefully, planning his strategy. He wanted to know her, wanted to show her he was serious, but he didn't want to be predictable. A woman like Kat would get bored with predictable.

"Do you ever have nightmares?"

"I did years ago. Not often, but once in awhile. Not now."

"What were they?"

"That's another question. You're going to have to take something off first."

He kicked his shoes off.

She rolled her eyes. "You know that's only prolonging things, right? For the guy who wants to jump way ahead, that's an interesting move."

"Take your shirt off," he said.

Her eyes widened. "What?"

"Take your shirt off."

"I didn't—" Then she clearly remembered using a question mark. She narrowed her eyes. "That might be cheating."

"Too bad there are no referees. Need another drink?" he slid the shot glass toward her.

Eyes narrowed further, she shook her head. "I'm fine."

She grabbed the hem of her shirt and pulled it off, tossing it on top of his on the floor.

Not that he watched it land. His attention was firmly on the woman across from him. The pale pink bra she wore was modest, covering everything it was supposed to cover, but he suddenly felt like there was less oxygen in the room. Her skin still showed light tan lines from her bathing suit that summer and he wanted to trace those marks. With his tongue.

He looked up to find her watching him watch her.

"The answer to your question," he said, "is yes, I know it's only prolonging things. But as quickly as I'd like some of this to go between us, making love to you is something I'm going to want to spend a lot of time on."

Heat flickered between them and she had to take a deep breath. He knew because he was carefully watching her face instead of staring at her breasts. With their very hard nipples pushing against the soft satin.

He raised an eyebrow.

"Now my next question. Where would you like me to kiss you first?"

His words hung, seemingly suspended in the air between them. She stared at him, then slowly smiled. "Glad to know the Q and A is over."

"Who said that?"

"I did. The answer to your question is left nipple."

He should have expected something like that but he still almost swallowed his tongue. He didn't hesitate even long enough to pull in a full breath. She must have seen something in his eyes as he stood and rounded the table because she tried to scoot back in her chair. Of course, she didn't get far.

Reaching down he pulled up on the lever that reclined the chair and pushed her back. She stared up at him. "I— *Holy—,"* she groaned as he went down on one knee, leaned in and took a nipple into his mouth through her bra.

Her other hand came up to cup the back of his head. He sucked, ran his tongue over the firmness and then sucked again.

God, she felt good. He wanted to have every inch of her against his tongue.

"Tell me what you are most proud of," he said roughly against her breast.

She let her air out on a groan. "We're really going to keep *talking*?"

"This is strip-get-to-know-you. We haven't finished stripping."

She sighed and Luke prepared for a smart-ass, sarcastic comment.

"The fact that I am completely, one hundred percent in charge of my life. I don't let other people influence what I do, how I think or how I feel about things."

It took him a moment to process the fact that she'd actually answered.

"That's really—" he started.

"I don't need your commentary on my answers."

She was so difficult. But worth it. "What do I take off?"

"Shirt."

He stripped his T-shirt off.

Her gaze roamed over him hungrily and he felt his skin heat several degrees.

"Do you like spaghetti?" she asked, not taking her eyes off his chest and abs.

"Yes. Which you know. This is supposed to be about learning things we don't already know," he chided.

"This is supposed to be about getting naked."

It wasn't supposed to be *just* about that but with the feel of her nipple still imprinted on his tongue he wasn't going to argue. "Take your bra off."

She arched her back as she reached for the hooks. The clasp gave and the pink satin fell away.

She was perfect.

The perfect size, the perfect shape, the perfect nipple color. Strangely, he hadn't realized that he had preferences in those things. But she was it.

He lifted his gaze to her face.

"Tell me about something you regret."

She moaned again, this time clearly in frustration. "Are you frickin' kidding me?"

"If you answer without arguing, it's all the sooner you get to tell me what to do next." He rested his hand on her tummy, running his palm back and forth over the silky skin.

"It's gonna involve your hand up under my skirt," she said.

"No more stripping?"

"If I can get your hand in my panties I don't care if the panties are on or off."

He grinned. He really liked her. And he wasn't about to argue about who was supposed to be stripping and when. His hand was going to be up Kat's skirt. "I can live with that.

Answer the question."

She sighed. "Fine. I regret telling Jennifer Owens what I really thought of her."

Luke knew Jennifer. She and her very wealthy husband lived on the West Coast somewhere. "What did you really think?"

Kat's eyes opened. "I believe that's another question and your hand hasn't moved a bit."

He chuckled softly and gladly put his hand on her knee, then slid it up under her skirt. "Better?"

"Gettin' there," she said.

He slid higher, her skin growing warmer as he moved. She shifted her thighs apart and Luke felt his erection press against the back of his fly. "How am I doing?"

"You're about three inches from getting any answer to any question ever," she said breathlessly.

He watched her face as his fingers found the satin of her panties, as his middle finger slipped under the elastic edge, and then brushed soft curls and hot, wet woman.

"And now?" he asked huskily.

"Just a little more." She arched her hips toward his hand and the pad of his finger found her clit. "*There.*"

He slid over it, then circled and pressed.

Kat's head dropped back against the chair and she said, "I thought she was the biggest bitch I've ever met."

Luke smiled. And stopped his finger.

She looked at him. "What are you doing? I answered."

"I have another question."

"Of course you do."

He slid his palm down over the front of her panties, over her mound.

She was hot and she pressed up against his hand as a long breath escaped from her lips.

"Just take your pants off," she groaned.

Her breathlessness made him smile. “Nope. You have to ask a question before I strip.”

She glared at him. “I can’t think of a question. I’m a pile of sexual frustration right now.”

“I’ll fix that if you keep answering my questions.” He bent and flicked his tongue against her nipple again.

She sucked in a quick breath. “Dammit,” she muttered. Then, “What do you want to know?”

“Why do you regret telling Jennifer you thought she was a bitch?”

She sighed. “Because Mr. Hawkins overheard me and I had to sit in detention for three days.”

He chuckled. Of course she hadn’t regretted actually telling Jennifer off, just getting caught doing it. “See, this talking stuff isn’t so bad.” He flexed his fingers against her. When she groaned, he thought about stopping with that and moving to the next question, but she tasted and sounded so sweet, he couldn’t help but take her nipple into his mouth again. She was wiggling and gasping when he finally lifted his head from her breast.

“Tell me about a time you were really disappointed,” he said gruffly.

She groaned in protest this time. “Damn you, Luke.”

She looked amazing lying there, breasts exposed, one nipple wet and hard from his mouth, her skirt hiked up with his hand under the edge.

“Answer it and I’ll make it worth it.” He moved his hand against her again.

Her thighs parted slightly and he almost told her to never mind. Almost.

“You really want to know this?” she asked.

“Yes.”

“Okay.” She looked at him directly when she answered. “I was really disappointed when you went to the courthouse with Sabrina to get married after you knew she was in love with

Marc." She paused and took a deep breath, then said softly, "You deserve to be somebody's first choice."

That was what first came to mind? And it wasn't about her being jealous of Sabrina, but about what *he* deserved.

"I, um—"

"I told you that you don't have to comment on my answers. Just move your damned hand," she said, arching her pelvis up to him.

He had a hot, amazing woman in front of him, and he was even considering talking about something from the past that would likely piss her off? He was much smarter than that. He slid his middle finger into her hot center.

Her breath hissed out as her eyes slid closed. "More."

He slipped two fingers into her heat, memorizing the silky tight feel of her as she gasped his name. He slid in and out, watching her face, trying to ignore the throbbing in his cock.

He stopped after only a few thrusts. Somehow.

"Tell me how you decided to be a doctor."

She moaned. "Are you kidding? Haven't we done enough?"

He started to withdraw. "Well, if you think so—"

"No." She clamped her thighs together around his hand.

He grinned.

"Fine. When I was a freshman in high school I was having these episodes where my ears would ring and I'd get really dizzy," she said, talking at three times her usual speed. "I was convinced I had a brain tumor and was scared to death. We went to the doctor and I remember walking in there and thinking 'this is the place that will help me'. Then the doctor came in and I got this calm feeling. It turned out it was only a bad ear infection, but that feeling of hope stuck with me, how good it felt to have somewhere to go, someone to turn to. I hated that scared feeling and realized that I wanted to be that person, to make people feel better when they're scared like that."

Luke was staring at her, nearly forgetting that she was mostly naked and where his hand was.

"I just think that's—" She was awesome. How had he possibly *not* been with her all this time?

"No comments. I just need your *hand*." She spread her legs a little wider.

Luke was the one to groan this time. His fingers sank deep and she gave him a heartfelt "*Yes*".

Watching her like this made him realize that he was done asking questions. He was done doing anything but sending Kat right over the edge. He pumped his fingers deep, pressed his thumb over her clit and sucked on her nipple at the same time.

He heard his name on her lips. Loving the way her hips met his thrusts, he increased the tempo, wishing like hell he'd gotten rid of the skirt first. He'd love to see this. But feeling was good. Very good. And as her orgasm hit, Kat gasped, and Luke felt her inner muscles gripping his fingers. Her fingers dug into the arms of the chair and her neck arched as she pressed her head into the headrest.

When the tremors passed, she slumped into her seat and slowly opened her eyes.

He withdrew his hand, holding her gaze.

They sat staring at one another for several seconds.

"See," she finally said, breathlessly. "Tequila isn't so bad."

He shook his head. "I'm not letting you make this about tequila."

"Of course you want full credit." She gave him a wobbly smile and thrust her fingers through her hair.

"Damn right." He stretched to his feet and held out his hand to her. "Let's go to bed."

She put her seat upright and vaulted from the chair. "Right with ya." She grabbed his hand and started for the bedroom.

He chuckled at her enthusiasm. "I've gotta park this thing for the night."

"We can't leave it here?"

"In the diner parking lot? I don't think so." He was quite sure of it, in fact. "We'll find the park and then we'll be able to spend as much time as we want to." He gave her a wink as he pulled his shirt back on.

She grinned. "I'll meet you in bed." She reached back and a moment later her skirt dropped to the floor, leaving her in only tiny satin pink panties.

He swallowed hard and stared, his blood pounding in his veins.

"Luke?" He looked up to find her smiling knowingly. "Drive fast."

A few minutes later, he turned into the town park, searching for an area for campers to hook up. It took a bit for him to get the RV ready for the night, and the dark and his inexperience didn't help. He scraped his knuckles, strained his shoulder and muttered several expletives but he finally had them settled in.

He started shedding his clothes the minute he stepped back into the RV, locking the doors as he tossed his shirt away. Shoes landed near the fridge, socks followed, pants fell on the seat where Kat had been at his mercy. Only a pair of boxers were still in place when he stepped into the bedroom. All the lights were on, the shades closed and Kat was...asleep in the middle of the bed. Snoring softly.

She was covered by the sheet to her shoulders, but he saw her panties lying on the floor next to the bed.

He groaned.

Frickin' tequila.

Then he sighed. She was here with him. That was what really mattered. They had days to make love. Years even. The rest of their lives.

He slipped under the covers and slid across the sheets, bracing himself for the first feel of her against him. The bed was a queen-size but there was no way he was going to resist touching her completely. This wasn't going to be the easiest night of his life but if she faced away from him and didn't move much... He had to tamp down a swear word when she snuggled up against him, her ass against his groin.

He lay stock-still for several seconds until he was sure she was done wiggling. Then he let the tension out of his muscles and settled into the pillow.

And she sighed and relaxed into him further.

His cock twitched as the shape of her, the heat of her, the smell of her surrounded him. He grit his teeth, willing her to lie still. It was great that she was comfortable with him in bed—even subconsciously—but his body didn't seem to understand that she needed to be fully coherent to do anything more than spoon.

When she wiggled again, her soft, naked back against his not-soft front, he sighed. He reached out, snaked his arm around her waist and pulled her back against him fully, trapping her so that she couldn't move as easily—or at least as much.

She stirred slightly. "This feels...perfect," she mumbled.

He chuckled into the back of her hair. "I know."

And it definitely did. Not that he was surprised. He was very seldom wrong about these kinds of things.

Chapter Five

Kat insisted on leaving at an ungodly hour the next morning. She was a physician, used to being up and ready to go at any and all hours. On top of that, she looked great. Totally put together.

Luke, not as much. He was an early riser, but he liked a relaxed start to the day. A run, a cup of coffee, the paper, some breakfast, *then* thinking, planning and doing. He was an organizer—too much so, according to many—but he organized things at a reasonable time of day. Like after nine.

But that morning he found himself behind the wheel of an RV, searching for the headlights through bleary eyes. He needed headlights because the sun wasn't up yet. Which was just wrong.

Kat sat beside him in the passenger seat, wide-assed awake in a flowing black skirt and a black vest over a fitted bright blue tank top. She often added some bright color to her perpetual black. And she wore boots of all kinds. He particularly liked the three-inch heels. But today—his eyes traveled over her smooth, bare calf to her slim ankle and down to the sexy arch of her foot—she wore flip-flops. Blue flip-flops. That threw him. Which she might have intended. Predictable was not a word used to describe Kat Dayton.

Sabrina had packed for her but he guessed there were only so many options in Kat's closet. Black, black and gray, or black. Still, the flip-flops were an anomaly.

Probably.

The truth was, he usually saw her at The Camelot. Not really a flip-flop place.

He snuck a glance at the woman in the passenger seat. Her

hair was dark, with one stripe of blue over her left ear, and spiked up behind a black headband. She wore a variety of earrings along the curve of her ears, at least seven in each side, but the tiny studs in her eyebrow and nose were blue as well. She was studying the map she had laid out on her lap and sucking on the straw to a travel cup full of fruit smoothie. He assumed she'd found the ingredients—and blender—in the back in the stuff Marc had packed. He wondered if there was any coffee back there.

"I think we can make it to Grand Island easily before we stop."

He glanced at the clock. It was five in the morning. Holy hell, she expected him to make some kind of strategy? "I'm just working on the ignition and shifting into drive," he said, his voice gruff.

Though it was god-awful early, he acknowledged that he'd slept better than he'd slept in years. In an RV. That wasn't even his.

Go figure.

He was sure it had everything to do with Kat being beside him.

She had slept well too if her warm, relaxed body and soft, steady breathing were anything to go by. Which was probably why she was up and at 'em, fully dressed, styled, made up and ready to go. At five fucking o'clock in the morning.

He was just too damned groggy to spank her like she deserved.

The idea of her turned over his lap picked his heartrate up enough that he felt a little jolt of energy. He looked at her again, focusing this time on her full lips around the straw. Yeah, this would work. Thinking dirty thoughts about Kat might just get enough blood circulating to help him get the RV on the road.

"Why are you looking at me like that?"

He looked from her mouth to her eyes. "Like what?"

Her mouth opened, but then she quickly shook her head. "Never mind."

He grinned. He knew that she knew that he knew exactly how he'd been looking at her. Funny that she didn't want to say *like you want to do me until I can't remember my own name.*

Because that was exactly how he was looking at her.

He wondered what she thought she was figuring out on that map. It would only take a couple of days to get from Justice to Nashville. If they drove straight through and really wanted to get there quickly. Luke didn't want to get there quickly. He wanted plenty of time with Kat. So there was no way they were getting to Nashville one minute before they absolutely had to be there.

But he wasn't going to mention that just yet.

They headed out of town, chatting idly about nothing. It was Tuesday. Barely, Luke noted with a frown. They didn't have to be in Nashville until Friday.

"What did you just say?" Kat pivoted on her seat.

"About what?" He'd been concentrating on not wrecking the RV while checking out the smooth, silky expanse of leg bared by the way she was sitting.

"When are Marc and Sabrina flying in?"

"Friday."

"When does the music festival start?"

"Friday."

She stared at him. "What the hell are we doing driving down *now*? It's only eighteen hours."

"Didn't want to have to rush." He pressed on the accelerator. She wouldn't jump out at fifty-seven miles per hour. Probably. But going sixty-seven wouldn't hurt.

"Rush?" she repeated. "We have four days to drive eighteen hours."

"Plenty of time for sightseeing."

"We're not sightseeing, Luke."

He could feel her glare, but refused to turn to look at her. He also fought his smile.

"Why not? We have plenty of time."

She practically growled, then turned to face the front.

After several seconds of glowering silence she said, "I can't be gone for that long."

"Yes you can. Diane and Nancy took care of everything. You don't have to be back until next Wednesday."

She swung to face him again. "*What?* They know? *Next* Wednesday?"

She was stammering. Kat also never did that. Luke tried not to look pleased with himself, knowing that would only piss her off at this point.

"Well, the band starts Friday and performs until Sunday. Then we have to drive back—"

"You said the festival was four days."

"It technically starts Thursday night. But Sabrina and the guys don't perform until Friday."

"I can't believe you butted in like that. This is...crazy. This is...too much. It's my practice, my *work*. I have people who depend on me. I have responsibilities—"

"You have vacation time too," Luke inserted. "You never take time off. That's not good either. Everyone will be fine. The doctors covering you are more than capable. And Diane was happy to handle it. Everyone knows how hard you work."

She worked horrible hours, took more call than anyone else, and covered everyone else. She hadn't had more than two consecutive days off in more than seven months. She worked holidays, weekends—it was ridiculous. He hadn't been surprised when Diane, the office manager for the entire practice, assured him that everyone would be glad she was taking some time for herself.

"It wasn't your right to—"

"Maybe not," he interrupted again. "But someone has to take care of *you*. And if I don't have the right, then I'll take the risk."

He dared to glance at her.

She was staring at him—which was an improvement over

the glaring—like she had no idea what to say. Another rare occurrence for Kat.

Again, he fought to not look smug.

She was a tough cookie. Everyone knew that. He suspected she enjoyed the label and worked at it. But he meant it when he said someone needed to take care of her.

And by someone, he meant *him.*

"No apology then?" she finally asked. "For butting in like that?"

He looked over at her. "Tell you what. When you apologize to me for assuming this trip is going to suck, I'll apologize for making you come along."

"Hmm. Why don't you hold your breath for that," she replied.

He chuckled. "That's what I thought."

She pulled out her cell phone and started to dial.

"It's barely after five a.m. You can't call Diane now."

She paused, sighed, then snapped her phone shut. She sat chewing on her bottom lip. Probably wondering if it was too early to call one of her covering MDs. It wasn't if they had been called in for a patient. It definitely was if they *hadn't* been called in and were trying to catch up on sleep.

They drove for a few minutes without talking. Finally Luke settled deeper into his seat, made sure the cruise control was set and decided to dive right in.

"Where would you most like to travel in the world?"

She looked over at him, seemingly confused. "What?"

"If someone was hypothetically going to take you on a trip, where would you most like to travel to?"

She shook her head and faced forward. "You're not taking me on a trip."

He smiled and rolled his eyes. What woman didn't want to be whisked away on a fabulous trip to the place she most wanted to go?

"You like pets, right? I would like to have a dog at some

point, but I like cats too and they're easier to have with crazy schedules like ours."

She glanced over. "What the hell are you talking about?"

"Pets."

"Why?"

"Isn't that something we should talk about before we live together?"

She sighed. "Live together? Really? It's five a.m. and you're dragging me along on a trip I not only did not agree to go on, but specifically said no to going on, and now you want to talk to me about living together?"

He knew it was a gamble but he shot her a grin. "Yeah."

Instead of yelling or even telling him he was an idiot or something, she pulled out her iPod, stuck the buds in her ears, opened her Kindle and propped her feet up on the dash.

"We're not going to talk?"

She pulled the left earphone out and looked over. "This trip was your idea. I never agreed to entertain you. And I didn't get sex last night, so you don't get conversation today."

"You fell asleep," he pointed out.

"Because you made me drink tequila."

"I made you?" he repeated.

"Yes."

He chuckled. "You did get an orgasm though. That's gotta be good for a little conversation."

He looked over in time to see her shift in her seat slightly. He grinned.

"Fine." She cleared her throat. "But we're not going to talk about crazy stuff like moving in together or how we're going to spend our first anniversary or anything bizarre like that. Just normal conversation, okay?"

"No talking about what kind of engagement ring you'd like or if you'd consider naming a child Anthony after my grandfather?" he said, sort of teasing. And sort of not.

It was no secret he was ready to settle down and start a family. The woman he wanted to do it with should certainly be a part of these discussions.

"I'm only doing this because of the orgasm," she muttered. "I want a small setting because I want to be able to wear it at work and not a diamond—too cliché. And I would absolutely consider Anthony, but only for a boy."

A sudden and new emotion hit Luke in the chest with her words. It was something akin to amazement. He'd never had this kind of conversation, joking or not, with another woman and hearing actual answers from Kat made him feel a combination of good old-fashioned happiness and relief—all of the things he wanted could really happen—with a good shot of something he couldn't name in hearing his grandfather's name being considered for one of his—their—children.

"Now shut the hell up so I can read." She replaced the earbud and looked down at her Kindle.

But he wasn't letting this go. Yeah, he was pushing, but he'd been waiting for these things for a long time and besides, where was she really going to go? They were traveling down the highway, well over the speed limit, far from home.

"That orgasm was worth more than that."

She huffed out an impatient breath and pulled both earbuds out this time. "Now what?"

"I want to know what the lottery analogy was about last night."

"The lottery analogy?" she hedged. "I was drinking a lot. I don't remember."

He snorted. "You hadn't drunk that much when you said it."

"It was nothing. Just mumblings."

"No, it was very clear. I heard you say, 'I just won the lottery, but I cheated'. What's that mean?"

"I have to go the bathroom," she said suddenly, pushing up out of her seat and then climbing over the middle console. She tripped on the bag of stuff she'd set behind the seat and lost a flip-flop, but righted herself quickly and disappeared in back.

Luke sighed, but grinned in spite of himself. He'd let her go for now, but he was going to find out about the lottery. And everything else about her. After all, he was going to be sure this trip took twice as long as it needed to. And he could always handcuff her to the chair if he ran out of other options.

Kat bypassed the bathroom and lay on the bed with the door shut between her and the incredibly tempting man up front. She was stubbornly determined to ride out the rest of the trip in back, far from him. She wasn't usually one to avoid things but she really didn't know how else to deal with this. Until she could get to a rental car, she was stuck in the RV with him and his insistence on talking about things that made her *want*. She wanted him, she wanted the emerald engagement ring she'd immediately pictured when he'd asked, she wanted... God, she wanted a baby boy they could name Anthony.

Yeah, so Luke was the lottery and she'd cheated by letting him believe she was all of the wonderful things he thought he wanted.

Eventually though, if they were truly together and she was truly honest, he'd find out that she was not as well-liked in town as he imagined, she had a past that was a secret only because the people who knew were scared of her, and—oh, yeah—she couldn't tell a rotator cuff tear from a stroke.

She grabbed a pillow and covered her face while she let out a scream of frustration. She had to avoid talking to, laughing with, kissing and *definitely* sleeping with Luke because she didn't need to want him any more than she did right now.

And she couldn't even begin to think about the orgasm from last night.

She somehow focused on her Kindle, managing to read three full chapters and retain at least sixty percent of them. When she was bored she dialed Marc's number—not caring if she woke him up early—but hung up before it rang so that she wouldn't wake Sabrina. Then she read another chapter, then tried unsuccessfully to nap, then wished for her laptop that was up front near Luke.

Just as she was about to go truly crazy from boredom she felt the RV slow and turn, then stop. She smiled and sat up. Whatever the reason for the stop she was getting up and out.

She headed for the front of the RV as Luke turned off the ignition.

He was across the dirt parking area and handling fresh fruit by the time she'd stepped out of the RV. He kept his attention—mostly—on the strawberries in front of him.

"What's this?" She came to stand beside him, looking over the bins of cucumbers, tomatoes, watermelon, sweet corn and strawberries.

"Fresh produce. Couldn't pass it up." He selected two baskets of berries and moved on to the watermelon.

"You're buying fruit."

"Watermelon to be exact. The food of kings."

She chuckled. "Kings. Really."

"In ancient Egypt they used to bury watermelons in the tombs of the kings to nourish them in the afterlife."

She didn't say anything to that and he turned to find her looking at him with amused confusion.

"What?"

"Why in the world do you know so much about watermelon?"

He moved in closer to her and dropped his voice to a whisper. "I'm a part of a secret society plotting to infiltrate the most nefarious circles and bring about the destruction of all evil with the seemingly innocuous watermelon."

She stared at him, then shook her head. "You're deeply disturbed."

He shrugged. "You're not even impressed by my use of nefarious and innocuous in the same sentence?"

"Did you see a show on the Food Network or something?"

"History Channel."

She rolled her eyes.

"Did you know watermelon is an aphrodisiac?" he asked, moving to the bin and picking up a huge specimen.

"It is not."

"It is. It contains a chemical called citrulline. It acts like Viagra."

She looked interested now as she regarded the huge bin of green melons. "No kidding."

He moved close again and waited until her gaze met his. "I would never kid about something like that. In fact, I'm feeling a little affected just standing next to them."

She swallowed hard before answering. "You have to consume citrulline for it to have an effect."

"Then maybe it's just you."

Her gaze dropped to his lips and she hesitated just a moment. Then she shook her head again. "We better get going."

"I need to buy the watermelon."

She took the heavy fruit from his hands and put it back in the bin. "No. You definitely don't."

She headed back toward the RV.

Luke was grinning and whistling as he followed her.

Thirty minutes later he pulled up at another roadside stand.

By the time she joined him from the back of the RV, he'd picked up a bag of peaches and had another watermelon under his arm.

Without a word, she took the watermelon from him and replaced it in the bin.

He paid for the peaches and followed her back to the RV.

"Are you planning to stop at every stand that sells

watermelon?" she asked as they reached the vehicle.

He shook his head. "I'm mostly just bored. I see a stand and some nice farmer sitting there and I figure it's a chance to talk to another human being."

She sighed heavily. "If I sit in the front seat with you, you'll quit stopping every few minutes?"

"You have to sit up front *and* talk to me," he clarified.

"Fine." She got up into the passenger's side as he got behind the wheel started the engine. "But no talking about weddings, babies or sex."

"Why not?"

"Because it's *ridiculous*."

"Ridiculous?" That was not the word he would use at all.

"We've spent one night together, you haven't put out yet, we haven't even been on an actual date, and you *proposed* to my *best friend* three months ago. I'm not sure we should be naming our kids just yet."

Of course he'd never jump ahead like that with any other woman, but this was Kat. "I don't need all of that to know that we'll work. And neither do you." As he said it he recognized the truth. He expected their history to not just help him recognize her as the one he wanted, but vice versa.

She turned to face him, just watching him for a moment. "You know, you have a point," she finally said

"Yeah? Well, that's good. Isn't it?"

She chuckled. "Yeah. Even though you're talking to me about how practical it is for us to be together, how it's not crazy and emotional, the truth is—this *is* kind of crazy."

Ah, the conversation from the diner. "Kat, I didn't mean that I don't feel anything. It's just—"

"I watched you with Sabrina for years," she went on over the top of him. "I saw you do all kinds of things that made no sense, put up with stuff no one else would, do crazy stuff that you wouldn't do for anyone else." She took a breath and then said softly, "And I wanted that."

Luke swallowed hard and looked at her, not sure what to say.

"And now you're talking crazy, doing crazy things—like blindfolding me, kidnapping me, talking about babies already."

"It doesn't feel crazy," was all he could think to say. He glanced at her again and found her watching him contemplatively. "What?" he asked.

"I'm just... It just occurred to me that you would never have done that with Sabrina."

"I already admitted that I wasn't rational about her." He could concede he'd made mistakes with Sabrina. But he didn't want to talk about her. As far as he was concerned it was settled and he was moving on. With Kat.

"But you would have never pushed her, you *never* would have kidnapped her," Kat said, almost as if she was figuring it out as she spoke. "You always treated her carefully. You never really fought. If she got upset you backed off."

He shifted in his seat. Sabrina had always been on the verge of flight and he'd known that pushing would never work.

"But you push me," Kat said.

He frowned and looked over at her. "Well, I—"

"And you'll fight with me."

"Only if—"

"And you're not afraid of me."

He started to reply but she sounded...pleased. When he looked over she was smiling at him.

"Of course I'm not afraid of you. I—"

"That's a good thing."

"It is?"

"Definitely. You're different with me than with other women, especially Sabrina. But you *are* acting crazy with me."

He really wasn't sure how to respond so he decided to be honest. "Okay, maybe it's a little crazy to talk about kids already." But it still made his chest feel warm to think about kids with her. Which was, okay, crazy.

She laughed softly. "Thanks."

"Can we talk about pets?"

She shook her head. "Not yet."

"I'm guessing weddings is a no too then?" He was enjoying this.

"Weddings come between pets and babies."

He laughed. "Got it. Sex?"

"Maybe."

He grinned. That was something. "We could talk about other people having sex if you'd rather," he said. "I heard that Susan and Tyler are dating."

"We're not talking about other people having sex." But she was smiling as she said it.

"How about sexual positions in general? I also saw a TV show about that. Do you know the five sexual positions women like most? I wasn't surprised by number one or two, on top and missionary, by the way. But standing and all fours were on the list and that *was* a pleasant surprise."

"You watch too much TV" was her only response.

He smiled, slowing down behind the farmer in the pickup in front of them. The man was driving fifty miles an hour, which would have normally irritated Luke, but on this trip he had no problem slowing down.

"Okay, tell me your favorite memory about your dad growing up," he said.

"My dad?" The change in subject clearly threw her.

"I'll tell you mine." He didn't smile but he had her exactly where he wanted her as long as they had to stay clothed—beside him, talking, getting comfortable. "When I was a kid my dad traveled all the time."

David Hamilton had quickly moved up the ranks of the printing company he worked for and had ended up as a senior vice president, a position that required travel forty weeks of the year.

"What I liked best was that when he traveled he always

took a book with him, a classic. Then when he'd call at night, after he talked to my mom, he'd read me a chapter. I read *The Adventures of Tom Sawyer*, *Catcher in the Rye* and *To Kill a Mockingbird* that way. Those are still my favorite books." He looked over at her. "How about you?"

"My favorite book? Wow, I don't think I could pick just one."

"What about a memory with your dad? Or mom?"

She looked suspicious when he glanced over. "You really want to talk about childhood memories?"

"Sure."

"Why?"

"I want to know everything."

She hesitated a moment before asking, "Because you think it will lead to talking about pets?"

It appeared that *talking about pets* had become code for *talking about more serious things*. He shrugged. "I hope it leads to something like that. But the truth is, I want to get closer to you. I want to be the closest person in your life. I want to know you, everything about you."

She didn't respond for a long time. When he glanced over, she was watching him.

"What's wrong?"

"You sure you want to know everything?" she asked.

"Definitely."

"Even the bad stuff?"

He frowned, not sure what she meant by that. But he nodded. "Everything."

She took a deep breath, then started. "When I was a kid I hated pizza—well, anything with tomato sauce. So when our family would go out to eat and it was pizza or pasta or something, my dad would let me buy a burger and fries at McDonald's and sneak it in."

Luke grinned. "We are going to talk about our childhoods then."

"You can ask me three questions about anything. Then we talk about weather."

"Three? That's not nearly enough."

"It's supposed to be sunny and in the upper sixties while we're in Nashville."

He chuckled. "Okay. Three." He thought about it, wanting to make the questions important. Not that he really thought in the next thousand miles he wouldn't have a chance to find anything else out, but he wanted her to know this mattered to him.

It wasn't like he knew nothing about her. He knew her family. Her dad was an insurance agent, her mom worked at the school and her sister, Isabelle, was a year older than Kat.

But there were plenty of things that he didn't know that he wanted to.

"Okay, what is the first Christmas memory you have?"

She looked surprised.

"You were expecting a question about sex toys or something, right?" he asked.

"Actually, yes."

"Did you have an answer ready?"

"Vibrating eggs."

He glanced at her quickly, heat unexpectedly shooting through him. "What was the question, exactly?"

"Nope, that's your part," she said, with a sly grin. "I remember going to visit my grandparents and everyone piling in the car to drive around and look at all the Christmas lights in town."

"No, no, we're not dropping the sex toy topic. I want a redo on question one."

"No redos. Especially since I already answered the Christmas question."

"But—" he protested.

"I also remember the first time I visited my grandmother after I dyed my hair and got my piercings."

That distracted him enough that he forgot—temporarily—about the vibrating eggs. He was pretty sure he knew what those were but he was going to be sure to Google it as soon he had a chance. "You didn't change that stuff before you went to see her?"

"Nope. I decided that I had to be fully committed to it, with everyone."

"What did she say?"

"That I pulled it off." She looked very pleased with herself.

This is more the Kat that he knew. She was getting more comfortable. This was good.

"Okay, question two. Which celebrity would you most like to meet?"

"I thought we were staying away from sexual topics."

"That's a sexual topic?"

She gave him a wicked little grin. "Definitely."

He did not want to know who she was fantasizing about. But he wouldn't mind a peek at a few of the activities that entered those fantasies.

"What do you hate most in the world?" he asked for question three.

"Shaving my legs."

His eyes dropped to the bare leg closest to him. "Really?"

"I have really sensitive skin. Every time is a battle with razor rash."

"I'm glad you make the sacrifice."

She narrowed her eyes. "Not sure what it has to do with you."

"I can explain. In detail."

"Nope. Forget it. My favorite subject in school was science, my favorite band of all time is Bon Jovi, my favorite color is pink, my—"

"Pink?" he interrupted. He remembered the pale pink bra from the night before. Vividly. Along with the dark pink of her nipples. He shifted in his seat as he grew less comfortable in his jeans.

"Yeah. Pink." Her tone was definitely wanna-make-something-of-it?

"Not black? You wear black all the time."

"You don't know that I don't wear pink all the time. Too."

"But I would have noticed—" His eyes dropped to her breasts. The bra. And panties. "Oh. Really?"

She shrugged. "As far as you know. My favorite food is—"

"Let's go back to the pink under black. I'm intrigued."

"Intrigued is not a synonym for horny," she told him.

He grinned. "Do your bra and panties always match or do you sometimes have one that's pink and the other something else?" He'd only seen her panties briefly but they'd definitely been pink.

"My favorite movie of all time is *It's a Wonderful Life,* my favorite family vacation ever was to Washington, D.C., my favorite holiday is the Fourth of July."

"Are the bras all pink, all the time, or do they sometimes just have a little pink on them, like stripes or something?"

"I'm scary good at Mario Kart, I actually love doing the Macarena, I can make a pot roast better than my mother's, and I can play 'Für Elise' on the piano by heart."

"And are we talking all shades of pink or just that pale pink or what? Any hot pink? You could pull *that* off for sure."

"I like Diet Pepsi but not Diet Coke, I like iced tea but not hot and I believe that iced tea should always be sweet."

Now she was definitely fighting a smile, and mostly losing.

"Fine, but now I'm just going to be imagining your underwear even more."

"Even more?" she asked. "More than what?"

"More than I do now."

"You imagine my underwear now?"

"Definitely. You're partial to thongs by the way."

"Um, no, actually I'm not."

"In my imagination you are. Of course I'm willing to alter those images, but you have to give me something to work with."

She raised that one eyebrow and waited until he looked over. "Good try."

He chuckled. "Guess I'm stuck with the mental picture of you in a pink see-through thong."

She shook her head and, though he glanced quickly, he could have sworn she was blushing.

"I'd rather go without than wear a thong," she muttered, smoothing her skirt down as she faced forward and put both feet on the floor.

"Done."

"Done?"

"My mental image was just altered to you wearing no underwear."

"Stop it."

"Stop what?"

"Thinking about me in my underwear. Or without my underwear."

"Can't do it. It's like a great commercial jingle that gets stuck in your head. No matter what you do it won't leave you alone."

"Then I get to ask you three questions. That'll distract you."

"I'm just realizing that without any underwear, you'll have fewer options for wearing pink..." He purposefully trailed off, waited two heartbeats, then said, "Nope, never mind. There's some pink after all."

"What are you—"

He knew the exact moment she realized what he was talking about. He looked over. She was staring at him, her mouth partway open, eyes wide.

"You are *not* talking about naked pink things."

"Oh, yes, I am." And getting even tighter in his jeans at the same time. Because there was no way to tease about thinking about naked pink things and not actually think about them.

She leaned over and punched his arm. "Knock it off. Stop thinking about my naked pink things."

He laughed and dodged the next swing at his arm. "Can't. And the more you talk about it, the more I think about it."

"Tell me about someone who died that meant a lot to you."

He looked at her, properly sobered. "That's a low blow."

"I had to get your mind out of the gutter somehow."

Luke focused back on the road. "My grandpa. He died when I was nine."

"Sorry," she muttered. She was staring at her hand in her lap, looking a little like she regretted the drastic measure.

"I think he was part of the reason I got attached to Bill so easily."

Bill Cassidy, Sabrina's father, had lived next door to Luke when he was growing up and had taken the young man under his wing, teaching him to hunt, upgrade the plumbing in an old bathroom and grill a perfect steak, as well as instilling a strong sense of community and public service in the boy.

Luke's father had traveled a lot and Sabrina had not shared her father's interests, so Luke had stepped into the role of protégée for Bill—a situation that benefited both men. And kept Bill out of Sabrina's hair. Some.

"My grandpa used to take me fishing and camping," Luke said to Kat. "He taught me to throw a baseball and football, he taught me about gardening and lots of stuff. After he was gone, I missed having that and Dad obviously couldn't do it." Dave was gone more than he was home and while Luke never blamed his father, he did miss him. "When Bill wanted someone to teach and mentor, it was a great match."

Kat sighed. "That's really nice." She sounded like she meant it.

"What else do you want to know?" This trip and time together wasn't just about him getting to know her better. He wanted her to know him too.

"Okay." She turned toward him.

Luke took that as a good sign as well.

"What is your most prized possession?"

He had to think about that. His restaurant, that he owned with Marc, was certainly important. He had some valuable baseball cards, and the like. But most of the things beloved to him were people and memories.

"I suppose the framed newspaper article announcing the opening of The Camelot."

"Not The Camelot itself?" she asked.

"The article has a lot of really nice things about me in black and white." He grinned at her. "And it's a really good picture."

He knew exactly why that article was important. Part of his dream was to have a business in his hometown that was integral to the community, that truly added something of value. The article in the *Justice Times* said exactly that about him and The Camelot. It was proof he'd met his goal.

"What's your worst habit?" Kat asked, moving on to question number two.

He considered that for a minute too. "I eat too much red meat," he finally said. He annoyed people with his seemingly endless supply of worthless trivia, was a little obsessed with John Cusack, and actually enjoyed Twitter, but those weren't really habits per se.

She laughed. "That's not your worst habit."

"It's not?"

"No. You do lots worse things than that."

He shot her a glance. "Such as?"

"You give away too many free desserts at The Camelot."

He grinned. "If that's the worst thing I do, I think I can live guilt-free."

"You quote eighties movies on nearly a daily basis."

He thought about that. "Twice a week I'll give you. Maybe

three times. Not daily."

"You drink that really dark beer."

"That's probably more of a preference than a habit."

"Well, your absolute worst habit is that you always have to be a hero."

He looked at her. "I... What?"

"You always want people to need you and you love doing stuff for everyone else. Even if it's a sacrifice for you. It's why you love your restaurant. At The Camelot you give people a great place to go and have fun. It's why you always hung out with Bill—and still do sometimes—because he needed someone to mentor to feel good about himself. It was the basis for your entire relationship with Sabrina."

Luke took a deep breath and actually felt—satisfied. It wasn't like it was a secret that he liked to help others. Still, he liked knowing that Kat had given so much thought to what he did and why. So he liked being a hero. He'd been raised by two generous, loving people who taught him a lot about giving and sacrifice and very little about taking.

"How is doing things for other people a bad habit?" he asked

"It's not the actual doing stuff. It's just that it's so..." She stopped, pressed her lips together, then shook her head. "Never mind."

"Oh, no. I want to hear this. It's so what?"

"It's nothing. I'm just running my mouth."

"I like it. We're talking. This is good."

She shook her head again. "You won't think this is good. This is what you get for wanting me to talk. I shouldn't have said that. Helping people out is not a bad habit. How about we talk about sex some more?"

He chuckled. "While that's tempting—and would be properly distracting—I want to know what you think about this habit of mine. You said it's not the doing that's bad. So what is?"

She sighed. "I never realized how persistent you can be."

"Katarina, I'll cuff you to that chair again if I have to." And he'd enjoy torturing the answer out of her—one silky inch of skin at a time.

"Fine. Just remember—you pushed."

"Right. Now spill." He loved talking to her and he loved that she'd spent time figuring him out. That had to mean something. And her read on things in his life would surely tell him a lot about her too.

"It's just that it's so one-sided," she finally said. "You do things for other people but you almost never have them do things for you."

He thought about that. "The people at The Camelot give me money for the things I do."

She shook her head. "That's not what I mean. You never think about *your* wants and needs."

"I want and need money." He knew that wasn't what she meant, but he wasn't used to people analyzing him. Frankly, it was rare for people to question why someone did something nice. Which was just fine with him.

She laughed. "Luke, I'm serious. You—deserve more than that."

He looked over at her. "I get more than that." He meant it. "Taking care of people makes me feel good. Seeing people enjoying themselves in my restaurant is enjoyable for me too. Hanging out with Bill taught me a ton of great stuff."

He paused with that and Kat was quiet, but he could feel her watching him. Finally he glanced over. "What?"

"What about Sabrina?" she asked. "You didn't mention what you got from her."

He shifted in his seat again. He should have known she'd notice that.

Out of the corner of his eye he saw Kat lean back against the passenger-side door, facing him, arms crossed. "Come on, Luke. What did you get from Sabrina?"

"Friendship." It wasn't like he and Sabrina had never had fun.

"Okay," she said agreeably. "That's true." A moment passed, then she sighed. "Nope. I should be a bigger person than this, but I can't help but take the chance to point out that you got nothing from her. Not really. You deserved better."

His chest ached. This was an awkward conversation to have anyway, but now she'd brought up Sabrina. And not being able to really look at her didn't help.

"I don't think it's about what I *deserved.*"

He just hadn't been what Sabrina wanted.

"Of course that's what it's about," Kat argued.

"So she should have married me, spent her life with me, because I was nice to her?" he asked.

"No, dammit," Kat snapped. "She should have...let you go."

The ache in his chest intensified. "Maybe I didn't want to be let go."

There was a long pause. Then Kat said softly, "Exactly."

He scowled at the road that kept him from really looking at her. "What the hell does that mean?"

"You didn't do all those crazy things for her because you didn't want to let *her* go. You did them so she wouldn't let go of *you.*"

Kat sounded a little amazed and Luke wondered if these were new revelations for her.

"That's always been what you're about," she went on.

"I—" He wasn't sure what to say to that.

Because she was right.

"That makes sense," she went on. "You were front row center in a home where you saw people—foster kids—who had been let go by someone." She nodded as if she was just getting it. "And then you had to let them go too. Roots matter to you, being stable and secure matter to you. And now you do everything you can to be important to people so they won't let you go." She stopped and took a deep breath.

He looked over to find her watching him.

"What you don't realize is that you don't have to *do* things. There are people who will care about you, want you, hold on to you just because of *you*."

Before he could speak, Kat swallowed and finished quietly. "So that's your worst habit—not believing that you're amazing, no matter what you do for people."

Luke stared hard at the road in front of them. His chest still felt tight but it wasn't with anger or frustration now—it was shock.

No one had ever said those kinds of things to him. He knew he was loved, he knew he was appreciated, he knew he was important. But no one had ever called him on his motivations—his fears.

No one had ever called him amazing.

He didn't consciously decide to do things for others just so he was significant to those people, but he could acknowledge that being *needed* fed his soul, made him feel happy. And safe.

And he could admit he had been more intentional in the things he did for Sabrina. As they'd gotten older and he realized that he loved her and wanted her, he tried very hard to be indispensable to her.

He'd given her everything.

And then she'd shown him that he wasn't indispensable at all.

Fuck.

He ran a hand over his face and took a deep breath. He wanted to be over those emotions. He *was* over those emotions. Kat was just bringing it all up to...

He thought about that. Why was Kat bringing all of this up? It seemed that some of his underlying motivations were a new realization for her. But she'd pointed out that Sabrina hadn't appreciated him. She'd claimed that his worth wasn't about the things he did.

She'd used the word amazing.

Those things didn't sound like they were new thoughts for her.

Sabrina hadn't held on to him. But Kat had. Even when he hadn't paid enough attention, even when he'd left her in his dorm room to pick up another girl, even when he'd been an idiot—she'd been there. As a friend. Wanting more. Thinking he was amazing.

Stunned, he decided that he needed some time to think, talk and *do* something about all of that without worrying about putting the RV in some guy's cornfield.

He flipped on the turn signal.

Chapter Six

Kat was still debating whether being honest about the whole Sabrina-never-appreciated-you thing had been a good idea, when Luke signaled for a left turn into the tiny town of Stuart, Nebraska.

"What are you doing?"

"Need to stop."

He didn't even look at her and Kat figured he was pissed. She sighed. Well, that was too bad.

He was amazing and he deserved to be with a woman who knew it.

She hadn't fully realized why he did all the things he did, but now that it made sense, she felt almost giddy.

The truth was—she really was perfect for him.

Not because she wanted to live and die in Justice, but because she felt for him the way he'd always felt for Sabrina.

She was head over heels for him and wanted to do over-the-top things to make him feel good. Regardless of the return on emotion.

Sure, that wasn't exactly playing hard to get. But he needed it. Luke deserved to have someone focused on him, what he wanted and needed, as much as he focused on everyone else.

Did she want to be that someone? Hell yes.

When the RV finally came to a full stop it was beside a sign that said *White Horse Museum.*

Okay, whatever.

She slipped on her flip-flops and tried to figure out what to say to him. Blurting out *I'm in love with you and will do anything you want me to do* didn't seem appropriate. True. But perhaps a little too much all at once.

"You've always wanted to know a lot about white horses?" she asked instead, as she joined him at the front of the RV.

He stared at her for several long seconds and Kat felt her skin beginning to heat. Weird.

"Something like that," he finally said.

She had to clear her throat before she spoke. "I'm beginning to think that you don't ever want to make it to Nashville."

"I'm beginning to think a lot of things about you too."

She wasn't sure she wanted to know what he was thinking exactly so she left that alone. At least he didn't seem incredibly angry. But she was concerned that he was hurt. She hadn't meant to bruise his ego with the Sabrina talk. Even if *she* thought he was great, it didn't change the fact that for years he'd wanted Sabrina to think that.

Kat wanted him to feel good.

Yes, she wanted him crazy in love with her. Yes, she wanted his feelings for her to trump the imperfections. Yes, she was afraid of ending up brokenhearted.

But suddenly she wanted him to know that she was crazy for him too.

In spite of *his* imperfections.

Maybe she should show him how it was done.

Maybe instead of fighting him on this trip and trying to avoid getting closer to him, she should just take the risk, take the leap of faith.

Maybe she should talk about china patterns and baby names.

Luke headed for the big, old two-story house with the white-horse statue in front and since she wasn't sure what she needed, or wanted, to say to him about how she felt, she simply followed him. Maybe what they both needed was a little time and space to sort through things.

As she took the first step forward her phone beeped in her pocket. A text message. It was so natural to grab it that she hadn't even really been aware she was holding it. She glanced down, saw it was finally late enough in the morning for someone to be doing something at the hospital and noted the number was the hospital in Alliance. She glanced after Luke. He'd already disappeared into the museum/house. She flipped the phone open and saw the message was from Britney, the ICU nurse.

Flying Tom Martin to Denver. Subarch hem.

Subarachnoid hemorrhage. Likely from the fall when he'd lost consciousness and surely right underneath the location of the skull fracture.

Dammit. Like the stroke wasn't bad enough. Like the hip fracture wasn't enough of a complication.

What else could happen?

Oh, yeah. They could need to fly him to a major hospital in Denver. A hospital that would have a full-time neurology staff and the experience to deal with these multiple serious issues.

But of course Dr. Brickham hadn't called her.

If she hadn't been nice to Britney, bringing her coffee when she knew the young nurse had been working overnight, she wouldn't know even now.

Dammit.

Kat fought against the combination of anger and hurt. It wasn't about her. She wasn't the attending physician. There wasn't a reason to call her.

She took a deep breath and looked up at the White Horse Museum.

Fine. She hadn't been the attending in Alliance and now that Tom was in Denver his physicians certainly had to obligation to keep her informed. Brickham would likely get updates but would clearly not share them with her and she doubted being there in Justice, or even Alliance, would matter—Brickham had cut her out from the beginning. Now Britney wouldn't have any information, or at least she'd have to dig to get it. Kat wasn't sure she'd bought Brit enough coffee for that.

So she was on vacation, with Luke. Luke, who thought she was perfect, loved being with her, and wanted to be closer to her.

She really should just enjoy that since the people who felt that way were dwindling in number.

She hit the *Off* button on her phone and started for the front of the museum.

The museum consisted of the main building and then a few additional buildings behind it, including an old schoolhouse, a church and a blacksmith, but Luke had gone up the front steps of the main house first.

"Welcome to— Wow." The greeting changed as the twenty-something guy at the front counter caught sight of Kat.

She watched him come around the counter, leaving behind a thick book and a highlighter. "Hi."

"Um, do you need directions or something?" he asked. He had shaggy blond hair, a scruffy goatee and glasses. His nametag said *Zach*.

"No. Just a pit stop." She scanned the immediate area but didn't see Luke.

"Well, whatever. I'm happy no matter what the reason. We don't get girls like you here very often."

She was used to varied reactions to her appearance and it was always a source of interest and amusement for her.

"Girls with blue hair?" she asked

"Yeah, sure, that's what I noticed first." He grinned as his eyes scanned her from head to toe.

She smiled back. He was too young and not her type, but a compliment was a compliment. And she could really use the boost right now.

"Stop noticing her at all." Luke came to stand just behind Kat's right shoulder.

They weren't touching but the tiny bit of air that was between them immediately heated.

"It's hard not to," Zach said unapologetically.

"Tell me about it," Luke muttered.

She rolled her eyes and Zach grinned again. "She giving you a hard time?"

"You could say that."

Kat didn't respond to Luke. "He's fine," she told Zach.

"What'd you do, man? Forget her birthday or something?"

"Would you believe it involves a blindfold—"

Kat elbowed Luke in the ribs. "It's not my birthday or anything," she said. "Everything is fine."

"You sure? There's some definite tension," Zach said.

Kat couldn't believe this. There was small-town friendly and then there was small-town nosy. It was a fine line.

Of course, he was right. There was tension. Major tension. Sexual tension between her and Luke for sure. Then there was Luke's-irritated tension. And finally her tension over trying to decide what dramatic look-how-I-feel-about-you gesture she was going to make for Luke and when. It was definitely throwing caution to the wind, considering he could change his mind about the whole damned thing when he found out a few of her secrets. But Luke deserved to have someone head over heels for him for a change.

And she was perfect for that role.

But whatever she was going to say, or do, to Luke wasn't going to be done in this tiny museum in Podunk, Nebraska, in front of an impressionable twenty-something anyway. "Hey, tell me about this book collection over here." She headed for the display of old texts.

"Man, looks like you've got some work to do," he said to Luke, ignoring Kat's request.

Luke responded, "Don't worry, I'm getting to her."

He definitely was. She didn't register even one title of the dusty books on the shelf in front of her, but she looked at them as if they were the most fascinating things she'd ever seen.

"You're not trying very hard," Zach said.

Kat stoically kept her eyes on the books she didn't care about. So they were talking about her as if she was on display with the other artifacts. That didn't bother her.

"What do you mean?" Luke asked.

"You haven't touched her once since you came in here."

There was a long pause and Kat knew that she was holding her breath.

"I have a good reason," Luke finally said gruffly.

Yeah, he was pissed.

"There's no reason good enough, man," Zach said.

Kat read the title on the spine of the book in front of her for the twelfth time without it registering. What was this kid? An undercover relationship counselor?

"I'm afraid if I start touching her I won't be able to stop."

Kat sucked in a quick breath as tingles spread through her body like she'd touched a live wire.

Luke was being pretty open with a complete stranger. Then again, maybe that made it easier. In Justice, all eyes were on him and he had to watch what he said and how he acted. And it was probably all kinds of entertaining for the guy working in a small-town museum on a weekday.

Zach chuckled. "That's an even better reason to do it."

Finally she heard Luke mutter, "You know what? I think you might have something there."

It took her three seconds to realize what he meant, but before she could move or form a single syllable Luke grasped her upper arm, spun her, pulled her up against him and kissed her.

It really wasn't fair. Being human with no superpowers whatsoever, she gave in immediately to the hot onslaught as he cupped the back of her head and opened his mouth over hers.

Okay, so her own dramatic gesture was going to have to wait, but she could most certainly react to his.

He lifted his head and stared down at her for a long moment. Then one of his hands went to her hip and he urged her closer, widening his stance and bringing her pelvis to pelvis. Then he kissed her again. Slowly and sweetly.

She was the first to moan.

She was also the one to turn up the heat. She went up on tiptoe, her arms went around his neck and her tongue licked along his bottom lip. When he opened with a groan she stroked along his tongue, with thoughts of other things she could stroke her tongue along. Then thoughts fled altogether and she concentrated only on the sensations coursing through her. She pulled his T-shirt up from his waistband and slid her hands onto the hot bare skin of his back.

He pressed his hips closer. And did the same with her shirt. His hands slid up her back to the level of her bra, then came forward to cup her breasts, his thumbs rubbing across her nipples, sending want zinging through her body, making her hot and wet and crazy.

When she curled her fingers into the tight muscles of his back he pulled his mouth free and stared down at her, breathing hard, desire clear in his eyes.

The kid behind them finally cleared his throat.

Damn.

Kat sucked air into her lungs and watched Luke struggle to focus his eyes on anything but her. That alone made her melt, arch closer to him and wish to dive right back into that kiss.

That kiss that not only made her want to strip down here and now, but that also gave her visions of waking up late on lazy Sunday mornings, drinking lemonade on the porch swing on summer nights, unwrapping presents on Christmas Eve, getaway weekends, stolen workweek lunch breaks, holding hands in the movie theater—all with Luke. Only him.

Crazy. Definitely.

That's what she wanted and that was definitely what she was getting.

Shouldn't she be imagining things like various naked body parts, the different positions she wanted him in and deciding if she wanted to go down on him or have him go down on her first?

But no. It was sweet, happily-ever-after, forever stuff she was thinking about.

Kat straightened her clothes, pressed her lips together and decided that the White Horse Museum was by far the best tourist stop in all of Nebraska.

"You were right," she told Luke. "I don't want to stop touching now that I've started."

"We better get back to the RV," he said.

She nodded. "Definitely. Don't want to stay in one place too long." Especially a place without a comfortable horizontal surface.

"Definitely." Luke gave her one last, long look, grabbed her hand, then pivoted on his heel and headed for the front door.

"Give me a minute." She pulled her hand from his.

He looked back at her. "Not long," he said simply.

"Not long." She dragged in a deep, long breath and ran a hand through her hair as she watched the museum's screen door bump shut behind him. She knew exactly what her first gesture would be to show Luke how she felt, but she had to get some control.

She didn't want to scare him off.

"What are you doing working here?" Kat asked Zach, who was grinning madly.

"I'm going to the community college in O'Neill but I help my mom out here once in awhile."

"What are you studying?"

He chuckled. "Diesel mechanics."

When she realized he was serious, she shook her head. "I hope you're as good at that as you are with relationship advice."

"Oh, even better."

Now that was saying something.

Luke was in the kitchenette when Kat stepped through the door into the RV. He'd just downed a bottle of water, trying to cool his libido and calm his system some. He felt ready to jump out of his skin and wanted to regain some control before she was here with him, in this tiny space, alone, being—*her.*

She'd rocked his senses before, but that kiss in the museum, so soon after realizing that she was the one person he hadn't tried to be close to and yet was the one who wanted him most, made him want to...*devour* her.

He didn't want to scare her off.

But she definitely didn't seem scared as she stepped through the side door, locked it behind her and then leaned over the front seat to hit the front locks.

Then she came toward him.

As she got closer, her breathing changed. She took a deep breath, which seemed to hitch slightly, then puffed out a long stream of air. "I hope you're not in a hurry to hit the road," she said.

He shook his head. "I don't think there's any way I could concentrate on the road."

"Oh?"

When she stopped in front of him, he lifted his hand, running the tip of his finger over her lips, her chin and down her throat until he came to the edge of the tank top, then he drew his finger back and forth along the neckline. "No way."

She licked her lips. "Good."

"God, Kat, every time I get within two feet of you I want you so damned much I can hardly think. Then that kiss—" He leaned in, determined to pick right up where they'd left off.

But she ducked.

Instead, she took his hand and lifted his index finger from the neckline of her shirt to her mouth. She sucked the tip into the hot wetness of her mouth, running her tongue over the pad of his finger.

He pulled in a quick breath as pulses of lust shot straight

to his cock. As he slid his finger free, the tip wet and glistening, he groaned and she leaned in and brought it back into her mouth, sucking hard. She curled her tongue under it and he slid along the silky flesh so similar to other places he wanted to slide. Then she took his wrist, pulled his finger out, and licked from the base of his wrist to the tip of his middle finger.

Just as he was about to reach for her with his other hand, she went to her knees, her hands skimming down his sides, over his hips and then around to the front of his jeans where she cupped him with both hands.

Holy—

Wordlessly she ran her hand up and down the length of the evident bulge behind his fly as she cupped his balls with the other hand, squeezing just enough to make him nearly lose his mind.

"Kat—" But he lost the rest of the words when she popped the snap and eased his zipper down.

She had his jeans whisked down his thighs and his erection free of his boxers in the blink of an eye. His cock strained toward her as she returned to the pattern of stroking, cupping and squeezing but now she was able to wrap her hand around his shaft, skin on skin, as she pumped him. Luke let his head fall back, a deep groan coming from what felt like his soul.

"Come here," she said softly. She stood, her hand still on his cock, and gestured toward the chair right behind him.

He was in no position to refuse her anything. The woman knew a thing or two about hand jobs. "Hang on." He reluctantly removed her hand and quickly kicked his shoes, jeans and boxers off so he didn't trip himself and cause a concussion—or worse. He'd hate to black out and miss one second of this.

"T-shirt too," she said huskily, running her hands up underneath the soft cotton like she had in the museum. This time, though, she took the whole shirt up, pushing it over his shoulders.

He yanked it over his head and tossed it in the direction of the bench by the table.

"Now you," he said.

But she gave him a sexy smile and shook her head, giving him a gentle shove into the chair. "I have a better idea."

As he sat, he reached for her. "There's no better idea than me getting deep inside you, babe."

She dodged his hand. "Oh, I don't know." She leaned over him, her hands on his shoulders, her breasts at eye level.

He turned his head just enough and sucked on a nipple through her shirt. She gasped and ran her hands down his arms, leaning closer. He could smell her hair, feel her heat and he wanted to grab her and strip her down.

She had her fingers linked with his though, so he settled—for now—for licking the soft, sweet skin along the side of her neck.

"Luke," she breathed.

He loved that almost helpless sound, like she couldn't think of anything but his name.

"This is going to be so good," she whispered.

"I know." He started to reach for her but—couldn't. He tugged and found that his wrists were held together. Behind his back.

Handcuffed.

"Kat?"

She leaned back, a triumphant, sexy smile on her face. "Yeah?"

With disbelief he tugged again. He was cuffed all right. And he didn't want to get free. "Okay. So now what?"

She pushed her hair back away from her face and let her eyes roam over him. He was as naked as he could get, as aroused as he could get, and completely—well, mostly anyway—at her mercy.

"This is all about you, Luke. How you feel, what you want, what you need. You're not going to think about me or doing anything for me or making me feel anything. You're just going to enjoy."

His cock throbbed with the unspoken promise there, but more, his heart pounded.

He stared at her. She'd claimed that he didn't let people do things for him, that his focus was always on everyone else, because he wanted them to need him.

Well, he *needed* her now and having her focus completely on him, with no expectations of him in return, made him feel...vulnerable...but also humble, and hot, and a bunch of things he couldn't even describe.

She didn't seem to be expecting words though because she knelt between his knees and took hold of him again, gliding up and down slowly at first, then pumping him with a little more pressure.

"God," he groaned. "You're going to make me come like this."

"Not quite like this," she murmured.

Luke watched as she leaned forward, then licked the head of his cock, then sucked the tip into her mouth as she had his finger.

"Kat," he groaned. "I want—"

He had no idea what he was going to say though because she took him deeper, stroking his base with one hand, massaging his balls with the other.

The heat and wetness were nearly too much, but then she sucked and Luke couldn't help tightening his glutes and thrusting a little deeper.

She'd lift her head slightly, lick, then slide down, his cock gliding between her lips, until he was deep. Then she'd start over.

It was heaven, pure and simple. No woman had ever felt like this. Watching her head move over him, feeling her pulling on him with her mouth and hand, it was almost as if she was enjoying it as much as he was. But when he lifted again, pressing deeper, and she moaned, he knew it was true. Holy crap, a woman who enjoyed giving head.

She really was perfect.

A few minutes later he felt the tightening deep in his balls.

"Kat, babe, I'm really going to come," he rasped. He wanted to be inside her. He had no trouble believing he could get it back up for her shortly, but he wasn't going to make it this time and she'd better—

She wouldn't move away though, even when he nudged her with his foot, and as he felt his climax start and quickly build she kept working him until he exploded, spilling into her mouth.

He slumped back in the chair. "Unbelievable," he breathed.

She sat back and grinned at him. "Yeah," she agreed simply.

"You were, are—"

"I know, unbelievable, right?" she asked. She stood, her hands running up his thighs, then up over his chest, sighing. Then she bent over and kissed the base of his throat, reaching back to unlock him. She turned and bent to grab his clothes, then tossed them on his lap. "This is definitely the best tourist stop in Nebraska."

Kat settled into the passenger seat and strapped her seat belt on even though Luke was in the bathroom cleaning up and getting dressed.

She took a long drink from the bottle of water she'd grabbed from the fridge, hoping to cool off some. She felt like she had a fever. It wasn't like she'd never given a blow job before but—wow. She'd never liked it quite that much.

"Seriously?" he asked as he put one long leg over the console between their seats and dropped into the driver's seat.

She took a long drink of water and turned to look at him. For a moment she lost her breath. He was so sexy and for a moment she could remember every detail of how he felt, looked, sounded—and tasted. And frankly, she wanted more. She felt herself blush. "What?" she asked as if she had no idea what he was talking about.

"That—" he gestured toward the back of the RV, "—and now we're just gonna start driving again?"

"What did you want to do instead?" she asked innocently.

"Well, I'd really like to put my mouth between your legs," he said as he started the engine.

Heat rushed through her and she had to concentrate on not fanning herself.

"Then I'd like to put my cock—"

"Okay," she interrupted. "So you're feeling cheated? You seemed to think that was a good idea at the beginning. And in the middle. And, oh yeah, at the end." She gave him a little smile she knew had to look wicked.

He didn't smile back but his gaze was hot and she couldn't look away.

"Oh, it was a fantastic idea. And let me just be clear—anytime you want to get on your knees in front of me, please feel free. I'm just feeling like there wasn't nearly enough naked-and-moaning time on your part."

"I'm fine." She tilted the water bottle back again and squeezed her thighs together. "We're even from last night." She'd be even better if she could steal a few minutes back there with her travel vibrator, but she could handle this.

"This isn't over," he said, but he shifted the RV into drive and pulled out onto the highway.

She knew it wasn't over.

She could barely sit next to him without thinking about how great he felt in her hands and mouth and imagining how great he'd feel deep inside her, thrusting over and over—

"I'll be right back." She almost took a nosedive trying to scramble over the arm of her chair, the tote bag she had right behind her seat and the console.

"You're going back there *now*?" he asked. "Without me?"

"Bathroom. I'll be right back."

She grabbed her overnight bag from the closet in the bedroom, rummaged for the tiny vibrator she kept in her bag—and yes, used from time to time when she traveled. She was a doctor and knew that sexual release was an important part of overall balance and health. It was a fantastic stress-reliever. She dated and had human-to-human sexual relationships too, but sometimes all a girl really needed was a quick orgasm to get a good night's sleep.

The little purple plastic toy only needed an AA battery and fit perfectly in her travel bag. With it clutched tightly in her hand she shut herself in the bathroom. Leaning back against the door she closed her eyes and thought of Luke. How he looked naked, how he felt and sounded as he slid in and out of her mouth, as he came, and then how he said he wanted to put his mouth between her legs. Then there was last night—

Strangely, memories of his hand between her legs flashed past quickly, moving to the feel of him just holding her in bed through the night. And it did nothing to quell the lust.

With one foot up on the stool and her skirt hiked up, she flipped on the vibrator. She always had good orgasms with her vibrator and with the added thoughts of Luke she came quickly and surprisingly hard.

In person, with him using more than his fingers, she'd probably last three seconds.

Several minutes later she was still trying to calm her heartrate. She still wanted more.

A lot more. Soon.

She cleaned up, tucked her friend away in her bag and checked her makeup and hair in the mirror in the bedroom. A quick reapplication of some eye shadow and lipstick, a ruffle to the hair and she was ready to head back to the front.

Feeling a little more relaxed and in control, she reclaimed her seat.

But as Luke shifted in his seat to look over at her, she felt even more aware of him than she had before the vibrator. Want

thumped through her like the bas
the wetness between her legs simp
to the orgasm.

At this rate, she was going to l
she could sit next to him comfort
sleep with him next to her for anot

"You okay?" he asked.

She looked at him sharply. "Of
Because of him.

"You look weird."

She did not. She'd just looked
fine. "I'm fine."

"No, really, you look...hot."

She frowned at him. "Knock
fifteen minutes ago. You don't have

He grinned. "I didn't mean it a
always look hot. But," he said qu
mouth to respond, "I mean you loo
need more AC?" He leaned forwa
without waiting for a response from

"I'm fine," she repeated again.
forehead and felt that it was a bit
too. And she was probably flushed.
person. So could lust.

"You're not sick, are you?"

"Why would you think I'm sic
blow job. Who did that when they h

"You just look hot. And you
bathroom. I was just putting two an

"Well, obviously there are ot
things. I'm fine. Drop it."

"Reasons like what? I'm just co

"The only thing I need is—" She
shut up, but instead she trailed off.

"Is what?" Luke asked.

He did
what she
uncomforta
sex. The o

"What
pants off."

He sta
the center

He pu
highway
oncoming
time too."

"Oh,
this time."

Screw
for that m
thought s
could ign
fantasies.

Screw

Luke'
thirty mi
but it mig

"Thir
at every
frustrate

"Hon
time and
while."

Her
wait thirt

"Wha

"I go

She

He

coughed again and said, "Battery-powered friend?"

Okay, maybe he hadn't heard the *again* part. "My travel buddy," she said easily. "Never leave home without it."

"You're killing me here," he muttered. He shifted in his seat. "What do you mean *again*?"

So he'd heard that after all. "Um, nothing." She squirmed in her own seat and looked over at the speedometer. "Sixty-five? That's it? Really?"

"Have you seen the size of this thing?"

She couldn't help it. It was her super-turned-on-rushing-hormone state, she knew, but everything was starting to sound suggestive. She giggled, slapped her hand over her mouth, but giggled again.

He was smiling when he looked at her. "What?"

"Actually I *have* seen the size of that thing and, wow, loved every inch."

He groaned and chuckled at the same time. "Girl, you're *seriously* killing me here. We have to get somewhere that it's safe to park this beast."

"I know, I'm sorry." She really tried to stop laughing. She pressed her lips together. But it wasn't working. She snorted again.

"Kat," he said warningly.

"Sorry." She raised her hands when he looked suspicious. "Really. I don't mean to."

After a pause he said, "You're thinking about it, aren't you?"

"What?" Feeling bold and brazen she leaned onto the arm of her seat. "Your cock? Oh yeah."

Luke choked and pressed a little harder on the gas pedal. "I've never heard you use that word."

"No, probably not. We're not usually in settings where that's appropriate."

"I knew you wouldn't be shy about all of this though."

"What's that mean?" she asked, seriously wanting to know.

"You're up front with everything. I knew you'd be a dirty-talker." He gave her a sexy smile. "I like it."

She thought about it. She wasn't necessarily *not* a dirty-talker. But she hadn't really been with men who made her feel like doing it. She hadn't used graphic language to tell them what she wanted. She didn't use it to turn them on. They'd all been turned on enough.

But now, looking at Luke and thinking of every dirty word she knew, she wanted to tell him exactly what she wanted because she knew he'd deliver. Every detail. That was who he was. Conscientious to a fault. She almost laughed again. His tendency to always make sure everyone else was taken care of was going to get him some great dirty talk and some hot sex.

She also wanted to get him beyond turned on. She wanted him wild, out of control, crazy.

Yeah, she could talk dirty. Definitely.

"What did you mean by *again*?" he asked.

"Again?"

"When you said you would go in back and use your little friend *again*?"

"Nothing. Just slipped out."

"Kat?" He looked over at her. "Did you use your vibrator when you went back there?"

For all the good it had done her.

"Yeah, so?"

"So, I think that's pretty fucking hot."

A flash of heat shot through her stomach and her eyes widened. "I haven't heard you talk dirty before today either." And, God help her, she really liked it.

"We're not usually in settings where that's appropriate," he said, repeating her words back to her. "What do you think?"

"Of the dirty talk?" she asked.

"Yeah."

"I think that earlier when you said you wanted to put your mouth between my legs I almost came right then and there."

"Hell," he muttered as he seemed to be making himself concentrate on the road. "I'm never going to make it another twenty-some miles."

She grinned, totally full of herself suddenly. She leaned back, propped her feet up on the dashboard and said, "It'll be worth the wait."

He glanced over, his eyes lingering on the bare leg revealed by her skirt riding up. "I have no doubt."

That was nice. The whole thing was really hot and for better or worse they were going to have RV-rattling sex pretty soon, but she truly felt like Luke was anticipating this, appreciating it even. She wasn't sure she'd ever had sex with a man who actually felt like it was...monumental in any way. Okay, maybe monumental was exaggerating things, but she still felt like Luke thought this was important. And it was nice. Really, really nice.

She rolled her eyes at that. Only Luke Hamilton would manage to pull off *hot* and *nice* at the same time.

"Let's talk about something else, to keep your mind off your cock for a while." She emphasized *cock* because she knew it would get a groan from him.

It did.

She really liked turning him on.

"My mind is more on your pussy than my cock, but okay."

Damn. She'd never in her life imagined Luke Hamilton would use the word *pussy*.

"What's a safe topic?" she asked.

He took a deep breath. "Okay." He seemed to be thinking hard. "What's your favorite food?"

She laughed. "That's the best you can come up with?"

"Sorry. My brain seems intent on replaying our last half hour or so, rather than coming up with interesting repartee."

Instantly her brain also replayed the highlights. Of course, all of it had been highlights.

"Okay, um..." She cleared her throat. "Of all foods of all

kinds I'd have to say manicotti."

"Your favorite—as in you'd do anything for it?"

She gave him a sly look. "Maybe."

"Might have to think about putting that on The Camelot menu."

She laughed. "Marc makes great manicotti."

He frowned. "When has Marc made you manicotti?"

"When he wants to get me to do something." She said it teasingly, really liking that he sounded jealous.

"Well, no more manicotti from anyone but me."

"What if I'm—"

"No."

She grinned. Yep, she really liked him jealous. "Even if I'm—"

"No. In fact, no one should be doing anything to get you to do stuff. Except me."

"Can you make manicotti?"

He hesitated there and she laughed. "So how are you going to get me to do stuff?"

Luke gave her a cocky grin. "I can be very...charming...when I need to be."

"Yes, I know," she murmured. That was one word for it anyway. It was safe to say that Luke could probably get her to do anything he wanted and it wouldn't take charm.

He did have it in spades too. Though it wasn't his charm per se that drew her, she did love watching him work a room.

Watching Luke in the dining room of his restaurant was truly a sight to behold. He was warm, sincere, taking time to talk to anyone and everyone who wanted to chat, taking compliments in stride, publicly acknowledging his staff's hard work. He was so genuinely happy when he was there that it was obvious he'd found his calling.

It was strangely sexy.

The Camelot was more than a restaurant, more than a way

to make a living. It was his way of taking care of the community he called home. There was no doubt the Camelot was a staple in Justice and the surrounding area.

It was something that would become a family business, passing from Luke and Marc to their children and beyond.

Suddenly she couldn't take a deep breath.

Damn. She sat up a little straighter and concentrated on moving air in and out of her lungs for a moment.

Oh, boy.

The thought of Luke's children had choked her up.

"Kat?"

"I'm fine. I'm just—" *Madly in love with you.*

"Kat, there's a car in the ditch up there."

There sure was. Every other thought fleeing in the face of the potential emergency, Kat was already unbuckled by the time Luke parked the RV along the side of the highway.

Chapter Seven

"There's someone in the driver's seat," she called over her shoulder.

"I'm right behind you, babe."

Her doctor-on-the-scene-of-an-accident adrenaline was pumping, but she still noticed and loved the *babe.* "Call 911," she told him, forcing herself to concentrate.

"You got it."

The decline into the ditch was sharp and Kat's flip-flops skidded in the dirt as she headed for the driver's side. "Ma'am?" she called as she knocked on the window. "Can you hear me?"

The woman turned toward her slowly. Kat could see blood on her forehead and could tell, even through the window, that she was dazed.

Kat could hear Luke talking to the dispatcher, giving them their location. "Tell them she's conscious," she called up to him. "Only one person in the car."

Luke gave the report while Kat pulled up on the door handle. It opened and she reached in to steady the woman.

"I think I know what happened," Luke said, skidding down the hill to Kat's side.

"Yeah?"

"There's a really dead deer a little ways up."

Kat wrinkled her nose. "That makes sense." There was always wildlife to contend with on the rural highways in Nebraska. Deer, obviously, caused more damage than raccoon or pheasants though. They could cause a hell of an impact and if the woman had tried to avoid the collision or had overcompensated after hitting the deer, that would explain how the car ended up in the ditch.

"So, what do you want me to do?" Luke asked.

"Just stay close." She'd been assessing the woman's breathing pattern and visually inspecting for other injuries. It seemed that the cut on her head was the only bloody area, which was good. The woman lifted her hand to her head—movement was a good sign. "I'm Kat. I'm a doctor. I can help, okay?"

The woman nodded, then winced. "My head hurts."

"I need a clean cloth, Luke," Kat said over her shoulder. "What's your name?" she asked the woman.

"Sandra," the woman answered softly.

"Do you have pain anywhere else, Sandra?" She would later if she didn't now, but the shock might be masking anything serious.

"Just my head. I think."

"Do you know what day it is?"

She did.

"Do you know where you are?"

She did.

Luke pressed a clean dish towel into Kat's hand and she applied it with gentle pressure to Sandra's head to help with the bleeding. "Can you hold this up here?" Kat asked her.

Sandra lifted her hand and was able to keep the cloth against the gash.

"Okay, so far, so good. I'm just going to do a little poking, see if there's anything else going on to worry about right now," Kat told her.

Sandra nodded her understanding and Kat ran her fingers over the woman's ribs, collarbones, neck and down her back. "Everything feel okay?"

"Yes. I just feel a little beat-up. Nothing horrible."

"Then let's get you out of here and we'll go from there."

Sandra was able to unbuckle her belt, slide to the edge of

her seat and swing her legs out. She stood, with help from Kat, and then Luke took over. He nudged Kat out of the way, looped his arm around Sandra's waist, talking softly to her.

"I have friends who cuss every time they see a dead deer," he told her. "They go out weekend after weekend hunting and never get a thing, but then nice ladies like you are just driving innocently down the road and *bam*, suddenly one's right there in front of you."

Kat smiled and shook her head as she followed them up the side of the ditch. Luke had a gift for making people feel better. She loved that about him.

Among other things. Many, many other things.

Luke helped Sandra into the RV where Kat wrapped her in a blanket to help with any shock symptoms that might set in, checked the cut on her head where the bleeding had slowed some and then gave her some water.

"I'd give you something for your headache but I better leave that to the paramedics," Kat told her. "They should be here soon."

"Rolland is only about eight miles," Sandra told them. "I know everyone on that crew."

Kat smiled. "Are they volunteers?" They were in most small towns, including Justice.

They chatted as they waited. Kat wanted to keep Sandra alert and awake. The conversation also allowed Kat to judge Sandra's mental status. If she hesitated to find words or couldn't think of something obvious, like the names of her children or what she'd been doing that morning, Kat would know there was a concussion that would need further assessment.

The ambulance siren wailed in the distance. While some of the symptoms of concussion could show up later, Kat felt confident that Sandra had a bump on the head versus a serious head injury. Thank God. She wasn't sure she could handle another head-injured patient right now.

Her stomach dipped as she was thrust back into thoughts

of what a mess her life and work at home were. She stretched to her feet keeping a smile in place.

"You're going to be fine, Sandra." She reached to help the other woman up.

"Thanks to you." Sandra gave her a weak smile as she stood.

Kat lifted the corner of the towel from Sandra's head. "The bleeding's slowed but you're going to need stitches. And a lot of headache medication." She squeezed Sandra's shoulders. "Could have been a lot worse."

"Still, you didn't have to stop. Who knows how long it would have taken for someone else to come along."

"Well, I'm glad we were there when you needed us."

"We're happy to help," Luke added. He held the RV door open.

They stepped out as the ambulance pulled up.

"Sandy!" The first person out of the back of the rig was a woman in her mid to late thirties. "My mom is going to freak out."

Sandra smiled as the younger woman hugged her. "I'm okay."

"You're bleeding."

"But I'm fine."

"Really, she has no signs of concussion, she's alert and oriented, she has no other apparent injuries, but a spinal x-ray would be a good idea."

The younger woman turned to her. "Who are you?"

Kat offered her hand. "Dr. Kat Dayton. I practice in Justice and Alliance. We came upon Sandra's accident and were the ones that called it in."

"Oh, thank you!"

Kat suddenly found herself enfolded in the woman's exuberant hug. Over her shoulder Kat looked at Sandra who smiled and shrugged. "This is my niece Lisa."

"Hi, Lisa." Kat awkwardly patted the other woman's back.

"I'm so glad you were here."

"Me too." It wasn't like they'd saved her life. Still, Kat appreciated being appreciated. Even more now, after everything with Tom.

And just like that she was back to thinking about that. She tried to swallow and managed it without choking.

Screw the whole thing, she thought stubbornly. They didn't want her? Didn't need her? Didn't trust her? Screw them.

That was her new motto. The motto that would give Luke heart palpitations if he heard it applied to his beloved hometown.

And to think that two weeks ago she thought the worst thing Luke would find out about her was that she wasn't a part of the newly formed women's book club.

He wouldn't like that much either.

Sandra was led off to the ambulance by one of the male paramedics. He attached a blood pressure cuff, checked out her cut and made her laugh. It was the last that was likely most important at the moment.

Lisa turned back to Kat, her eyes filled with unshed tears. "You have to come to town. My mom is going to insist on meeting you. And Dr. Haken might have some questions."

Kat knew that having family involved in an accident, even a minor one, could be scary, but there was no way that Dr. Haken needed Kat's report.

"Oh, we were just on our way by. We had to stop but we have to—"

"We'd love to come into town and meet everyone," Luke said, looping his arm around Kat's shoulders. "Any chance there's a place we could park the RV and get some lunch?"

"We have a great camping area." Lisa's eyes brightened and she smiled. "I know the perfect thing for lunch. Oh, this is great. We're having a big family reunion over the next few days. You have to come to tonight's barbecue too! I'll call Carl and tell him you'll be at the park overnight."

"A family—" Kat started. "Oh, no, we can't—"

"That sounds great. I love barbecues."

Of course he did. Anything to prolong this trip. If she didn't know better she would have thought Luke had planned the deer running into Sandy. Not that she minded prolonging the trip now. It was completely chicken, of course, but the longer they stayed away from Justice, the longer it would be until Luke found out the whole story about Tom. If his ignorance could last until Tom stabilized and was back home and recovered, she'd consider it a favor from fate.

Tom's recovery wouldn't happen that fast, if it happened at all—Kat forced herself to swallow again—but the longer Luke went without knowing, the better for her heart.

She wished she were confident enough to just be satisfied that she'd done her best and that it didn't matter what everyone thought. But it did matter. And it especially mattered what Luke thought.

Lisa stood grinning at them and Kat realized what this was—the chance for these people to show their appreciation, to say thanks. That was important, she knew.

"I love barbecues too," she finally said.

"Great! We'll see you in town." Lisa turned and joined the rest of the crew.

"I didn't think it was possible," Luke said as they made their way to the RV.

"What? That we'd get invited to a barbecue by a bunch of strangers in a town we didn't even mean to visit?" she asked.

He took her arm and stopped her, turning her to face him. "That I could want you even more."

She felt her mouth fall open.

"I've never really seen you work before," he said. "You were in charge, decisive, knew exactly what to do, how to do it. Very sexy."

He was sincere. She could see it in his eyes. She smiled up at him. "You weren't too bad yourself. You made her smile, you were right there with whatever we needed."

"I'll always be there with whatever you need, Kat," he said, his voice lower now as he moved in close.

God she wanted that. She bit her lip on saying so, though. She also resisted asking, *Are you sure? What if Tom Martin doesn't get better?* She gave him a smile that she knew was wobbly. "When we decided to pull over and park the RV for a while, this wasn't what I had in mind."

He gave her the sexy half smile. "Babe, I don't care who or what's around. Your mouth—both what you've said and what you've done with it—got us here. This is going to happen before that RV leaves this town."

"What...exactly?" She wanted to hear it. Once it was out loud he couldn't take it back. No matter what other phone calls might come in. To either of them.

It might have been completely selfish, but she wanted—needed—to make love with Luke at least once. And she was afraid that it wouldn't happen if he heard what was going on back home.

Right there was the problem she'd been worried about all along. She wanted unconditional love from him. She wanted him to want her, to be with her, no matter what went wrong—even if it was her fault.

She did not, however, want to test that quite so soon.

"I'm going to strip you down," Luke said. "Kiss every inch of your body and then make love to you until you never want to be anywhere but in my arms."

She was already there. And she wanted to cry.

She pressed her lips together and nodded. Heat flared in his eyes.

He looked at her for another heartbeat then said, "I think the barbecue can wait." He turned away before she could say anything and called out, "Lisa, I need directions to the campground."

"Stay on the highway until you come to the lumberyard on

the left. Turn on the road just past it, go about half a mile and you'll see it. I gave Carl a heads-up that you're coming and not to charge you a thing."

"Oh, no, we'll pay to stay. That's not negotiable," Luke told her.

"Please. We want to do this for you."

Kat could see it mattered to Lisa, and she trusted Luke would understand too. It was important for people to feel that they'd properly expressed their appreciation. Sometimes it was hard to do that. This was a way for Lisa and Sandy to feel like they'd adequately thanked Kat and Luke for their help. While neither of them would ever expect it, they did understand.

She was right. Luke nodded and said, "Okay, thanks."

The smile Lisa gave them was proof that it was the right thing to do.

"The barbecue starts at four. You can hang out at the park, or feel free to come downtown. There's some shopping and Marcy's café has great lunch specials."

"That sounds perfect," Luke assured her. "We appreciate it. I'm glad to have a chance to get out from behind the wheel."

He didn't even glance at Kat, but she knew the comment was directed at her. She could only imagine what he thought he was going to be doing out from behind that wheel.

Her body—and heart—had a few ideas.

The town of Rolland, Nebraska was only ten minutes from where they'd found Sandra and was small enough that the park was easy to find. There were four other RVs already parked and the doors banged open as Luke eased to a stop. Several lawn chairs had been grouped together under a tree a few yards from the parking area, and Luke and Kat were greeted by waves and grins from the people gathered there.

"Friends of yours?" Kat asked Luke.

He chuckled. "No, but it looks like they want to be."

A black extended-cab pickup drew up next to them, honking. The woman in the driver's seat was also waving madly and grinning, the man next to her climbed out with a huge cardboard box.

"You go first," Kat said, eyeing the couple with trepidation.

"No way. We're in this together."

He got out and rounded the front of the RV as another car pulled in, also honking. Oh boy, this was going to be interesting. Kat took her time getting out of the RV. Meeting new people sometimes made her pulse race. Yes, she was the one who did her hair and makeup and she dressed the way she did on purpose. She always stood out, and people's reactions were fascinating to her when she could be detached about it. But every once in a while she flashed back to high school and felt self-conscious and, yes, weird.

She watched as first one woman, then another, hugged Luke and the man shook his hand. Others from the lawn chairs started in their direction.

There was a huge sign hung on the fence surrounding the tennis courts that read *Haywood Family Reunion.*

Yeah, definitely interesting. They either thought she and Luke were some long-lost cousins, or they were crazy. Or both.

"I can't tell you how happy we are to meet you!" the woman from the pickup was telling Luke. She peered around him to Kat. "This must be Dr. Kat."

Luke turned to her with a big smile, brought her forward and wrapped his arm around her shoulders. "It is. The gorgeous lifesaver herself."

Kat met the woman's gaze directly. Her eyes were full of admiration—in spite of the streak of blue in Kat's hair—and Kat felt the tension in her body loosen a bit.

"Lisa called us from the ambulance, told us everything you did for Sandy and that you're staying here tonight," the woman said. "I'm Sandy's sister, Donna. This is Michael."

The woman from the car enfolded Kat in a huge hug. "I'm Connie. Another sister. I can't believe that this all happened when we're here for the reunion and everything. But thank God you were there."

"It was no problem," Kat insisted. It hadn't been. She'd given Sandra a cloth to put against the gash in her forehead. It wasn't like she snatched her from the jaws of death.

Kat mentally shook herself. She had to quit thinking like that. There was nothing she could do from here and worrying about it was only going to steal from her time with Luke.

"Where do you want this?" Michael asked his wife, nodding at the box in his arms.

"Over here. We can get things laid out before everyone else gets here." They headed for the picnic tables at the edge of the grass.

Kat turned wide eyes on Luke. "Everyone else?"

He shrugged. "Family reunion barbecue."

"We were thrilled to hear you were sticking around," Connie said, gathering her bags and starting after her sister. "And that you haven't had lunch."

Kat gripped Luke's shirt as he started to follow. "We're not really *sticking around.*"

"We told them we would hang out for the barbecue, remember?" he said, curling his fingers into her shoulder. He again started in the direction of the picnic tables, tugging her with him.

"What happened to the wild RV sex?" Kat asked for his ears only.

Maybe she could entice him away. This family reunion lunch had the makings of something that could drive her nuts and take hours out of their schedule. She was great one on one, especially in the ER where she didn't spend much time with the patients, in the hospital where she had the definite advantage of being in a position of authority and in the Justice clinic where she'd known everyone her whole life. But in large crowds, full of strangers, she was definitely not her best.

He stopped and turned to look down at her as his mouth

tipped up. "If it makes you feel any better, I can't stop thinking about how you look and feel and sound with my hand between your legs and how you look and feel and sound on your knees in front of me—"

"Okay," she interrupted before taking a big, shaky breath.

"I promise we'll get to the wild RV sex."

"When?"

"I can honestly tell you that if you head back to the RV and tell me that you're getting naked, I will—without question—get rid of some of the nicest people I've met in a long time."

Kat's gaze went from his face to those nice people and then back again. She sighed. These people were sincerely happy to see her, were accepting her into their group and wanted to feed her. And they didn't even know her. They wanted a chance to show her their appreciation.

She wasn't a total bitch. At least not usually.

"I guess I could eat something first."

"I think Donna would be completely devastated if you didn't," he agreed.

He threaded his fingers with hers and held on as they joined Donna, Michael and Connie. And Kat let him. She didn't pull away. In fact, she leaned into him a little as they stood and chatted, watching their hosts and hostesses lay out paper plates and plastic silverware, along with container after container of salads and side dishes. Five grills had been pulled into a half circle, and burgers, hot dogs and chicken breasts were placed over the heat. Lemonade, iced tea and beer were poured and everyone talked, laughed and included Kat and Luke in the commotion.

Kat didn't let them get separated though. Luke was the kind of guy to talk to anyone about anything. He could have been pulled into any of the smaller groups and fit right in. Kat wasn't as good at that. She was fine in Justice where she knew everyone and knew what to expect from everyone. Not every person in Justice was a fan of hers the way they were of Luke's, but she knew who to avoid.

Here, it was a free-for-all. It was possible that they would all think she was weird.

Well, no, probably not. She'd "saved Sandra's life" so that had to get her a few points. Still she wished she'd checked her eye makeup before she came out.

Instead, she stuck close to Luke. Which wasn't exactly a hardship. He felt great, smelled great, looked great, sounded great.

It was all just great.

About an hour into the party, Kat had gotten Luke within ten feet of the RV and had high hopes for getting him away from the family reunion, when Sandra showed up with her husband.

"Sandy!" One of her many cousins rushed forward. "Are you okay?"

"Better than the deer." Sandra gave the woman a small smile. "I'm fine. My headache is even better."

"Oh, my goodness, I almost peed when Lisa called and said you were at the hospital!"

Kat fought a smile and she heard Luke choke a little.

Sandra hugged the woman back and then turned to Kat and Luke. "This is my husband, Dennis. Dennis, this is Luke and Kat, the ones who got me out of the ditch."

Dennis grabbed Luke's hand, pumping it up and down, then turned and hugged Kat. "Thank you so much. I don't know what to say. Can I get you something?" He noticed their empty glasses. "More beer? A margarita?"

The empty plates and glasses had been working in her favor since she was trying to convince Luke the party was over. For them anyway. But Kat could tell Dennis desperately wanted to give them something in exchange for their part in Sandy's drama.

"I'd love some tea," Kat said.

"That's my girl," Luke whispered. Then he said to Dennis, "A beer would be great."

"You haven't tried my brownies yet, Luke." The woman

approaching with the huge plate of dessert was one of Sandy's sisters-in-law, Peggy.

"You're right, I haven't," Luke agreed. "Dennis, I'll have tea too. Beer doesn't go so well with chocolate."

Peggy's eyes brightened and her smile was huge as he chose the biggest brownie on the plate, and Kat wanted to kiss him. Luke didn't like chocolate. But he knew this woman wanted to cater to them for what they'd done and he rolled right along with it.

Kat and Luke ended up seated with Sandy, Dennis, Peggy and her husband and they each ended up having two glasses of tea while Luke ate two brownies, earning him even more beaming smiles from Peggy.

"Tell me everything," she said to Kat. "Sandy never complains, so she could be bleeding internally and never tell us."

Kat smiled at Sandra, who gave her an apologetic shrug. Kat didn't mind. She was blessed with family and friends who loved her and would be similarly concerned if her car ended up in a ditch. She glanced at Luke. He was one of them. He would be at her bedside in the hospital if she was ever there as a patient and he'd want to know all the details of what had happened and her medical status. He'd stay in the waiting room all night during a surgery if he had to and he'd personally see to it that she had any book, magazine, snack or other essential she needed.

She'd known all of that deep down for as long as she'd known Luke but for some stupid reason she was suddenly choked up by it.

Like most people, she took it for granted that she had people who cared about her and she realized that Luke was one of the people who cared most. She did believe that.

And if he got married to someone else, some of that would have to change.

That thought seemed to come out of the blue and hit her directly in the chest.

Dammit.

They'd always be friends, but it would be less appropriate for him to sit by her bedside, bring her flowers, and...kiss her.

Crap.

She'd only kissed him a few times in her life but she would really miss it if he was no longer free to do it.

Shaking her head and focusing on the people around her, she recapped the scene of Sandra's accident. "She'll be just fine. Her head might ache on and off for a couple of days, but she'll have no residual effects."

"Oh, thank God!" Peggy gushed. She turned to Sandra and hugged her. "Honey, you have to be more careful."

"These things happen," Sandra murmured but she seemed to gladly return Peggy's hug.

Again, Kat was choked up at the sight and filled with a strong desire to hug Luke. And be hugged back.

His future wife wouldn't like a lot of hugging between them either, she was sure.

"You have to stay," Peggy insisted as Kat tuned back in.

"It sounds like a fun time," Luke said. He turned to face Kat. "What do you say?"

"You want to stay?"

"The party sounds like a great time."

"The party—"

"We planned the family reunion this weekend because there's a big annual celebration going on this week too. They're using the party tonight as a fund-raiser."

How had she missed all of that? Fussing about Luke's future wife.

But it was a party and Luke was an even bigger sucker for fund-raisers than he was for barbecues. They would be staying for a while. Which meant they'd be together longer. Which sounded great.

"It sounds great," she agreed.

"We'll be sure you have anything you need." Sandra said, sitting up straighter and seeming more animated than they'd seen her.

They'd stay the night. All at once, Kat's heartbeat sped up. Tonight it wouldn't be like last night. As much as she'd loved sleeping in his arms, she wanted more. She knew somehow that spending the night with Luke tonight would change her life forever.

It sounded dramatic, but she was certain of it.

"Okay." Luke stood and patted his stomach. "We'll be there. I've got to get away from this food and get some physical activity right now though. Where do the festivities happen?"

He didn't look at her but Kat had all kinds of ideas about what kind of physical activity she was interested in.

"Oh, right here in the park," Peggy said. "Just over the hill. The band will be in the pavilion and the movie will be shown up against the wall of the equipment shed by the baseball diamond."

"Wonderful." And Luke seemed to truly think that it was. He was grinning at the two women like they'd just invited him to the Academy Awards.

Typical. Luke loved this kind of stuff, even if it wasn't happening in Justice.

He put his hand on the small of Kat's back as they headed for the RV. When they were out of earshot of the Haywood family he sighed. "I love this kind of stuff. Even if is isn't happening in Justice."

Kat rolled her eyes but smiled. "I know."

"This is what it's all about, Kat."

"Outdoor movies and barbecues?" She pulled the door to the RV open and started to climb in. Her heart was pounding. Surely they wouldn't just go at it with all these people right outside. But then again, the door had a lock and the windows had shades—

"People coming together to help after disasters. This is why

I can't imagine living anywhere but a small town. It's like you have a family that's the size of a town."

"Disaster?" she repeated, turning back to face him. Sandra's encounter with the deer could have been serious but it wasn't quite to the level of disaster in her opinion. "What do you mean?"

"The tornado."

"The...what?" She blinked at him.

"They were hit by a tornado here three nights ago. Remember how stormy it was on Saturday?"

There had been a lot of warnings of severe weather that night, all over the northern part of the state. She nodded. "Something hit here?" Wow, she'd missed a lot of conversation today worrying about if these people would think she was strange and thinking about how much she liked Luke. And how much she was going to hate his wife.

"They had a touchdown. It took the roof off the church and blew a tree from one yard through the garage next door. And the nursing home was hit. There are several people in the hospital. One died."

"Oh, my God. That's terrible."

"But they decided to go ahead and have the party, raise some money and make some plans for repairs and cleanup. To keep everyone's spirits up, come together as a community."

"How many are in the hospital?" Her mind was already jumping ahead.

He shrugged. "Didn't say. Several."

"Maybe I should go up and see if they need some help. It's a really small hospital. Wonder what their staffing is like."

Luke smiled at her. And it was a different smile than the many others she'd gotten from him over the years. This one was full of tenderness and...pride.

"I think that would be awesome. I think *you're* awesome." He moved close. "It sounds so strange, I know, but that turns me on almost as much as when you talk dirty."

She put a hand on his chest. "Easy, tiger. I'm a doctor. I can't help it."

"No. You're you. That's why you can't help it," he said.

She stared at him. She had no idea how to respond. Because she wasn't sure anyone had ever said anything quite that nice to her. And because she really needed to hear that kind of stuff right now. And he was looking at her with tenderness and desire at the same time.

"Will you take me up to the hospital?" she asked, trying to do the right thing *before* jumping on him.

"Yeah. And I might go and see if I can help with any cleanup or anything. As long as we're here."

"Right. Might as well." She knew that they both naturally felt compelled to help if they could. There was really no *might as well* about it. "So, we better go."

"After I kiss you for a while."

Kissing. For a while.

She wouldn't be able to think. She might not do the right thing.

Still, she went up on tiptoe, meeting him halfway as he lowered his lips to hers.

The kiss was sweet. At first. It started with just a meeting of their lips, a silent communication that felt strangely like reverence. They liked each other. They believed in the same things. They understood each other.

But they also wanted each other. Badly. The kiss reflected that as well when it went from sweet to spicy, close-lipped to openmouthed, satisfied to hungry.

Luke cupped her face between his two hands, she grabbed his hips and pulled him forward and they both groaned as they took the kiss deeper, harder, faster, *more.*

Several moments later, they broke apart as another RV's door slammed, reminding them they weren't alone.

"Or we could just go inside the RV and—"

She pushed him back, laughing. "Let's at least spend a

little time being good people before we go at it like lust-crazed nymphomaniacs."

"But we *will* go at it like lust-crazed nymphomaniacs, right?" he asked, not moving back more than a millimeter.

She didn't think there was any way to avoid it. "I'm having a hard time coming up with any other options."

The heat in his eyes flared at her words. "Glad to hear it."

They didn't need Kat's help at the hospital, but Dr. Stan Haken, the physician on call, verified Kat's credentials and then asked if she'd be willing to go up to the nursing home and check on a few people he wanted to keep an eye on. She readily agreed, and as Luke pulled the RV up in front of Sunshine Estates, he found the perfect way to spend his time too.

The west end of the building was badly damaged, with windows blown out, one wall crumbling and no roof. A large team of volunteers was already making some headway but Luke reasoned they could always use more help.

After Kat completed her rounds, she also pitched in, helping with hauling debris to the backs of the pickups parked around the area, boarding up windows and taking measurements for the supplies needed for repairs. It made it convenient to have the RV with them wherever they went so she could just hop in back and change into more appropriate clothing.

Or so she'd said when she'd headed that direction.

Once she emerged, however, Luke had to wonder what she thought was appropriate.

She now wore a fitted black T-shirt and black jeans that made Luke's mouth go dry. They were the exact opposite of baggy work jeans. They molded to her waist, hips and butt, making Luke's hands itch to follow the curves. She'd also changed into boots, but not her usual—these were chunky black boots with thick soles. Luke had no idea what Sabrina had been thinking when she'd packed those for Kat, but he was glad she had. They were much more suitable than her black leather, lace-up, three-inch heels.

Though Kat could, apparently, make chunky look hot too.

"Holy sh—"

Luke swung to face the man behind him. Eddie was the unofficial leader of the group of volunteers. A local contractor, he was able to use the well-intentioned group to actually get some repairs done.

"You okay?"

Eddie looked at Luke. "Um, yeah, sorry."

Luke realized that Eddie had been looking past him and he turned to find Kat bent over filling a bucket of water from a garden hose. The view was certainly noteworthy.

"I'm tryin' not to look, man," Eddie said, giving him a sheepish grin. "But doesn't she have some baggy sweats or something?"

Luke sincerely doubted it. "I've known her since we were kids and I haven't seen her wear anything baggy since we were about twelve."

"How have the men in Justice survived?" Eddie asked. His attention flickered over Luke's shoulder, then back to his face.

"There's a lot of looking but no touching," Luke said honestly.

Kat was gorgeous but she was intimidating. Not to him—he'd always been comfortable around her—but he knew that many of the men and women their age found Kat hard to approach. He'd wondered about that with her medical practice, but she was great with kids and older people and Justice was the kind of place where word spread quickly and people trusted each other. It had only taken a few patients to seek care from her and soon everyone knew that Kat Dayton had beauty, brains and a great bedside manner.

"But not for you, right?" Eddie said with a grin. "You're looking and touching. Lucky bastard."

Luke grinned back. He was definitely looking and touching.

"Hey, I've earned every touch."

"Yeah, she has handful written all over her," Eddie said with a nod.

Luke thought about that. Handful wasn't entirely inaccurate.

She was tough to impress, hard to get close to. He'd always known that being close to Kat was a special place to be. He'd understood that innately, but he'd never really thought about why. Her appearance—and even more her attitude—held people at arm's length. A lot of people in high school and college had decided it wasn't worth the effort and she'd seemed fine with that.

Being close to Kat was a privilege. One he intended to appreciate. For a very, very long time. "Well, she's taken, so nobody needs to worry about if she's a handful or not." He'd take her on. Anytime, anywhere. And Kat needed to know that.

"Yeah, that's pretty obvious," Eddie said, bending to hammer nails into his end of the two-by-four they were putting up.

"Yeah?" Luke liked the sound of that.

"Even if we hadn't noticed the way you've been watching her, she's only got eyes for you, man."

Luke felt emotion—pride, want, affection, possessiveness—surge through him.

"She worth it?" Eddie asked, leaning for more nails.

"Absolutely," Luke answered. She was worth whatever it took to convince her that she could be close to him, that he'd be there.

"That was quick," Eddie said with a chuckle. "How can you be so sure?"

"I've—" He stopped. How could he be sure? There were so many very practical reasons. Because practical was what he was doing this time. This time was going to work. It made sense with Kat.

But just then he realized that when he thought about her

and how it felt, it didn't feel practical. It felt, well, pretty damned emotional if he was being completely honest.

"Did I stump you?" Eddie asked, looking up.

"No. She's the only woman I know that wants exactly what I want." He and Kat had already covered this. There were numerous logical reasons that she was The One. She knew the same people, liked the same things, lived in the same place. With Kat it would be easy. Basically, she was living the life he wanted, just across town. All he had to do was move her in with him and the happily-ever-after would commence.

Most importantly, he could count on her to stay the same. She'd proven that. She'd gone away, but come back—on purpose—and settled in. She wasn't looking for anything else. He could give her what she wanted.

The emotions were just a bonus. They were good. She made him feel alive and crazy and real. It was nothing to worry about, nothing to cause concern. He had feelings for her, feelings that were very much bordering on *I'll do anything for you.* But that was okay because they still made sense too.

A huge raindrop splashed against Luke's forehead. He looked up to find dark gray clouds had rolled in.

"We better get stuff covered up," Eddie said, pounding two final nails. "Plastic's in the truck!" he called to the other guys.

"Got it," Luke said. He looked over to where Kat was putting the lids back on paint cans. "Be back in a second."

As soon as he was close enough he had to touch her. Hands settled on her hips, he leaned in close. "I think you're about to get very wet."

She turned to face him with a big smile. "Tell me—in great detail please—how you're going to do that."

He grinned, heat exploding in his gut at her words and her smile. Sure, feelings could be good. These feelings, for instance, were great. "As much as I'd like to, I don't know that I have a lot of control over this, actually." He pointed up at the sky. "At least right now."

She looked up and a drop hit her cheek. "Oh." A flash of

lightning streaked from one cloud to the next.

"I'm going to help them finish covering everything up and then I'll meet you in the RV." The drops began falling closer together.

Suddenly he had to kiss her. This woman was going to give him his dream life. She was perfect for him. He kissed her, not lustfully but with tenderness and affection and everything he felt for her.

When he let her go, she stared up at him. Then pressed her lips together. "Wow."

"Exactly what I wanted to hear," he said. He dragged his thumb over her bottom lip. "I like that look on your face."

"I like how you put it there."

"Me too." He let go of her reluctantly. "I've got some work to do. See you soon."

She moved off, helping to gather up paintbrushes and tools and store them in the back of Eddie's truck. Luke kept his eye on her—he couldn't help it—as he worked. So he noticed when she ducked under the edge of the roof out of the rain and pulled her phone from her pocket.

He also noticed the look on her face as she listened to whoever was on the other end. Her expression went from nervous to worried to almost...sad.

What the hell?

He quickly threw tarps over the last pile of wood and started in her direction but just as he got close he heard, "Dr. Dayton! Kat!"

They both turned in the direction of the nursing home's front doors. A nurse was in the doorway.

"Yeah, Linda?" Kat called.

Luke smiled. Of course she already knew the nurses' names.

"Can you come back in for a minute? Marge said she forgot to tell you about the time Jack took her dancing." The nurse gave her a smile that said she understood it might be a silly request.

"Of course. I'd love to hear that," Kat said. She turned to Luke. "Jack was the resident who was killed the other night by the storm. This might take me a bit."

Luke got it. Even if they had no external injuries, there were still plenty of things that needed to heal. In a small nursing home like this—or the one in Justice—all the residents knew one another well. Most of them had been neighbors, even friends, before they'd come to live at Sunshine Estates. The fact that one had died hit them all hard.

"Take your time."

"Thanks." She paused and smiled up at him. "This is going to happen between us eventually, you know."

He knew she was referring to sex, but he knew a lot more than that was going to happen between them. "Count on it," he promised. Before he let her go, though, he grabbed her hand. "Hey, are you okay?"

"Yeah." But she didn't quite meet his eyes.

"You sure?" She wasn't. He could feel it.

"Yeah, of course."

Dammit. "Can we talk about it later?" he pressed.

"It?"

"Whatever's bothering you."

She shook her head. "I'm fine. And I have other plans for later. Not talking."

He faked a small smile and let her go, but he didn't like it. He could tell something was wrong. For now Marge needed her, but he would find out if Kat was really okay or not.

And if not, he'd make it okay.

Chapter Eight

Luke jogged across the parking lot toward the RV as the rain picked up and thought about Kat and the phone call as he toweled his hair dry. It bugged him for some reason. But that was typical for him—he liked to fix things.

She'd seemed happy at the barbecue. She was completely comfortable with the nursing home residents and staff. She'd willingly pitched in with the cleanup duties. But he could tell that she hadn't been happy since the mysterious phone call.

He wanted her to tell him when something was bothering her. He wanted her to come to him with her problems. He wanted to be the person she opened up to, leaned on. Sure, it might just be an error on her bank statement, or maybe she'd forgotten to call the pharmacy for a patient, or something else that was easily fixed.

But he wanted to know even the silly, minor things. And certainly the serious, major things.

"We're gonna have those repairs done in no time," Kat said with a grin as she climbed into the back of the RV.

He breathed deeply and turned to face her. "You love this stuff as much as I do, admit it," he said, trying for light and friendly when he really just wanted to grab her and hug her until she promised to lean on him, and let him help her.

"Okay, I do."

He was pleased, though surprised, when she came toward him and stopped close enough that she had to look up at him. "We should probably stay another day. Just to be sure everything's under control."

He raised his eyebrows but nodded. "I think that's a great idea."

"Me too."

Looking at her he could tell that she meant it. It wasn't a test, or a joke. She thought they should stay. He lifted his hand to her cheek. "That's one of the reasons I love you."

It came out so naturally. He felt like it had been just under the surface and couldn't wait any longer. But he held his breath waiting for her reaction.

She didn't have a reaction.

She blinked. Then said, "Do you want me to make you some lunch?"

"Lunch?" he repeated.

This was her reaction to him saying he loved her?

"Yes, lunch."

"We had lunch in the park." He lifted his hands to her upper arms and rubbed up and down. Was she in shock or something? "Maybe we should talk." He wanted her to open up, to let him close.

"But you've been working so hard. I thought you might..." She sighed. "Never mind."

"You were going to cook for me?" he asked. Instead of saying *I love you too* or telling him what was bothering her? Okay. Maybe she needed to work up to the rest. He could go with that, for now.

"No. I was going to get out some of the food Marc packed for us."

"Still, it could be construed as a play to soften me up," he teased gently.

"Soften you up for what?"

"Sex." That, he knew she'd reciprocate. And they had to start somewhere.

She snorted at that. "All I have to do is snap my fingers and point at the bedroom."

He walked forward, backing her up against the countertop. "Snap your fingers, babe. *Please.*"

She stared at him with her mouth open. "I um..." She

finally swallowed and said, "We're in the parking lot of a nursing home."

"I loved working with you here today, Kat." He moved in even closer, pressing hips to hips. She was going to know exactly how turned on he was. "I know it sounds weird but you were so sexy as you were hauling garbage."

She actually returned his grin. "It doesn't sound weird. You were too."

"The fact that you jumped right in there, that you didn't even hesitate, that you understand why I wanted to stay—that's all part of why I want you so damned much."

Desire lit her eyes and her voice was almost a whisper when she said, "I feel the same way."

He dropped his voice. "Snap your fingers, Kat."

She licked her lips and lifted her hand. And snapped her fingers.

Luke groaned. "One of my favorite sounds."

He moved away only far enough to close the blinds. As he did, he heard the lock on the door click and he turned, ready to tell her everything he was feeling. But she'd already taken her T-shirt off and thrown it over her shoulder into the front seat.

Her bra was simple cotton—in hot pink. The only decoration was the two hard nipples pressing into the cups, begging him to touch.

But he had so much to say to her first. So many things he wanted to be sure she knew.

"Kat, I just want you to know..." He blanked on the words he wanted and had to start again. "I have to tell you that..."

She was watching him, a sexy, confident almost-smile on her face. It was the look of a woman who knew exactly what she was doing to the man before her—and loving every minute of it. She didn't say a word as she undid the button at the top of her jeans and pulled the zipper down before pushing her jeans to the floor and kicking them to one side.

Her panties were also hot pink cotton. They weren't

skimpy, high cut, low cut or otherwise risqué. In fact, they were very normal, likely on two hundred women at this very moment. But Luke felt his blood rushing through his body and gathering hot and heavy in his cock.

"Pink." Even though she'd told him it was her favorite color, he still was trying to wrap his mind around that. He would have never guessed pink.

"Pink," she said.

He wanted to rip them from her body.

"I'm in love with you, Kat," he said gruffly stepping forward. "I'm sure of it."

Kat sucked in a quick breath but said nothing. Instead she reached behind her and unhooked her bra.

As it fell forward on her arms, revealing her breasts and nipples, Luke was the one to suck in a breath. She was...beautiful didn't fit, gorgeous wasn't right...

Then it came to him...she was the only woman he wanted to see like that ever again.

He had to get the rest of this out before he lost all ability to think. "It's not about your favorite dessert or what music you listen to. I love that you argue with me and fight back. I love that you're not afraid to tell me I'm being a dumb-ass or to go to hell if I try to tell you something you don't want to hear. I love that you know exactly what you want and where you want to be. I love that you're sure of yourself and what you can, and even what you can't, do. I love that helping other people is second nature to you. And I love the way you feel, look and sound when you're sucking on me, and I'm going to love sucking on every inch of your gorgeous body."

She didn't say a word as she hooked her thumbs in the top of her panties and pulled them down, also kicking them away when they reached her ankles. She stood before him, completely bare and just let him look. She didn't talk and she'd definitely taken his words away.

There were no piercings he hadn't seen before. She had body paint swirled around her upper arms, her wrists and ankles but there was nothing marring the perfect skin from collarbone to midthigh. It was as if she only decorated the surfaces that people could see. Underneath her clothing she was all natural. And he loved that he was getting to see it.

She moved close enough so she could grab the bottom of his shirt, pulling it up and over his head. When he moved to help with his jeans, she pushed his hands away, stripping the jeans and underwear down together. He wondered for a moment if she was going to suck him again, but she stood and he kicked his clothes to the side.

Keeping her eyes on his, she lifted her hands, but instead of touching him, she cupped her breasts. He blew out a breath at the erotic sight. She played with her nipples, rolling and pulling, the tips lengthening. Then she slid one hand down over her stomach and lower, through her curls, until the pad of her middle finger disappeared into the hot folds. She rubbed her finger back and forth, then circled, watching him watch her.

He thought he was going to die.

He wanted to talk about his feelings and she seemed determined to get straight to the sex.

God. He'd turned into the girl.

But he'd said he loved her. She hadn't responded. Other than the fact there's no way she could have missed it, he didn't even know for certain that she'd heard him. But he'd said it. And he'd say it again and again.

Comfortable with the fact that he'd put the feelings first, he reached for her and pulled her up against him. As their bodies bumped together, her hands dropped and he moved to kiss her, but before he could, she'd taken his cock in hand and began stroking him. He lost all train of thought.

She walked him backwards until the backs of his knees hit the bench by the kitchenette table. She pushed and he sat, but she quickly crawled up, straddling his lap. This seemed like a fantastic idea.

"Don't be shy, babe." His palm spread on her back, he urged her forward, determined to take her mouth. Again she changed things, moving up on her knees and putting a nipple to his lips.

Luke wasn't going to argue. He swirled the firm tip with his tongue, then pulled it into his mouth, sucking long and hard. She groaned and tangled a hand in his hair to keep him where he was. Her other hand continued to stroke him, so he moved his hand too. Right up her thigh and into the hot slick center of her.

"Oh," she moaned, her head falling back and her eyes closing.

"I want to see and touch and lick every inch of you," he said against her throat. "Let me lay you back on the bed, spread you out—"

She lifted her hips, moved forward and sank down on him.

"Or this will work," he ground out, his hands going to her hips and pressing up into her. "God, Kat."

"I don't care about anything but both of us coming as hard and fast as we can," she murmured by his ear.

His fingers curled into her hips, slowing her lifting and lowering. "Whoa, babe. I appreciate the sentiment, but we can take a little time." He wanted to enjoy it, feel every centimeter as he slid in and out, watch her breasts bounce, see her face as he gave her the best orgasm of her life.

"I want you, Luke. I want you now. Hard."

She rolled her pelvis and Luke almost lost it. He braced his feet against the floor and lifted his hips, driving deep. Fine, if she insisted, he'd take her hard and fast. This time. They had all night for slow and sweet. They had the next several days. They had the rest of their lives.

Kat reached between them, her middle finger circling her clit and Luke felt her muscles clench around him. The pace increased exponentially from there and soon they were climbing the peak. She came just moments before he felt his climax crash over him.

She slumped against him a moment later, dragging in deep breaths.

Luke ran his hands up and down her back, breathing deeply of the scent of her, loving how she fit against him.

"That was incredible," he told her. "You're amazing."

She had her head on his shoulder so he couldn't see her face. "Thanks. Ditto."

She sighed deeply and pushed back to sit up.

He was still deep inside her and as she shifted he swore he was getting hard again.

Then he realized...condoms had been the last thing on his mind.

"We're getting married right away if you get pregnant."

She rolled her eyes and shifted back farther until she could slide to the floor. "Don't panic, I'm on the pill. I wouldn't have just climbed on if I wasn't." She headed for the bathroom and pulled two towels from the rack.

He fondly remembered how she'd climbed on. He also hadn't been particularly worried and certainly not panicked about the idea that he'd just gotten Kat pregnant. Which just went to show how far gone he really was.

She looked suspicious as she tossed him a towel and wrapped the other around her. "You're nearly weak with relief right?"

He shrugged as he tucked the towel around his hips. "I intend to get you pregnant eventually. I wouldn't be devastated if it happened now."

She gaped at him. Literally widened her eyes and let her mouth drop open. "Are you *insane*?" she demanded.

"What? You want to have kids, don't you?"

"Kids?" she repeated. "You're talking to me about having *kids*?"

He frowned at her. "Do you want to have kids?"

"Of course. Some day. Eventually. With someone."

He frowned harder and took a step closer to her. "Not with someone. With me."

She shook her head. "We have sex for the first time and

you're already talking about babies and—"

"Marriage."

Her eyes got rounder. "Seriously?"

"Of course."

"Of course?" she repeated.

"What did you think all of this would lead up to? We were talking about engagement rings just this morning."

She narrowed her eyes. "We've never been on a date. We've had sex once. We've been on the road together for *two days*, Luke. It's not like we've been together for two years or even two months. We—*you*—can't talk about marriage already." She turned and started toward the bathroom.

He couldn't let her walk away with that. "I hope you are pregnant."

She whirled, her eyes flashing. "I'm not pregnant."

"I can still hope." He dropped his voice. "And keep trying."

"That's what you think."

"Oh, that's definitely what I think."

"Right," she scoffed. "You're going to force me."

"Honey, I'm not gonna have to force you. Remember, *you* climbed up on *me* a minute ago."

Her cheeks reddened, but he suspected it was from anger versus embarrassment. "Why are you making this so difficult?"

"That's the beauty," he said, reaching out and pulling her close. "You and I are the easiest thing ever. Nothing difficult, nothing complicated. Natural." It was so true. Even now, when she was pissed at him, he wanted to be with her, felt happy, knew things would be okay.

She sighed and let him wrap his arms around her. "I'm not going to get pregnant," she said with her cheek against his chest.

"Maybe not tonight."

"You're nuts," she told him.

He just grinned. "Let's take a shower."

She pulled back. "I'll go first."

"Together." He put his hands on her butt and pressed her against him where he was ready for her all over again.

"I don't shower with people. Besides, that bathroom's barely big enough for one."

"I'm okay with standing really close." He lifted a hand to tug the towel down over her breasts.

She grabbed it before more than the upper slope was revealed. "Nope. I'm a solo shower act."

"I could make you okay with sharing."

"My makeup will wash off."

"I don't mind."

"I do," she said firmly. "Nobody sees me without makeup."

He looked at her, puzzled. "No one?"

She shook her head.

"Kat?" He knew that she'd had other boyfriends. She wasn't a virgin. Surely—

"You've never been without makeup around a man?"

"Not since I was fourteen."

"Has anyone seen you completely naked before?"

She narrowed her eyes. "Why do you ask?"

"I'm just imagining you going at it hard and fast and maybe not bothering to fully undress." It made sense. He didn't think that Kat let people see her plain pink underwear.

"Why do you think that?"

He traced a finger over the swirling pattern of body paint she had on her right shoulder. "Seems like there's a difference between what's on the surfaces that people see and the ones they don't."

She shrugged his hand away and turned toward the bathroom. "Whatever."

He knew he'd hit on something and even if he didn't fully understand it he felt pretty good about being someone who'd seen her bare-assed naked.

How did he know that stuff about her? As she shut herself in the bathroom Kat made sure to lock the door. Luke wouldn't hesitate to let himself in, she was sure, and she needed a few minutes.

He understood that seeing under her makeup meant something. He said he loved her. He thought they were getting married. He wanted to get her *pregnant*. And not necessarily in that order.

He was overwhelming her.

She wanted all of it. When she was in his arms, and he was filling her body and heart, she believed it could happen.

Kat was amazed. Not that he'd noticed her body decor only went as far as what her clothing revealed, but that he knew there was more to it.

She stepped into the shower, which ironically was going to wash all the paint, makeup and hair dye from her body. The stuff that Luke had realized was more than a simple fashion statement.

There were always reactions to how she looked—positive or negative—and that kept people on the surface, focused on what they could see, rather than noticing the deeper stuff, like mistakes or flaws or insecurities.

In Justice, everyone was so used to her appearance that she wasn't regarded as strange anymore. Which made practicing medicine a little easier. It was tough to be aloof and rebellious when taking care of someone's fever or split lip.

Still, no one asked *why* she dressed the way she did. Some people accepted it, some didn't, but no one had asked. Luke hadn't actually asked, but he'd hinted that he had some questions.

And she kind of wanted to tell him. The potential malpractice suit hanging over her head made her feel even more vulnerable and—

She let her head thunk against the shower wall. There was a potential malpractice suit hanging over her head. Luke had helped distract her from it for a little while, but it was still there. It still made her feel sick to her stomach.

She wanted someone she could talk to about it. She wanted to confess that she was scared to death, that she felt terrible about Tom and that she felt guilty. If there was even the smallest chance that she could have prevented Tom's stroke she didn't think she'd ever get over that.

But she couldn't tell Luke. She couldn't tell him that she might have done something wrong and that not everyone in Justice loved her anymore.

The phone call just before Marge needed her had been from Marc—who knew everything that happened in Justice and would be honest with her.

Tom was still in the ICU and there were murmurings in town that there was more to the story than just a sudden stroke. Tom's son was also in town. He'd flown in from Indianapolis and was, in Marc's words, pissed and raising hell at the hospital over his father's care. He wanted to know what had been done, why, what had not been done and why, and everyone who had been involved. She didn't know for sure that her name or Tom's visit to the clinic would come up, but Tom's wife knew about it and she'd mentioned it to Brickham. It stood to reason she'd mention it to their son.

Kat needed to call her lawyer. She knew that but had been putting it off until she could find several uninterrupted minutes alone. So far, thanks to Marge and Luke, that hadn't happened.

Luke.

Pretty soon the only thing on his top ten list that she could fulfill would be the blow jobs.

Stepping out of the shower, she quickly dried off, leaving her hair wet with the thick, extra-strong-hold gel in it, spiking it up in an easy style. She made some of the tips of the spikes pink—Luke seemed to be fascinated with her affection for pink—and quickly applied her eye makeup.

It was funny really. Her eye makeup and lipstick were always so dramatic that people didn't look closely enough to notice that she barely wore anything else on her face. Her skin was naturally pale and smooth without being too dry or too oily. She had no freckles, no blemishes, no uneven spots. She knew she was lucky and appreciated the fact that a simple face powder was enough. It meant she could spend more time on her eyes.

Satisfied, she started to turn away, then couldn't ignore the body paint. It allowed her to be creative and feel fun or sexy but wasn't permanent like tattoos. She liked changing it up every day. Luke was right—she never painted where people wouldn't see it. The paint was part of her "costume". So the elaborate swirling design on her left inner thigh was new. No one saw her left inner thigh. Until now. She added an arrow at the top pointing right to where she wanted Luke's attention later on.

She dressed quickly, then gave Luke the bathroom.

"You sure you don't want to come in?" he asked, moving past her, close enough that his whole body rubbed against hers.

She did, she really did. "I just redid everything. Wouldn't want all this color to go to waste," she said, her hand running over the pink tips of her hair.

Something that looked a little like frustration flashed over his face, but disappeared as he smiled. "I'll be quick. The party's going to start without us."

He showered but didn't shave, leaving stubble on his jaw. He'd also pulled on new jeans and a T-shirt. It was nice to see Luke this way. She usually saw him at the Camelot where he wore khakis and dress shirts, often with ties. This was a more relaxed Luke. He was completely comfortable in his restaurant, but he was also focused on making sure everything ran smoothly and that his patrons had a fabulous experience. Here in Rolland, he could just enjoy. He looked fantastic in a tie, but this look was equally sexy.

They drove to the park and then, holding hands—something she *never* did with men—joined the group that had gathered near the pavilion where the band had already started playing. Beer and wine were flowing from the stand set up by the local bar and Luke deposited fifty dollars in the jar marked *$10 Suggested Donation* as they each took a glass of beer and headed for a picnic table where some friendly faces were sitting.

"Luke!"

"Kat!"

They were greeted enthusiastically and Kat couldn't help but smile. It was nice. She wasn't that different from Luke in that she preferred to hang out with people she knew well. People she was sure liked her, accepted her...

With that her stomach knotted.

She might need a new group to hang out with. The people in Justice might not like or accept her now that she'd almost killed someone.

Kat took a deep breath and tried to forget about the mess at home, not overreact, and just enjoy the evening. The trip with Luke that had seemed so long yesterday was suddenly going by quicker than she liked.

But she couldn't do it.

She couldn't forget about the mess, not overreact or convince herself it was no big deal.

She had to call her lawyer. Like right now.

"I'll be back in a minute," she said to Luke.

"Where are you going?" He wouldn't let go of her hand.

"Just need to make a phone call."

"To who?"

He was watching her closely and she looked at his earlobe instead of his eyes.

"Just checking on some things back home."

He leaned in. "What things?"

"Just some stuff with the clinic. No big deal."

Luke grabbed her chin between this thumb and finger to hold her still. "What stuff?"

"Luke, I can't tell you." Couldn't he let it go as a confidential medical issue?

"You can tell me anything."

She pressed her lips together. She wanted to tell him. So much. But she felt like she needed more details—like just how fucked up her life was actually going to be—before she filled him in.

"I need to make this phone call, okay?" she asked. She let her vulnerability show in her eyes. "Please."

He looked at her for a long moment. Then sighed. "Fine."

But she could tell that he was very hesitant to let it go.

Before she could change her mind and blurt the whole damned thing out, she headed off to one side of the party, away from other ears. She quickly dialed Brad Conner's cell number. Thankfully she still had it in her phone from when they'd served as co-chairs on the committee to redo the landscaping at city hall.

"Dr. Dayton."

He picked up right away and didn't sound surprised to hear from her. That couldn't be a good thing.

"Hi, Brad." Brad had been a classmate. He was also Marc and Luke's lawyer. He'd never called her Dr. Dayton in his life.

"Dr. Brickham called to say that you'd spoken with him," he said.

"Yes, he filled me in on the situation with Tom Martin."

"I've been expecting your call."

So she did need to talk to him. "I was afraid of that." She was also afraid of Brad's formal tone.

"I'm going to advise you not to speak about it to anyone else. Especially Mr. Martin's family. They may be trying to get ahold of you. I feel it's a good thing you're out of town, and I would encourage you to stay in touch but not return to Justice until things are stabilized and the partners decide how to handle this. I don't want you in a position of saying something that might hurt the medical practice or the other physicians."

And what about her? Did she have a say in how things were handled? Did he care about protecting her? "Brad, do I need to have you present if I speak with anyone?"

He cleared his throat and Kat felt her stomach tighten.

"I don't know that I'm going to be able to represent you, Dr. Dayton."

"So I need representation."

"It wouldn't be a bad idea to have someone familiar with the situation."

"And why can't that be you?"

"I represent the medical practice and the partners."

"But I'm..." She wasn't a partner. "Their legal counsel doesn't extend to their physicians?"

He cleared his throat again. "You should know that Dr. Taylor informed me this morning that they've chosen to rescind the offer of partner."

Dr. Colin Taylor was another of the partners. She wished she were shocked. But no matter how things turned out with Tom, her reputation as a physician was tarnished. Yes, she'd grown up in Justice and knew everyone, but now there were questions about her abilities. There was nothing in her past that would definitely protect her in that regard. She'd been valedictorian, never gotten picked up by the town cop and served as head of three committees in the past year, but that didn't mean that she could save a life. Which was, obviously, something they were counting on her to do.

"But as an employee—" She stopped and took a deep breath as a thought occurred to her. "Are they firing me?"

"They would like you to take a voluntary leave of absence," Brad confirmed. "The family has reported this to the state licensure board. If they suspend or revoke your license, your employment will be terminated. The partners will also have to investigate the situation further and decide if there was any breach of company policy and procedure. Decisions will be made at that time."

She'd been turned in to the state licensure board. And she had to take a leave of absence.

Awesome.

"The leave of absence won't look like an admission of guilt?"

"Are you admitting guilt?" Brad tossed back.

"No."

"Then it's just a leave of absence. And that's the story you should tell anyone who asks."

Which would be everyone she knew. Even more awesome.

"I assume you'll be in touch?" she asked dryly.

"Yes. But when you get an attorney, you should give him or her my number."

"Right." Sure. When she got an attorney. How did one go about doing that? She'd never needed one before and Brad was the only one she knew personally.

She realized there was nothing more to say to Brad except good-bye. They disconnected and she shut her phone off. There would only be people calling with questions. Questions she wasn't supposed to answer. Not that she really had any answers. Except that she'd never meant to hurt anyone.

She was surprised her parents hadn't called yet. If they hadn't heard yet, that wouldn't last much longer. This would be terrible for them to hear.

She took a deep breath, then another. Then she wiped her eyes.

The window of opportunity to enjoy her time with Luke was getting smaller. She was going to take full advantage of it.

"Are you okay?"

She wasn't surprised Luke noticed that she seemed out of it. Or that he asked about it.

"I'm...not great," she admitted.

"Let's talk about it." He took her hand and started to tug her away from the group.

She resisted. "I just need to think about it myself for a

while."

He looked so frustrated. "Kat, I—"

"Just give me some time," she said. "I need some time. Let's enjoy the party. Everyone's having such a good time. Let's stay for a while." She couldn't deal with this right now. She wanted him, was pretty sure she was falling in love with him—and not the crush-in-college love that she'd felt before, but actual real love—and had just started believing that he might feel the same way about her. Now she was going to have to tell him something that would change what he thought of her.

Luke's jaw tightened. "I want to know what's going on."

It was inevitable. She was a little surprised he didn't know already. She'd made Marc swear he wouldn't tell Luke, but that left at least six hundred other people who would hear the rumors and who would tell Luke anything he asked.

That he hadn't called anyone, especially Marc, asking what they knew said something. He really did want *her* to tell him.

"You'll find out."

"Promise?" he asked.

There was no way to avoid it. "Yes."

He grudgingly returned to the picnic table with her. They sat and visited with the others for a while, then Luke moved off to refill their drinks and got stalled by a group of men. He was talking and laughing, much as he did in his restaurant's dining room each night, and she knew he was happier there than with her when he knew she was keeping a secret from him.

Kat was fine sitting by herself, thinking. She hadn't lied to Luke when she'd said she wanted some time to sort through things in her mind. How did she tell him? And what exactly? The whole sordid story? Just the facts she knew? Or her fears and guilt too?

She took a deep breath and looked around. It was nice here. These were nice people, who thought she was great because she'd taken care of a gash on Sandy's forehead and had spent some time at the nursing home. She liked people who thought she was great. She should definitely spend more time here.

"Mrs. Benton told me that I should hire you. Apparently you're much sweeter than I am and know more about Jane Austen than I do."

Kat looked up to find Stan Haken standing next to their table with a beer in hand.

"Mrs. Benton told me that you used to play football with her son and that you bring her your wife's copies of *Cosmo*. I think she likes you just fine," Kat told the other physician. She slid down to give him space to sit on the picnic bench.

"Thanks for pitching in today," Stan said, settling in next to her.

"It wasn't a problem," Kat told him. "I checked in on some really nice people. No one had any issues, so I got off pretty easy."

"It was still a big help. I'm short-handed on a good day and when something like this happens—well, it's not a good day."

"It was my pleasure."

They both took a drink. Then Stan turned to face her more fully. "What's your background, Kat?"

"Family practice. Small town. I cover the ER in Alliance so we see a little bit of everything there. Not too different from here really."

She was happy and settled in Justice. But that might change when she got back. And there wasn't much she could do about it. She hated that. Her stomach knotted and she felt her eyes sting. Knowing that people were talking about her hurt. Knowing that people were doubting her hurt. Knowing that there was a man in the hospital that she should have helped and hadn't, really hurt. And the idea that she might not be able to go back to her life in Justice as it was before made her feel like curling into a little ball under the covers and not coming out. Ever.

She could defend herself. She could try to explain that strokes were tricky and could happen suddenly without warning. She could remind people that even with the best medicine sometimes bad things happened. But it wouldn't change the fact that Tom Martin had suffered a stroke while under her care. That was just pure fact.

"You ever think about relocating?" Stan asked.

"I may be looking at options," she answered. "Why do you ask?"

"I'm shorthanded and you've made a great impression. Just couldn't let you go without at least asking if you'd be interested in staying."

Kat's attention went to Luke, where he was still talking with the guys. Would Luke consider— But she couldn't even finish that thought. Luke said he loved her, but if it came down to choosing between her and his hometown...

No, if she left Justice it would be alone.

Which did not make her stomach, or her heart, feel any better.

"You don't know how much I appreciate that, Stan."

He looked surprised, then pleased. "I can offer you a smaller salary than anyone else in your med school class, horrible hours at least half the time and a pager that will go off on every major holiday." He paused and looked around the gathering. "But I can also offer you some of the most honest, caring, hardworking patients you'll ever meet."

She smiled. "Sounds like home."

"Maybe it will be."

Her throat tightened and she looked again to Luke.

"Are there any good attorneys in Rolland?"

Clearly surprised by the question he said, "As a matter of fact, there is one."

"What kind of law does he practice?"

Stan chuckled. "Small-town law is a lot like small-town medicine. A little bit of everything."

She smiled, then sighed. Stan was a nice guy, a seemingly caring doctor who was offering her a job. He deserved to know about the baggage she would be bringing with her. He might not want her once he knew but suddenly she wanted to talk about it, to *someone.* "I don't suppose he's ever handled a malpractice suit?"

Half an hour later, she'd told her story to Stan and to Larry Tripp, attorney at law. Thank goodness Luke had been asked to act as a judge in the chili cook-off.

"Well, Kat, sounds to me like you need a lawyer, and without some research, I'm just talking off the cuff here, but you have a good case. It's certainly not a slam dunk *against* you."

"I agree," Stan said. "You could get any number of expert witnesses to testify on your behalf. If that's even necessary. Honestly, the attorney for this patient's family should be advising against suing you. It would be difficult to prove negligence."

"Thanks." Kat really did appreciate the words of support. "My bigger problem is my reputation."

"That's another story," Larry agreed. "Not sure if I can help with that."

"I'm not sure anyone can," she said honestly. "Would you still be interested in hiring me, even with my spotty background?" she asked Stan.

Stan smiled. "I wouldn't hire you if you were perfect. You'd make me look bad." He slid off the bench and stood. "I think Luke's impatient with two other men monopolizing your time."

She looked over her shoulder to find Luke stalking toward her. Frowning hard.

"Um, yeah, okay."

"Let me know what you decide and if I can help," Stan said.

"Me, too," Larry added, also stretching to his feet.

She felt like crying. "Thanks. I really appreciate that."

They both greeted Luke. Luke, for probably the first time in his life, was less than gracious and friendly. He simply gave them each a nod as they moved past.

He dropped onto the bench beside her, leaned back and

braced his elbows on the picnic table behind him. He continued to watch the party casually, but Kat wasn't fooled. He was not feeling casual.

"I thought maybe you were discussing patients until I asked someone who the other man was and I was told he's a lawyer."

"That's right. Been practicing here for about ten years. Nice guy." She took a sip of beer.

"It looked like more than just a friendly conversation about the weather."

"The weather wasn't even mentioned," she admitted.

Shit. She was going to have to tell him about what was going on. It was confusing her to have Luke be the person she most wanted to tell and least wanted to tell at the same time.

Luke pivoted toward her. "Kat, I want to know what's going on. There's obviously something bothering you."

"I don't want to talk about it." She stared ahead at the trees and drank again.

"Too bad."

"I could distract you with sex."

"Not this time."

Okay, so he'd caught on that she'd done that before. That wasn't the only reason, of course, that she'd stripped down for him. But it had worked.

"Why's it matter so much? I'm here, naked when you want me to be. Isn't that enough?"

He was quiet for a moment. Then said, "No."

She looked over at him. Something in his tone caught her attention. "Are you surprised by that?" she asked.

He met her gaze. And shook his head. "Not surprised. I just hadn't really thought about it—about stuff beyond, well, the obvious."

"The whole me-being-perfect-for-you thing," she said.

"Right." He shrugged. "It seemed easy and natural and like a great idea. But I've realized that I want the not-so-easy stuff too."

Her heart flipped but she kept her expression calm. "And you've admitted there might be not-so-easy stuff. I'm impressed."

He gave a self-deprecating grin. "It didn't take me long."

None of this had taken long. That should also be a red flag. They'd been together on the road in the stupid RV for twenty-four fricking hours.

But it didn't feel like a warning sign. It felt...right. Like if they'd ever spent twenty-four straight hours together before this, it might have happened sooner.

It clicked. *They* clicked. And there was no use denying or ignoring it.

She'd evidently been quiet too long because Luke muttered, "Fuck," and then grasped her shoulders and spun her to face him.

"This is crap, Kat. I love you. I want to be there for you, but you're shutting me out. You're telling everything to Stan and the lawyer. Well, it ends now. I want it all. Starting now. All of it, everything you've got."

She knew she was staring. She knew she looked like an idiot with wide eyes, breathing hard.

"What if it's bad?"

"Especially if it's bad," he exclaimed. "Christ, Kat, what do you think this is? Me just wanting to play house?"

She bit her bottom lip and then slowly nodded. That was kind of exactly what she'd been thinking. "You wanted me because I would be easy, because it made sense. Well...this isn't easy."

He frowned at that. "What's hard about this is realizing that you don't want to let me in. *That's* hard. Being there for you, helping you, wanting to fix this for you—whatever it is—is easy."

Her heart was pounding even harder, but it wasn't about her now. Luke needed her to share this with him. He needed to be her hero. He needed to be a hero for someone who would treasure it. And even reciprocate from time to time.

She could do that.

She'd loved focusing on his physical needs earlier. She would love taking care of his emotional needs as well—even if it meant exposing her own mistakes.

And having someone want to help her fix this felt good. Stan and Larry wanted to help, but Luke's help would be...more. Stan could testify that she'd done what she could, Larry could argue her case, but Luke could assure her that she was loved no matter how it turned out.

"It's bad," she whispered.

"Tell me."

"Tom Martin had a stroke. A bad one. He also has a hip and skull fracture from the fall he took when the stroke happened. He's being flown to Denver."

Luke frowned. "That's terrible. How's Julie?"

"A mess, I'm sure. Dr. Brickham has actually taken over the case. I don't know much more right now."

Luke just looked at her for a moment. Then he took her hand and asked, "Why did you want to talk to a lawyer?"

She took a deep breath. "I might have been able to prevent Tom's stroke." There. She'd said it. He knew. It was out there.

He started shaking his head. "No. How's that possible?"

"He was in the clinic with arm weakness and a headache the same day."

"Are those the sure signs of stroke?"

"No, but they are symptoms."

Luke frowned. "But they can't know for sure that something was going on."

"They confirmed a previous stroke on CT scan, along with the one that put him in the hospital."

"No," Luke said firmly. "You wouldn't miss something like that. Something else happened."

She smiled at his defense of her but squeezed his hand. She needed to be sure he heard this. "Luke, I missed it. That part isn't up for discussion. He had a stroke causing the arm weakness that he saw me for and I diagnosed it as a shoulder injury."

He pressed his lips together, frowning. Finally he asked, "What is up for discussion?"

"If I was negligent in missing it. They're wondering if I really did everything I could. If it was an honest mistake, I'm fine. If not, if I didn't do something I should have, then I could be in trouble."

She told him about Tom's family, her leave of absence and the licensure board.

Luke was staring at her when she was done.

"What?" she asked. "I told you it was bad."

"You've been dealing with all of this alone? You weren't going to tell me?"

"I don't like admitting to the guy who thinks I'm amazing that I'm not actually amazing at all, okay?" she said with a frown.

"Kat...I think you're amazing no matter what."

"Tom could die."

"Not because you're not amazing."

"There are..." God this was almost worse than what she'd already revealed.

"What?"

"People are talking. Justice knows that I missed the first stroke. They know Tom's son is upset. They're—" her voice thickened suddenly as she fought the hurt. She swallowed hard and finished, "—questioning me."

Luke slid until the entire side of his body was against the entire side of hers, and he put his arms around her.

She let the tears run.

"They're just talking. We'll tell them the truth. We'll be sure they know—"

She shook her head, even though her cheek was against his chest. "We can't. Brad Conner said not to talk to anyone until it's sorted out."

"You've talked to Brad Conner too?"

"And Marc."

Luke swore under his breath. "No more of this, Kat. You tell me everything. First."

She smiled in spite of her tears. He was jealous. And on her side. And hugging her. This wasn't so bad.

"I can give you something to do that I really, really need that no one else can do," she said, pulling back and looking up at him.

"Anything."

The sincerity in his voice and expression made her absolutely certain she was in love with him.

"Make love to me."

Chapter Nine

Instantly heat flared between them. Without a word, Luke rose from the bench and held out his hand.

"So, I was thinking," he said casually as they climbed into the RV. "We should break those handcuffs out again. They've been pretty handy to have along."

She grinned. "I keep thinking about you in that chair."

"You ever let anyone tie you up?"

"You mean besides all the times I've been kidnapped?" she asked dryly. "No. You were definitely the first." She'd barely let the guys be on top.

Luke stopped by the bed and started undressing her. "Ever thought about it?"

Only in her fantasies about Luke. For some reason, she could completely imagine him tying her up—not on a chair and not fully clothed—and her loving every minute. But she wasn't going to tell him that. "Nope." She lifted her arms so he could pull her shirt over her head.

"You wouldn't be willing to try it?"

Her skirt hit the floor.

What was he thinking? Her pulse kicked up a notch, but she tipped her head casually to the side. "I'll cuff you anytime. Gladly. But I'm not interested in being the one restrained, no." That was a very vulnerable thing and while Luke was the only one she'd consider it with, it would be a big step even with him.

"Anytime, babe." He left her in her underwear and yanked off his shirt. "You can do absolutely anything you want to me."

Several hundred scenarios ran through her mind. She licked her lips.

"I think next time I tie you up, it will definitely be in a chair in this RV again," she said softly, leaning in until their lips nearly brushed. "I'm going to not tell you a thing about what's going on." She slid her hand down over the firm length of his erection. "I'm going to turn the radio up, and not let you loose until..." she ran her tongue over his bottom lip and reveled in the tremor that went through him, "...I've driven at least an hour with you sitting there wondering what's going to happen and when." She kissed him with open lips and bold strokes of her tongue. When she pulled back he was breathing hard. "Then I'm going to take you into some dumpy little diner and buy you pie and coffee."

Suddenly she found herself on her back. "You're a big talker," he said, climbing up, a knee on either side of her thighs. "You think you want payback, but I think once you had me at your mercy, you wouldn't be able to resist undressing me." He pulled her bra cups down, exposing both breasts. His hot gaze on her nipples, he continued, "Then you wouldn't be able to resist putting your hands on me, which would result in a hard and fast erection. Then you wouldn't be able to keep from taking me in your mouth." He lowered his head and sucked her nipple into his mouth.

Kat moaned and arched. The pressure shot heat directly to her clit and she felt herself grow wet.

"That would excite you so much that eventually you'd be climbing up, lowering yourself down on my cock, letting me fill you up, stretch you wide." He slid down her body, ran his tongue over her ribs, then down the middle of her stomach to her belly button. He swirled his tongue there. "Then you'd ride me, lifting up and down like you did on the bench a little while ago." His hands finally pulled her panties down to her ankles, revealing all of her to his eyes...and his mouth. He ran his tongue from hip bone to hip bone, then slipped her panties off her ankles and ran his palms up her inner thighs, gently urging them apart. "But unlike on the bench, I'd be laying back, watching you move up and down on me. Watching my cock appear, then disappear in you. And I'd get to see it when you reached down and found your clit."

She felt like her whole body was hot liquid. She wiggled on the bed, but not hard enough to move away from him. In fact, she felt like she was straining toward him, toward something. He was taking her over, controlling how fast she breathed, how fast her blood pounded through her veins. Luke bent her knees and then urged them wide, revealing her most intimate area.

"I really like this," he said gruffly, tracing a finger over the hot-pink paint on her inner thigh. "And I can follow directions." He gave her a naughty grin, then licked the point of the arrow mere centimeters from her hot center.

Kat threw her head back. She never let men do this. She'd only received oral sex one other time and it had been...well, great. She'd liked it. But it made her feel so vulnerable that she always distracted the guys before they could go that far. Which wasn't difficult to do. She wanted Luke to do it. Bad. But she didn't. He was the one person in the whole world that she already felt more vulnerable with than she ever had with anyone else. Intimacy with Luke compared to anyone else was like the Kentucky Derby compared to pony rides at a birthday party. It was bigger, more exciting and there was definitely more risk of someone getting hurt.

Though she couldn't really remember if she believed he might hurt her.

Or whatever.

It was really hard to think straight when he was tracing the swirly-arrow design on her thigh with his tongue.

"Luke, I want you inside me," she gasped. Which wasn't untrue. "Please."

"Like this?" He slid two fingers into her together.

Her hips lifted from the bed. That was good. Really good. But not enough. "More. I need more."

He slid in and out, his other hand lifting to tug on a nipple. "Like that?"

"No. Yes..." Fine, she'd have to pull out the big guns. "Fuck me, Luke."

She heard and felt his groan. That always did it. Guys loved dirty talk, especially explicit dirty...

He licked her clit as he pressed deep with his fingers. She gasped and her eyes closed. His tongue flicked over her again and again and she couldn't for the life of her remember why she'd thought they should do something else.

For the rest of her life he didn't have to do anything else at all. He could just stay right there, doing...

He sucked instead of licking. She cried out his name, her hands going to his head. She certainly wasn't trying to pull him away. She thought maybe she even pressed him a little closer. But mostly she couldn't even think anymore. Luke sucked on her, then licked long and bold, then sucked again all the while his fingers worked her deep inside and suddenly an intense tightness pulled her body in, then all at once let her go, and she was unraveling, losing it, shattering.

Moments later he lifted his head and crawled up her body.

She immediately reached between them and took his heavy, hard cock in hand, guiding it into her.

He closed his eyes and breathed out of his nose, but quickly took over, thrusting deep and long into her. He paused, as deep as he could go, and opened his eyes, staring down at her.

"We fit perfectly."

She didn't want to hear the word *perfect* or *easy* or *right.* She just wanted him pounding into her and giving her another orgasm. She pressed her heels into the mattress, lifting up to him. "*Now,* Luke."

He made a growling noise in the back of his throat, but couldn't keep from responding. His hands gripped her hips and he held her as he thrust into her hard, deep and fast. Her second orgasm came on, swift and hot like the first, and he was right behind her, losing himself before her muscles even finished milking him.

"God, Kat," he groaned against her neck as he rolled to one side, keeping nearly every inch of her body against his.

She took a deep breath, trying to slow everything. Her body hummed, her skin tingled, her mind spun. Sex was not supposed to be that...overwhelming. It was sex. She knew, for a fact, that it was a combination of nerve stimulation, circulation and hormones.

But this was Luke, and everything with him was *more.*

Even little things. Things that shouldn't really matter. Like conversation. Talking to him was more fun and interesting than talking to anyone else. Watching TV. He knew the most bizarre, funny trivia about actors and actresses. Eating a meal was even more fun and interesting than it should be.

Good grief. How had she not expected sex with him to be mind-blowing?

Luke ran the pad of his finger over the painted design that ran up and down the inside of her thigh. She'd painted it just for him, he knew, and he'd intended to explore the swirls fully, slowly, but what was he supposed to do when the woman he burned for was begging him to take her? He was only human.

Now he was feeling mellow, happy, satisfied. "I remember when you showed up to school that first day with your hair cut and dyed," he said.

"Everyone remembers that."

She was probably right. They went to a small school where everyone knew each other—and each other's grandparents for that matter. And the girls in high school tended to look like they'd been produced with a cookie cutter. The hair color varied a little but everything else was practically predestined. Except for Sabrina and Kat.

Sabrina had been different but almost...accidentally. It was like she was too distracted to pay attention to current styles or fashions.

Kat was another story. Her style and fashions had to be purposeful. They were so different, so off the norm, it had to be intentional.

"Everyone probably does," he agreed. "You stood out in the crowd."

She laughed lightly. "That's an understatement."

"You liked it."

She shifted and he was afraid it was to move away from him. Instead, she just turned onto her side to face him. "I was so nervous that first day."

"Yeah?" Kat Dayton was never nervous. Or at least never seemed to be.

"Definitely. Justice isn't a great place for diversity, you know?"

That was certainly true. "I remember when I first saw you. I was standing by the lockers with Marc, with my back to you. He suddenly stopped midsentence and his eyes got huge. I turned to see what he was looking at and there was this hot girl all in black coming toward us. It seriously took me ten seconds to recognize you."

"By the time I got to you, you'd realized who I was," she said, stretching an arm over her head.

Luke was momentarily distracted by the new view of her breast.

"You said *holy shit*. I remember it distinctly."

He had. He remembered it distinctly as well. "It was amazing." She'd had long, dark brown hair, big brown eyes and dressed...like a normal teenage girl. That morning she had cropped black hair with purple streaks, blue contact lenses and a fitted black T-shirt paired with a short black skirt and knee-high black boots. She'd also had a piercing in her nose, four new ones in each ear and bold, dark eye makeup.

It had been a total transformation.

It had been awesome.

She'd looked amazing, confident, intimidating.

"I wanted to make an impression," she agreed.

"It worked." Had it ever. All the guys had been talking about it. He assumed the girls had too. But there was something he'd wondered about for awhile. "Who were you trying to make an impression on?"

Kat had dated in high school, for sure. Lots of guys thought she was hot, everyone thought she was funny and smart and cool, but few had the guts to actually ask her out. They also quickly figured out the whole signal thing. If Kat didn't seem interested, they didn't dare. The ones who did, however, had been smitten.

He'd always wondered, though, whether there was someone Kat really wanted. If she'd had a big crush, it hadn't been obvious. There had been one party in high school when he and Kat had almost kissed. It seemed that all he could think lately was—had she wanted him, even back then?

He couldn't deny that he'd really like it if that were true.

"Sherilynn and Heather."

That took him a second. "You... What do you mean?"

She looked at him and then laughed. "Did your mind go to something lesbian there for a second, Luke?"

"No... I mean..."

She pushed against his shoulder, but he didn't allow her to move him far. "Sherilynn and Heather were the popular girls, the ones who always got their way, the ones who made the rules, who reigned supreme."

Sherilynn Conner and Heather Mayfield had, indeed, been the queens of Justice High.

"So?"

"They made my sister miserable."

Kat's older sister Isabelle had been a shy, sweet girl. She'd been smart, normal, though a little timid. Luke thought about her for a moment, but nothing really came to mind. She'd seemed to blend into the crowd.

"Miserable how?" He didn't remember Isabelle running with Heather and Sherilynn.

"Literally miserable. They made fun of her, teased her, pretended to be her friend, then stood her up or left her out."

Luke rolled his eyes. "You know, I'm glad Sabrina's drama was with her dad. That I could understand. Females make no sense."

Kat sighed. "Women can be mean, no doubt about it. Some never grow out of it. But they used Isabelle to make themselves feel more important. And I hated that she let them. I told her all the time that she needed to just cut them out of her life completely. But she wanted to be a part of their crowd. She did anything they told her. It made her depressed. And bulimic."

"Bulimic?" Luke frowned. He hadn't known about that.

She nodded, her eyes downcast on the sheets. "It started when they told her that no one in their group could be more than a size four. God," she said looking up at him. "Can you imagine? A size four? Those bitches."

Luke felt tight through his chest. "She still have problems?"

"She's much better, but yeah, she still has trouble worrying about how she looks, what others think of her. She still has to fight the urge to binge sometimes when she's stressed."

"I never knew."

"We kept it really quiet." Kat's voice was soft, her eyes back on the sheet. "I hated them, Luke. I wanted to beat the crap out of them, sleep with their boyfriends, steal all their shoes..."

He couldn't help it. He knew it wasn't completely appropriate, but he chuckled. "You didn't do any of those. Did you?" It occurred to him that there might be some things about Kat that he didn't know and that the small-town grapevine hadn't provided.

"I, um..." She wouldn't meet his eyes. "I didn't steal any shoes."

He coughed. "Oh?"

"Isabelle was in the hospital right before I cut my hair and everything."

"That was connected?"

She nodded. "I wanted to be a person that they wouldn't mess with. I wanted to be kick-ass, intimidating, above their influence. So, I put on this tough-girl image." She wiggled, as if getting more comfortable for her story.

He spread his palm wide over her rib cage, content just to touch her, feel the warmth of her skin.

"And it worked?" He didn't remember anyone giving Kat a hard time in school.

"It worked. It worked even better after I approached Heather in the parking lot after school and told her that if she ever fucked with me or my sister, or any other girl in school, I would kick her ass, sleep with her boyfriend and put itching powder in her cheerleading uniform."

He chuckled again in spite of himself. "Wow."

"And then I proved it."

He pulled back slightly to look down at her. "What do you mean?"

"She cornered Isabelle in the locker room one afternoon after school. So I followed her out to the parking lot and punched her in the face. Then that Friday after the football game her boyfriend, Troy Anderson, ended up getting to third base with me in his backseat."

"Um. Wow. Again." What else could he really say? "I don't remember hearing anything about you and Troy Anderson." He frowned. It had been years ago, but he still wanted to kick Troy's ass.

"I only had to do it one other time when they picked on Molly Stevens."

Luke vaguely remembered Molly. She was a couple of years younger than they were.

"Heather again?"

"Yeah. She was dating Jake Carter."

He wanted to kick Jake's ass too. "So you defended everyone?"

"You bet. Those bitches would have messed with anyone and everyone if they could. But they couldn't mess with me. I could deliver a right hook and get any guy naked that I wanted to."

He felt his scowl deepen. He didn't doubt that for a moment.

She went on. "Usually I just had to give them an evil eye, a reminder note in their locker, a little nudge in the hallway. I was watching them and they couldn't get away with being mean."

Luke shook his head, a little impressed in spite of himself. "You were like a superhero—defending all those girls against the bullies."

"The most fun I ever had."

He ran his finger around the swirl on her thigh. "How did I not hear about Troy and Jake?"

"I don't know. It was big gossip."

"Maybe not. Maybe the guys I hung out with..."

"No," she cut him off. "Everyone. You just weren't listening."

He frowned. That couldn't be true. "I honestly don't remember any of this. About your feud with Sherilynn and Heather, your messing around with those guys, your sister... How's that possible? I thought we were friends."

"So it's my fault that you weren't paying attention to me?"

There was a coolness in her tone that made him prop up on his elbow. "What's that mean?"

He felt her pull away even though she didn't seem to move. "You were distracted. I wouldn't expect you to know anything I—or anyone else—was doing."

O-kay.

"What are you talking about?"

She sighed. "It's probably not really your fault. You were inside the Sabrina bubble. You spent all your time either with her dad or with her."

"I didn't spend *all*—"

"You did."

And she was right.

"Okay, I did," he admitted. "But..." he snuggled in closer, putting his lips against the sweet skin of her neck, "...I'm firmly inside your bubble now."

He felt the tension leave her body. "You're damned right you are," she whispered as she pressed into him. "And I'm going to make it so you never want to leave."

Already there.

Later that night, Kat awakened, tangled in the bedsheets and Luke's limbs.

She sighed and snuggled closer. God, she liked this. She wanted to be held by Luke like this every night, forever and ever amen. She wanted to feel, touch, taste him all the time, any time. She wanted to have the right to look across the room and know that she could pull him into the nearest coat closet and have her way with him, or simply know that at the end of the night, he was going home with her.

She wanted him to tell her all his secrets, and she wanted him to know all of hers.

And she had. He'd been sweet, supportive, so quick to believe only the best of her.

Kat sighed and turned over onto her back. It all seemed so perfect, so easy. He kept saying he wanted it all, with her.

And he knew what was happening back in Justice.

But she couldn't shake the niggling doubt that it wasn't quite the mad, head-over-heels, climb-the-highest-mountain-swim-the-deepest-sea love that she'd need if life crumbled once she got home. If she didn't have a job—worse, if she had a bad reputation—what would he do? Still want her? Even love her? Yes, maybe. But would he choose to be with her instead of being in Justice?

Not bloody likely.

Fuck.

She was going to lose everything.

Luke rolled to his side in his sleep and his arm tightened around her, pulling her closer. He buried his nose in her hair and sighed contentedly.

She felt tears prick her eyelids.

She was running out of time with Luke.

Suddenly something banged against the side of the RV, making her sit straight up in bed. It sounded like a gunshot.

Luke groaned and sat up slower. "What the hell was that?"

"I don't know."

She became aware of the fact that something was pounding on the roof of the RV as well.

Luke yawned. "That's rain."

Another loud bang sounded against the side, sounding right outside their window. "That's not."

They rolled to opposite sides of the bed simultaneously and reached for their clothes. They hurriedly dressed and headed for the door.

Luke went first and pushed the door open a crack. It was instantly flung wide, banging against the side of the RV as the wind caught it. Diagonally falling sheets of rain hit them, soaking the front of their shirts with cold water.

"Holy crap!" Kat gasped.

"We'd better get back in..."

Just then a lawn chair went tumbling past before slamming into a picnic table. It was clear that's what had smashed into their RV. The party had broken up before much cleanup had been done and the area around them was covered with tipped lawn chairs, overturned trash cans and garbage, a plastic tarp, even jackets and blankets, and several branches and piles of leaves. Everything was drenched, actually floating in some areas where there were depressions in the landscape, and scattered even farther than the party had strewn it.

"We've got to gather some of this stuff up," Kat said over the sound of the storm. "One of those chairs could go through somebody's window."

A cooler—obviously empty—tipped off the picnic table closest to them, landing so that the lid snapped off.

Luke looked from the cooler to Kat with an eyebrow up. "Let's get this over with."

As they took deep breaths and plunged into the storm, another RV door opened and Matt and Sheila Carson emerged, ducking against the rain. The wind was too strong to really talk with anything less than a shout, but with some pretty creative sign language they spread out and began chasing blowing chairs and picking up sodden paper.

It took about ten seconds to become completely wet. After ten minutes even her underwear was soaked.

Kat's hair was plastered against her head, her clothes clung and she was freezing, but as they ran and splashed she found herself breathless and laughing. She caught Luke's eye as he stepped in the middle of a huge puddle trying to grab a bag of aluminum cans that was rolling across the grass. He looked sexy. He was drenched but grinning and she realized that she loved that about him. Luke did what had to be done and managed to enjoy it—even in the cold rain.

By the time they'd gathered everything, the other couples from the surrounding RVs had materialized as well and they had the area, if not clean, at least secure from blowing metal and hard plastic objects.

Luke grabbed her hand and pointed to the RV. She nodded and they turned to wave at their temporary neighbors, then sprinted for warm, dry shelter.

Bursting into the RV panting and laughing, they slammed the door shut and stood shivering and dripping.

"I guess we might as well just strip down here," she said, looking at the puddle forming around her feet.

"I'm not going to talk you out of stripping, ever, for any reason," Luke said, getting out of his clothes quickly.

She was literally shaking with cold but still appreciated the naked man who headed for the bathroom and towels, and she peeled her clothes off, turning them inside out.

He handed her a towel and she quickly wrapped up. He wiped his arms, shoulder and hair, then draped the towel around his waist. Then he took a smaller towel and stepped close.

"You're going to hate what I'm about to tell you." He lifted the towel to her face and patted her forehead and cheeks.

"What?"

He pulled the towel back and held it up for her to see. Pink streaks colored the white terry cloth.

Her hand flew to her head. Her hair dye was washing out. Then she covered her eyes. "My makeup washed off too?"

"Um..."

She swiped a finger under her right eye. The pad of her finger turned black.

She groaned. "I must look terrible."

Luke took her hand and pulled it away from her face. "You're gorgeous," he said softly.

She looked into his eyes. She loved him. She wanted him. And she had only a few days to really show him before they went back to Justice and...whatever awaited.

She took a deep breath, dropped her hands and let him wipe the rain, makeup and hair dye from her face. He did it in gentle strokes, a half smile curling his lips, a tender look in his eyes.

"I love how you look," he said. "Always."

Then he kissed her.

She thought he'd rocked her world before with the hunger and passion and heat they always produced, but this kiss—sweet, almost reverent, full of affection—was like nothing she'd ever experienced. Or even imagined.

She pressed close.

She was going to make love to a man as herself—completely naked, with no makeup, no armor—for the first time ever.

Her towel dropped to the floor, Luke's towel ended up in the driver's seat and they left wet footprints all the way to the bedroom.

Luke woke up alone in the morning.

He didn't like that. He'd realized yesterday she'd awakened before he did on purpose, to avoid his seeing her without her hair and makeup done.

But after last night he'd hoped that was over.

Well, he was going to have to find her and reiterate how this was going to go.

She was his. All of her. And he wanted to know everything. Every good deed, every quirk, every mistake.

The bathroom still smelled of her soap and her towel was wet, indicating she'd been there not long ago, but the small counter was devoid of makeup and hair products.

He showered quickly, determined to find her and figure out how to handle the forced leave of absence and, maybe worse, the town gossip. He knew Justice, loved it, and had spent his life there. But while it was the perfect place for him to live and work, it was not full of perfect people.

Besides, Tom Martin's stroke was a big deal.

There would be long-standing effects on Tom's health and function, and there would be long-standing effects on Kat's reputation.

He didn't really believe that anyone expected her to be flawless but... Well, okay, they expected her to be flawless in doing whatever she could as a physician. She could pick out the wrong color paint for the concession stand at the baseball field or order too many plastic spoons for the chili feed, but in her role as physician it was different.

Kat was a hometown girl. Everyone liked her. But she wasn't cutting their hair or selling them tires—things that could be redone or corrected if they were wrong. She was taking care of their health and, maybe more importantly, the health of their families and friends.

They would, understandably, be less forgiving in those instances.

He sighed. He loved her, he knew she felt terrible, he knew she'd do whatever she could now to make it better. But she'd missed something and that was going to be hard for people to get over.

But he could help.

That was a perk of his position in town for sure. It wasn't arrogant to say that everyone loved him, trusted him, looked to him. It just was. He could help smooth this over for her.

He emerged from the RV, dressed for the day and determined to find a way to fix this thing.

"Luke, join us for pancakes!"

He turned to find their RV neighbors seated at the picnic tables, pancakes—amazingly—cooking on the grills.

"Grilled pancakes?" He chuckled. They smelled pretty damned good.

"Coffee?"

He turned toward the familiar voice with a big smile—that quickly changed to an amazed "o".

Kat stood behind him, dressed in a simple sundress—importantly, a *pink* sundress—with her hair curling naturally around her face without a single unnatural color streak. She also had no makeup on. Her big, brown, naked eyes looked back at him with a combination of curiosity, amusement—for the stupid look he was sure was on his face—and nervousness.

He was vaguely aware that everyone around them was completely quiet as he slowly turned completely toward her.

"Where'd you get that dress?" There was no way that was hers.

"Borrowed it from Lisa."

"Sandy's niece?"

Kat nodded.

He just stared, though he knew he looked like an idiot.

"I wanted you to see what you're really getting," she said softly.

His heart turned over and as of that moment was completely hers. He stepped close, until he was nearly on her toes, and said, "I'll take it."

"For sure?"

"No doubt in my mind." He lifted a hand to her face. "God, Kat, you're..." He wasn't sure what he meant to fill in there.

"Plain? Boring?" she asked.

There was something in her eyes that made him take the coffee cup from her, give it to the closest person—he didn't even look to see who it was—and then take her hand and pull her away from the group.

He didn't stop until they were at the gazebo where the band had played the night before. "What are you talking about?' he finally asked.

"People have ideas about what I'm like based on how I look. But I'm not tough and outgoing and sexy when all of the makeup and stuff comes off. I'm pretty plain and boring."

He frowned. She couldn't really believe that. "Seriously?"

"Seriously. I prefer to hang out in my pjs—my loose, baggy pjs—at home watching TV at night and I would rather read a book by myself than do it with a book club and I hate getting up in front of groups of people and I..." She took a deep breath. "I do actually care what other people think about me."

He cupped her cheek and looked into her eyes and the realization hit him—when he looked at her he didn't see the color—or lack thereof—of her hair or her eyelids or her clothes. He just saw *her*. And she was the same person with or without the makeup.

"Who you are doesn't come from how you dress, Kat. You feel differently in those clothes because you've told yourself that you're different. But the mind and heart you have—that made you stick up for all those girls who were being picked on and that made you want to help at a nursing home where you don't know anyone just because it's the right thing to do—those are the same no matter what you're wearing."

She frowned at that. "I'm not intimidating dressed like this."

He smiled and drew her closer. "I'm going to tell you something, Kat. It's not your clothes that intimidate people; it's your attitude. And you've got plenty of that no matter what you're wearing. I'm pretty sure that even if you're dressed in sweatpants and a T-shirt without makeup you won't hesitate to tell me—or anyone else—to go to hell if needed."

She rolled her eyes. "Maybe with you."

He liked the idea that she might be more comfortable with him than most people, but he knew she'd do what she needed to do whether she had tough-girl hair or not.

"Listen, I get that when you were thirteen you felt more kick-ass when you looked more kick-ass, so you *acted* more kick-ass. But now you're an adult. First off, why do you have to be intimidating? You've more than proven yourself. And second, you know that what you've got underneath—your brains, your heart, your *attitude*—matters more than what's on the surface."

She looked up at him, a tiny frown line between her eyebrows. "Because it's easier," she finally said softly.

"What's easier?"

"The status quo. Doing things the way I've always done them."

"Sure." He shrugged. "That's always easier. But that doesn't mean doing things differently will be bad. For instance, I love the way you look right now. Strangely, this is as much you as the black boots and piercings."

The frown line deepened. "I'm not sure you know what you're talking about. You can't even use a new color of paint at The Camelot."

Yeah, well... "I can change too. I would have never kidnapped a woman before this, and look how great that's turned out. Maybe I'll paint the lobby of The Camelot red. I might even get new centerpieces."

She gave him the fake gasp he was expecting. "I wouldn't want you to go too crazy all at once."

He chuckled and hugged her. "I think this is just the beginning of all the crazy we're going to have together."

She hugged him back, but didn't say anything.

They stayed that way for a long moment. Then she pulled back and looked up at him. "I think I need to go back to Justice."

He frowned. He knew she was feeling guilty but...hell, he really wanted to avoid her being hurt. Which he was really, really afraid was going to happen. "You sure? You don't want to let things settle first?"

She shook her head. "I've thought about it a lot and I'm not sure it will settle until I go back, face it and have a chance to be involved in what's happening. I feel helpless here just waiting to hear what other people decide."

Every protective instinct he had was riled up. He'd felt this before—the need to shelter and defend—but never this strongly. Lord knew he'd gone to bat for Sabrina a few thousand times, but this was different. This felt as though, if Kat was hurt, *he'd* be wounded and in pain right along with her.

He wanted her to smile, flirt, laugh and know she was wonderful. "Let me take you to Nashville. Everybody here is doing well, let's go on with our trip and we'll check back here on our way home." In fact, part of him wanted to never take her back to Justice. He wanted to wrap her up and keep her safe from anyone who might possibly upset her.

She took a deep breath and shook her head. "I have to go back, Luke. Staying here, avoiding it, letting Brickham and the rest handle it is...the easy way out."

Ah, hell.

"Nobody's going to blame you for going on vacation."

She gave a little smile. "But they're going to blame me for other things. I have to go back."

Okay, he was going to have to make this better for her in

Justice. It would be—okay, *easier*—to protect her feelings in Nashville, but they would have to go back to Justice eventually.

"When do you want to leave?"

"Right away. But I can rent a car in O'Neill and drive back. You keep going. Sabrina still needs the RV in Nashville."

"No way. I'm going with you."

She paused and tipped her head, watching him. "What about Sabrina?"

"Sabrina will just have to figure something else out. That's not my problem."

And he meant it. For maybe the first time in his life. Sabrina wasn't his problem.

But Kat was.

The trip back to Justice was strange. It went far too fast and it seemed like they'd been gone for weeks.

That probably had something to do with the fact her whole life had changed in those few days.

Her career had changed. She wasn't sure what, exactly, she was going back to but she knew it would be different.

And her love life... Well, *everything* had changed because of Luke. She'd left Justice with a crush and come back with a true love. And a future. With Luke anyway. She wasn't so sure about the medical group.

Luke pulled into The Camelot's parking lot so Kat could retrieve her car.

He looked at the front of the building and sighed, then gave her a little smile. "I wasn't supposed to be back to work for several more days."

She smiled and shook her head. "But you've missed it already, I bet."

He looked back to his restaurant, his dream. "Surprisingly, not as much as I would have guessed."

Kat took that as a compliment. It meant a lot to be able to distract Luke from his work. She turned and looked into the back of the RV. The RV she hadn't wanted any part of in the beginning. The RV she'd been forced into. The RV that now held some of the best memories of her life.

"Feels weird that this thing actually belongs to someone else," she commented. "It feels weird to give it back."

Luke was watching her intently when she swung her attention to him.

"What?" she asked.

"You," he said simply.

She frowned and smiled at the same time. "What about me?"

"It feels amazing that you actually belong to me now."

Her heart stuttered and she had to pull in a quick breath.

"You haven't been *mine* here in Justice, at The Camelot, in our real world until now." He took a deep breath, then let it out with a satisfied sigh. "I love it."

She did too. The whole concept of being Luke's—and vice versa—made her toes curl.

"I so want to take you in back and rock this thing one more time," she said.

Heat flared between them. "Don't let me stop you, darlin'," Luke said.

Kat sighed. "I have to go to Alliance. I have to talk to Brickham before he leaves for the day."

Luke shifted in his seat. "Yeah, that idea works as good as a cold shower."

"I know." She didn't want to go. But she wanted to get it over with. If she was going to get yelled at, sued, fired, whatever, she had to know today. She wouldn't be able to sleep until it was decided.

"I'll go with you." Luke opened his door and jumped to the ground.

She wanted him to. She couldn't deny it. And yet she

didn't. This was going to be the low point of her career and she really didn't want Luke to witness that.

"You stay here," she told him as she got out and met him by her car. "I don't know how long it will take or what will happen. I'll call you when I get back."

"Just come over." His hands went to her hips and he pulled her close.

"You'll be here?" Coming to The Camelot—and its bar—after meeting with Brickham seemed like a great idea. She wound her arms around his neck.

"I'll be at home. I'll make dinner."

She just stared up at him for a moment. "You're not going in?"

He glanced at the restaurant. "Nah. If I go in now I might get caught up in something and not be home when you get there."

She was in awe of this. Luke Hamilton hadn't missed a day in The Camelot...until they'd hit the road in the RV. As that truth sank in she stared at him. Taking her away to Nashville had been the first time Luke had been away from The Camelot for an entire twenty-four hour, or more, period of time.

That was big.

"I better get going," she said, stepping back before she started undressing him right here in the parking lot.

She dug her car keys from her purse and unlocked the door. Just before she climbed behind the wheel she gave him a grin. "You know I never mind ending my day here at the restaurant. In fact, I love it."

He cocked an eyebrow. "You think I won't be able to stay away? That I'll go in to check on one—okay, two—things and then lose track of time?"

She lifted a shoulder. "I think it wouldn't be the worst thing to happen."

He stepped forward, cupped her jaw and kissed her long and sweet. Then said, "I love you."

Her heart clenched and she swallowed hard. He was a dream come true—at the worst possible time.

"I'll find you when I get back," she promised. Then she kissed him again before slipping into the driver's seat and heading for Alliance and Dr. Brickham's office to see how much more her life was going to change.

Chapter Ten

The trip between Justice and Alliance was long even on beautiful sunny days. In crappy western Nebraska winter weather or when she needed to be there especially early in the morning—or when she was dreading what waited for her on the other end of the trip—it seemed endless. By the time she walked through the clinic doors she was so tense she wondered if she'd ever be able to move her neck fully again.

The Alliance Medical Partners main clinic was gorgeous. It housed not only the heart of the practice—the offices of the original partners, the scheduling and billing specialists, and the practice manager—but it also had twenty-four exam rooms, radiology, and lab.

"Hi, Lori," Kat greeted as she crossed the huge waiting room.

"Dr. Dayton," Lori exclaimed. "I thought you were on vacation."

"Cut it short," she said simply. "Is Dr. Brickham in?"

"He is. He has patients though," Lori said.

She'd figured that. She also figured he would torture her by making her wait. "I'll be over here." She headed for one of the waiting room chairs and pulled out her Kindle and iPod.

An hour and a half later, she sat across from Henry Brickham, his huge mahogany desk between them. He looked tired and frustrated.

Right away, he'd filled her in on Tom's condition—not good—then gave her the next news. Also not good.

"Probation."

"What does that mean exactly?" She didn't like that word. Or the tone in his voice. But at least it wasn't firing.

"You'll be working with another physician instead of being on your own," he said. "Someone who can give input, provide guidance."

She had no idea what to say. He was putting her on *probation*? Someone would be looking over her shoulder, judging what she did, watching for mistakes?

Bullshit.

"I don't need guidance or input, Henry."

"The partners disagree."

"*You* disagree." But it didn't matter. He was senior partner. The most experienced and respected of them all. And he owned a larger share of the practice than the others. What he said went.

"Yes, I disagree." He leaned his arms on the desk. "We have to do *something*, Kat. We can't just say *oops* and move on. We have to show that we're taking this seriously."

"Who am I serving my probation with?" she asked, recrossing her legs and folding her arms across her stomach. The tension in her body made her feel like she had tremors. She was holding herself so tightly she was shaking.

"Me," Brickham answered.

That figured. He was senior partner. And thought he knew it all.

"You're going to come to Justice? How often?"

"Of course not." He gave her a frown. "You'll come here. You'll practice with all of us here, but you'll be my responsibility."

"Here? Your responsibility?" Kat echoed. She wasn't sure what to say to any of this.

"I'll review your cases, we'll meet regularly about your patients. You'll be here, in the main practice, where you can observe procedures, ask questions."

"You are completely overreacting," she exclaimed. "I've already been a student and a resident." She was torn between wanting to throw something or throw up. "I was the top of my class, flew through residency. Do you really think this is necessary?"

He sighed. "I think it's in the best interest of the practice to publicly show that we are taking measures to ensure all of our providers are the best they can be. I don't want to fire you. I don't want you to have to defend yourself in court. We're hoping these measures will prevent both of those things from becoming necessary."

"It's in the best interest of the practice?" she repeated. "What about me?"

"You'll still be practicing medicine. You'll still be employed. Is that not in your best interest?"

The entire town of Justice would know, of course, that she was no longer working there and it would take about ten seconds for them to find out why. She'd be humiliated.

"How long is the probation?"

"A year."

She felt her eyes go wide. "A *year*?"

"Practicing general medicine in a small town is a challenge," Brickham said. "You have to know something about everything. In a single day you could deliver a baby, set a bone, diagnose a tumor and put in stitches. You have to be everything to everyone." He shook his head. "This is partly my fault anyway. I thought you were ready. I was wrong. I should have kept you here longer before putting you out there on your own."

"I was ready," she insisted. "It was a mistake. Surely I'm not the first to make a mistake in making a diagnosis."

He shook his head. "No, of course not. And this isn't the last diagnosis you'll miss. But your relative lack of experience is working against you in defending this situation. It can easily be argued that a more experienced physician wouldn't have made this mistake."

"It can also be argued that stroke symptoms mimic a number of other conditions and causes."

"Of course." He pinned her with a direct stare. "But do you

really want to have to have these arguments? Over and over? And I'm not even talking about court. You'll be having this conversation on the sidewalk in front of the grocery store and at the post office and when you go out for dinner."

He was right. The realization hit her directly in the chest. Strokes had been missed before, but Justice had never had its own medical clinic, its own doctor before. A stroke had not been missed before in Justice by the person they all trusted with their health, their lives.

This might not be the last time, but it was the first. And it would be remembered.

She didn't want to have to have this conversation at The Camelot.

That thought sent a cold shaft of dread through her. Could she even go back to The Camelot? That was where the bulk of the population of Justice could be found on any given night. If she didn't want to talk about her reassignment and the reasons for it, could she even step foot there?

Sure, it was chicken. Sure, she would be hiding. She hadn't done anything *wrong* or evil, but would they understand that? If they didn't, it would devastate her.

"What will happen in Justice?" People were just now getting used to seeking care in their own town, but it had taken awhile. If they shut the clinic now, even temporarily, it would obviously set the business back.

"Marty Davidson will be covering Justice," Brickham said. "He's excited about it."

Marty Davidson. The guy who'd covered her vacation. Brickham had known that Marty would be taking over even when he'd sent her on vacation.

Marty had only a couple of years more experience than Kat.

"It's a long drive."

"They're buying a house."

Kat's stomach pitched. Her fill-in was *moving* to Justice? That didn't sound temporary at all. She fought to hang on to her temper and professional façade.

"So this is not a temporary arrangement?"

"I think we need to see what happens in the next few months," Brickham said.

"You mean, we need to see if they end up yanking my license or suing me," she said bluntly.

Brickham didn't even blink. "Yes."

She took a deep breath. "I see."

And she did. She'd lost the Justice clinic.

Holy hell.

"This is partly my fault," Brickham said.

As far as Kat could tell, all of this was his fault.

"I'm sorry, Kat."

She jerked her head up, stunned that Henry Brickham was apologizing for something.

"I let you sell me with your confidence and your grades and the fact you were a hometown girl. But those things don't replace experience and objectivity."

"Objectivity?" she repeated. "What do you mean?"

"Sometimes when you treat people you know and care about it's easier to miss things. We don't want to see serious threats. We want everything to be fine. We want to fix everything. It's why physicians shouldn't treat family. It's impossible to be objective. In a small, close-knit town like Justice the same thing could easily happen."

Kat didn't reply. She wasn't sure what to say. She'd known Tom her whole life. Was it possible that her relationship with him made her see a sore shoulder instead of a more serious condition?

"So you don't think I'm the right choice for Justice? Even after the probation?"

Brickham didn't answer directly. Instead he said, "We would understand if you choose not to stay with AMP."

She stared at him. An invitation to leave? "Is that what you think would be best?"

"Not necessarily. Unless the probation and working in Alliance will affect your attitude and job satisfaction."

She narrowed her eyes. Of course it was going to affect her job satisfaction. She'd always wanted to be the physician in Justice, to take care of her friends and neighbors, contribute, be integral.

But it would not affect her attitude. She was a professional.

And what choice did she really have? She definitely didn't have the experience or knowledge to open her own practice at this point. And how would that be different exactly? If she was in Justice they would still know about Tom, about AMP and her mess-up. It was likely she wouldn't have a single patient seeking her care.

And there were no other hospitals or medical practices for hours.

She'd have to leave Justice, move, start over.

Leave Luke.

She pulled in a deep breath. She couldn't do that. And he'd never leave. Justice was the only place he ever wanted to be. Even without The Camelot, Luke planned to grow old and be buried in Justice. With The Camelot it wasn't even a question. It was his dream, his livelihood. It wasn't exactly something he could just pack up and move somewhere else.

"I'll stay."

"It's a long drive from Justice," Brickham said.

"I'm aware."

"I'm going to work you hard, give you a lot of exposure to a lot of things."

"Okay." Hard work didn't scare her. And he wasn't *entirely* wrong. She didn't have a lot of experience. She'd come to him with confidence—which was a little shaky at the moment—and volumes of book knowledge. But textbooks simply could not prepare her fully for how conditions presented in real people. So many factors came into play that it would be impossible to capture it all on book pages.

"You'll be covering more hospital visits, more ER, more of everything" he warned.

She took a deep breath. Being with Luke, being in Justice, having the life she'd always dreamed of was worth it. "Bring it on."

It was almost five hours later before Luke heard his front door open.

He strode down the hall toward the foyer. "Kat?"

"Yeah."

She tossed her purse on the table next to the door as if she'd been doing it for years. He smiled in spite of his concern. He loved that she was comfortable here.

"How'd it go?"

"I don't want to talk about it." She pulled her shirt off and tossed it toward the living room, then reached back to unhook her bra as she walked toward him. Her skirt and panties were gone before she wrapped her arms around him and pressed close. "Take me to bed."

There was something almost desperate in the way she kissed him. It was hot and wild, as usual, but it was like she was searching for something, needed something from him.

He was completely committed to giving her whatever it was.

"So no food?" he asked lightly when she let him breathe again. He ran his hands down to her butt and pulled her close. Even if she did want dinner he wasn't sure he could let her go now. This hunger that he felt whenever he touched her seemed to grow stronger every time and it made him feel pretty damned desperate too.

"I can get food anywhere from anyone, I can get conversation and friendship from a lot of people. Give me what I can only get from you." She started unbuttoning his shirt.

There was something in her words, in her tone, that nagged at the back of his mind. But once she started opening his fly he forgot all about it.

Her hands were hot and insistent as they pushed his jeans and underwear out of the way. The moment she took his cock in her hands, he groaned. "Bed?" he asked gruffly, his hands cupping and teasing her breasts.

"Floor," she said.

He managed to step her through the doorway to the living room, and the carpet, before she tugged him to the floor.

"Hard and fast," she panted. "I need you."

There was something in her eyes, something that pulled at him, made him want to give her everything, that made him nod. "You got it, darlin'. Whatever you want." Then he grabbed her hips and flipped her to her stomach. "Hard and fast. Make you scream."

"God yes," she breathed, bracing her arms.

He ran his hands over the sweet curves of her hips and ass, then reached to knock her knees apart. "Open up."

She complied, moaning slightly as she did, arching her back.

"I don't think I've ever seen you quite like this," he said huskily, cupping one breast, the hard tip setting the nerve endings in his palm tingling. Then he ran the pads of his fingers over her ribs and the soft skin of her stomach then slid over her mound. "You want me just to take you? Just move in and take over?"

"*Yes*," she groaned. She pressed back toward him, her butt against his stomach. "Take me, Luke."

"You're all mine," he reminded her, slipping his middle finger into her hot wet folds. "When you beg for this it will always be me. When you cry out a name when you come it will always be mine."

"Yes," she breathed. "Always."

She was ready. She was beyond ready. And knowing that he could have her, every night, over and over, forever, was enough to make him thrust hard and deep.

"Luke," she moaned. She widened her knees even farther, taking him as deep as he could go.

He fought to catch his breath. She was incredible and he knew that he would always give her anything and everything he could. Having her want him, having her need him, was more than he'd ever imagined.

He pulled back, then thrust again. Her body pulled on his, unwilling to let him go, massaging and drawing on him whenever he tried to withdraw. The tension around his length was heaven, the friction amazing and he pumped into her, hoping she could feel the heat and pressure he felt.

"Kat, Kat," he panted. He ran his hands up her back and pushed her forward, her chest toward the carpet, sinking even deeper. "This is so. Damned. Good."

She was making beautiful gasping, moaning sounds and he could feel her tightening even further around him.

He found her clit and circled, wanting to bring her up and over the edge of release but it only took one stroke of his finger and she came apart. And she did cry his name.

Luke continued to thrust, his hips moving, his cock absorbing every ripple of her orgasm until suddenly he shot over the edge too. Even as his climax swept over him, he couldn't stop moving within her and he pumped for another minute after his orgasm had quieted.

Finally he withdrew and slumped to the carpet, one arm around her waist, pulling her up against him to lie side by side.

They just breathed for several minutes.

When she finally wiggled in his arms, he loosened his hold and she turned to face him.

"Is it just me or is sex with you in Justice even better than in the RV?"

He grinned. "I'm definitely not complaining."

She kissed him, then pushed to her feet. "Okay, well, I'll see you."

"What?" He stood as well. "You're not staying?"

Something flickered in her eyes just before she shrugged. "I have to be in Alliance at six tomorrow."

"Six a.m.?" he asked.

"Yeah. And I don't know when I'll get home."

He tipped her chin up so she had to look at him. "What happened?"

"We met. He thinks I need to spend more time in Alliance. I need more experience."

Luke frowned. He knew there was something she wasn't telling him. "Kat, what happened?"

"Just...we're working some things out."

"How's Tom?"

Her eyes clouded. "Not good. Things are just...complicated. So I should get home so I can get up and at it tomorrow."

"Stay here. You can get up and leave from here." Not only did he want her in his arms all night—just a few days of it on the road and he was addicted—but he sensed that she needed him. He loved that in a way, but he wasn't sure what to do.

She was watching him. "I want to," she admitted. "I really do. This is so good. This is what I've wanted for so long." She put her hand against his cheek. "I just..."

"Stay. We'll go over and get some more clothes and stuff for you and then you'll stay here."

"Stay?"

Stay. With that word a warmth spread through him like he'd taken a shot of whiskey. "Stay. For good. Move in."

Her eyes got wide. "What?"

"Move in. Live with me."

She took a deep breath. "Are you serious?"

"Of course. Why not?" It was perfect. "We both want it. There's no reason not to. Move in."

She pulled her bottom lip between her teeth. "Things might be a little crazy with work for the next...few weeks."

That little pause made him frown. "That's okay. We'll figure it out."

"You sure?"

"Kat, I want you. Forever. For good. All the time. We'll figure the bumps out."

She looked sad for just a moment before she covered it. "Okay."

He didn't like that flicker of hesitation or whatever it was either. Every protective instinct was coming awake. But he didn't understand it. He needed to get her in his house, in his life fully, their routines and dirty laundry all mixing together, and he was sure he could take care of her—of it—whatever it was. She was his now and nothing was going to change that.

"Let's get you moved in," he said decisively heading for the door. Something in him drove him to want this *now.* Before anything could happen to mess it up.

"Luke, wait—"

"No waiting. Let's do this." He jerked open the door.

"Maybe putting some clothes on would be good," she called as he reached for the screen door.

He looked down, then back at her.

"Oh, right," he said with a sheepish grin. "But clothes are the only thing I'm taking time for."

"So, let me get this straight," Marc said, setting down his whisk and leaning his hands on the countertop. "You're madly in love with Kat, you're sure she feels the same way, you're having nearly constant sex with her and you're *upset* about this?"

"Only about the sex part." Luke sighed and braced his hands on the counter behind him, leaning back. He sounded like an idiot. He felt like one too. But it was true. He was upset that he was getting so much sex from Kat.

"You're going to have to talk slow and use small words," Marc said. "'Cuz I don't get it."

"It's been a month since we got home and moved in

together. But I barely see her," Luke started. "She's in Alliance all the time. When she does come home she's exhausted. All she wants to do is have sex. She doesn't want to talk, to come here, to just...be."

"And you want to just...be?" Marc asked.

Luke scowled at him. "I thought you, of all people, would understand."

"What's that mean? I like sex. I *love* sex."

"You never just want to sit and watch TV? Have dinner and talk? Hang out at a barbecue?"

Marc chuckled and started whisking again. "Yeah, I was just giving you a hard time. But it's not *bad* that she wants to have sex a lot, is it?"

Luke shifted. "It's just that...I think she's using it to distract me."

Marc grinned at him. "And it's working?"

"Well, yeah." He was a human male after all.

"What's she distracting you from?"

"Whatever's really going on."

Marc looked up from pouring whatever he'd been stirring into a pan. "What's really going on?"

"I don't know," Luke said impatiently. "I've been distracted."

Marc laughed at that. "Right. Sorry. What do you *think* is going on?"

"It's something with work."

"I can imagine she's a little stressed. Tom Martin is still out in Denver. Dr. Davidson is still covering the clinic here. I heard the licensure board decided she was fine though."

Yeah, Luke had heard that to. From Sabrina, not Kat. "But she won't tell me about it. The last time I brought it up she..." He trailed off, realizing that he didn't want to share every one of these details.

"She...distracted you?" Marc offered.

With whipped cream and her magical mouth.

He cleared his throat. "Anyway, she won't tell me about it. Claims there's nothing to talk about. She won't let me help her."

Marc bent to push the pan into the oven. "And you have to constantly be helping someone," he muttered.

"Really? Judgment from the man who *forced* the woman he loved onto an airplane to Nashville?"

"I get it. I do," Marc said as he straightened—and failed to acknowledge or deny his crazy behavior when it came to Sabrina before they figured out how to be together. "You want her happy. You want her to have everything she wants. And you want her to lean on you."

Luke nodded. "Yes. Exactly. How do I do that?"

"Since you want to see more of her, I guess forcing her on an airplane would defeat what you're going for."

"Right," Luke said dryly.

"I think you need to talk to her. Make her listen. Fully clothed. Maybe someplace where she can't seduce you."

The truth was that Kat could probably seduce him in the middle of a church sanctuary.

"Okay."

"Then don't let her leave until you've convinced her that she can tell you anything and you have the truth."

An hour and forty minutes later, Luke was sitting in the waiting room of the Alliance Medical Partners clinic flipping through a *Cosmo* magazine from 2009. Still, he couldn't argue with the seven ways to seduce a man outdoors and the position-by-position guide to "The Best Sex of Your Life" seemed timeless.

The receptionist, Jill, had assured him that Kat was finishing with her last patient when he'd arrived forty minutes ago, but he was waiting. No matter how long it took.

He was reviewing position number three, making sure he had all the details, when Kat finally emerged. He watched her for a moment before she saw him. She looked exhausted. And pissed off.

What was going on?

It also hit him that he missed her. He'd seen her every night. He'd made love to her every night. Yet he missed her.

He hadn't seen her laugh, hadn't really talked to her, in a month. It was driving him crazy.

"Kat."

She looked up from rummaging in her purse. "Luke?" She looked stunned for just a second, then her face lit up and she practically launched herself at him. "What are you doing here?"

He wrapped his arms around her, loving that he could make her so obviously happy just by showing up. "Can't stay away from you."

She pulled back to look up at him, her expression a combination of affection and amusement. "I know how you feel." Then something mischievous flickered in her eyes and she glanced around. The waiting area was deserted of patients as it was nearly an hour past closing time. The front office staff had also left for the day. She took his hand. "Come here."

She pulled him through a door just behind the potted tree. The restroom.

"Kat, I..."

"Oh, shut up and do me already," she said with a light laugh as she started unbuttoning her shirt.

He wanted her. He always wanted her.

But he wanted more than this. And he suspected she did too.

"Stop." He grabbed her hands and held them in his, trying to get her to look at him.

She did. "What's wrong?"

"I came to take you to dinner. Maybe a movie."

"You came...to take me to dinner?" she repeated, looking genuinely confused. "Why?"

"I've never really taken you on a date. And I want to spend time with you, talk."

"I have to be here really early tomorrow. And I have some

research tonight—"

"I brought the RV," he said. "We'll stay here tonight. You won't have the long drive tonight or tomorrow. I want the two hours I just saved you."

She stared at him. "You brought the RV? So you could spend time with me?"

"Yes. And not sex time. Real time."

The corner of her mouth curled. "Sex isn't real time? It's fake?"

"It's fantasy," he said, his voice a little gruff. "And very real. And I love every second. But I want to talk to you."

"About what?"

"Nothing." He blew out a frustrated breath. "I mean, everything. Nothing specific. I just want to talk."

She propped a hand on her hip, her blouse gapping and showing a hint of pink satin. "Why?"

Luke pulled his eyes from the peek of her bra. "Why what?"

She gave him a knowing smile. "Why do you want to talk to me?"

"Something is going on with you," he said, again focused. "And I want you to tell me about it. I want to know about work. I want to know why Dr. Davidson is still covering the clinic in Justice. I want to know how Tom Martin is doing and how you feel about the licensure investigation going in your favor. I want to know what you had for lunch, for God's sake." He thrust a hand through his hair. He sounded like an idiot. "Enough with the sex already." A complete idiot.

Her eyebrows were up by the time he finished. "Okay. Davidson is covering the clinic because I'm here. Tom has a feeding tube but came off the ventilator. I feel great about my license. And I had a turkey sandwich and barbecue chips. And iced tea."

He sighed, actually feeling—stupidly—relieved to know all of that. "Thank you."

"Now can we have sex?"

He sighed. She didn't get it. "No. I want to *just* talk."

"Well, *I* want an orgasm."

His blood heated in spite of himself. "No."

She moved in closer. "I really, really want your hands on me, Luke." She started unbuttoning again. "I want your mouth on me. I want my mouth on you. I want to suck and lick and—"

He was weak. He needed help. "I was afraid it was going to come to this." In fact, he'd been pretty sure it was going to come to this. He reached in his pocket and pulled out the handcuffs. "We're going to *talk*."

He grabbed her wrists before she could react and linked them together.

She recovered quickly. "You cannot lead me out of here handcuffed, Luke."

"Why not?" He'd throw her over his shoulder if he had to.

"People will notice."

There weren't any people left to notice. Thank goodness. "You brought this on yourself."

"By wanting to have sex with you? Well, gee, I'm so sorry." She was clearly irritated.

"By distracting me with your body and mouth and..." He focused on her lips. What had he been saying?

"You've enjoyed every single stroke," she purred, leaning in close again.

"I have. Which is why I handcuffed you and we're going to a restaurant where you can't seduce me."

"You're going to keep me handcuffed in a restaurant?" she asked. "Are you crazy?"

"I'll uncuff you once we get there."

"What if I try to put my hand down your pants under the table?"

He shifted as his cock responded without input from his brain. "You won't."

"Try me."

"We'll sit on opposite sides of the table." He took her hand and headed for the door of the restroom, then out the front of the clinic.

He drove her car to the Italian place he remembered from trips long before he'd built The Camelot. As he opened the car door for her, he unlocked the cuffs but slid them into his pocket for safekeeping. He might need them again to get her to behave. And it definitely wouldn't do for *her* to get ahold of them.

"You can make me come to dinner and you can keep my hands from taking my clothes off, but you can't make me talk," she said once they were seated and had ordered wine.

He leaned his forearms on the table. Yes, he could. If her feelings were as strong as he thought—and hoped—they were, he could.

"I love your body," he said. "I love that I know that you have an erogenous zone on your left ankle and that I can make you come apart with my hands and mouth before I even take my pants off. I love the sound you make when I first kiss you, I love the feel of your hair in my hands when you take me in your mouth."

He watched with satisfaction as her lips parted and her pupils dilated.

"That all matters to me, Kat. Connecting with you physically is unlike anything I've ever experienced before. And I love that it's true for you too."

He knew it was. He could tell even without her words, but she'd also confirmed it in breathless pants as he pumped deep.

"But there has to be more here."

She took a deep breath and looked down at her fork. She slowly turned it tines down, then tines up, again and again. "What if there's not?" she finally asked.

"What if there's not what?" He couldn't say why exactly, but a cold trickle of unease started down his spine.

She lifted her eyes and met his gaze. "What if there's not more? What if that's all I can give you?"

Chapter Eleven

Wine.

That was the answer right now.

Along with more wine.

"What are you talking about?" Luke asked with a frown.

She drank down half her glass.

"That's ridiculous, Kat. There's so much more between us."

She finished the glass and reached for the bottle.

It was a good thing he'd brought the handcuffs because this whole situation was exactly what she'd been trying to avoid for the past month. She didn't want to talk. Because once she started, it would all come out.

Instead, she'd been focused on proving to Luke that what she *could* give him—limited as it may be—was *really* good. Really worth it.

She loved living with him. What little of it she had experienced. She was never there, it seemed. She shared his bed, his toothbrush holder and his closet, dresser and fridge. But she hadn't sat on the couch, watched his TV or even used the oven.

So, she also hated living with him. It was like being able to see and smell chocolate chip cookies baking but not being able to eat them. Very tempting and very unsatisfying.

She was being constantly teased with *almost* having what she wanted.

"I've been trying to distract you," she finally said.

"I knew it!" he exclaimed. "The sex was to keep me from prying."

He looked so triumphant, for a moment she just smiled at

him. Then she realized his look of happiness was about to change. As was hers.

But she was tired. So tired. Physically and mentally, yes, but also emotionally. Keeping Luke at arm's length was zapping her because she didn't want him at arm's length. She wanted to be as close as two people could get. She wanted to tell him everything and then have him hug her and hold her and tell her it was fine—that she was still the woman he wanted, no matter what else.

Tom was progressing very slowly in Denver. Marty Davidson was doing a great job in Justice. She still had her license, thank God, but Brickham was either really punishing her or he truly believed she knew nothing. She was working long, horrible hours and he was constantly over her shoulder.

Something had to give.

Now Luke was here, demanding she do what she really did want to do—talk to him.

Okay, fine.

"I was trying to distract you from realizing that all I have to offer you is the blow jobs, the vibrator and the dirty talk."

He frowned. "What do you mean?"

"On your top ten list," she said. "I don't fit very many criteria anymore."

"Kat, you... Yes, you do," he insisted.

Of course.

Luke Hamilton always had a plan and he was the most stubborn man she'd ever met when it came to making his plan fit.

"No, I don't," she said with a sigh. "I technically live in Justice but I'm barely there, I'm certainly not able to socialize or be on committees, or spend time at The Camelot, or see our friends and family. I don't have a job there anymore and..." She broke off as she realized what she'd said.

He frowned. "What do you mean you don't have a job there anymore?"

She took a deep breath. She wanted to tell him this. Kind of. At least she wanted to stop wondering about his reaction.

And she was about two seconds from finding out what that would be.

"I lost the clinic, Luke."

"For now. For a while."

She shook her head. "No. Marty wants it. He's doing a great job and Brickham wants him to stay. He's buying a house."

"So what if Marty wants it. You're from there. Doesn't that matter? What about—"

"No," she broke in before she lost her nerve. "No, it doesn't matter. What matters most is having someone who will do a great job and everyone will trust."

"And that's not you?" He looked angry. Really angry.

She sighed. "The great job part is me." She believed that. She was a good doctor. She cared about her patients and she would do whatever she could for them. But Marty was a good doctor too. With more experience. "The trusting part is an issue."

"That's bullshit," he said. Loudly.

She glanced around. "Luke, calm down." People were staring.

He clearly didn't care. "Did you misdiagnose Tom on purpose?" he demanded, his voice still louder than necessary. "Did you want to hurt him or his family?"

She frowned. "Of course not."

"And do you think you need Brickham's help? Do you need mentoring? Do you need to be here in this clinic every day?"

"No." Not that she knew everything, but she could—would—learn. She'd make sure of it. She didn't need Brickham, or anyone else, watching her. She wanted to collaborate. She wanted someone she could talk to as a colleague—not someone who was testing and judging her. "Definitely not."

"Then stop feeling guilty."

She focused fully on Luke, realizing she'd let her thoughts

run and her blood pressure rise thinking about Brickham and her situation. "What?"

"Stop feeling guilty. You're letting him do this to you because you've let him convince you he's right. But he's not, Kat. You're amazing. You don't deserve this."

Wow. Luke was defending her. To her. It sounded good. And looked good. His gaze was intense, his jaw tight and he looked dangerous, like he was ready to do battle. For her.

It definitely made her want to put her hand down his pants, restaurant or not. She breathed out through pursed lips, then said, "Thanks. And you're right," she admitted. "I've let him do this. I have felt guilty."

Luke looked pleased. "So, go in there and tell him that you want the clinic back."

She blinked at him. "Um, no, that's not going to work."

"Make him listen. Tell him that you—"

"Luke, that discussion's closed." She might be in the right—Brickham might even acknowledge that—the thing was...

"I don't really want to work for Brickham. Even if it's in Justice."

Luke frowned. "Okay. Why?"

"He didn't support me at all. He assumed I did something wrong before he had the facts. He never asked how I was. He didn't keep me in the loop with Tom. And nothing about this past month has been encouraging. I've felt belittled and disrespected since day one."

Luke sat back in his chair processing the information. "Who else can you work for?"

That was part of the problem right there. "There's no one else. AMP has all the small towns covered. They contract to the hospital. I could work directly for the hospital but—"

"That's not Justice," Luke pointed out.

"Exactly. Doesn't solve every problem," she said with a nod. "Besides, Brickham is on the Board. They might not hire me anyway."

"Then you can open your own clinic in Justice. You don't have to be a part of a bigger practice, right?"

"Not technically," she said. She'd thought of this, but there were so many reasons it was a bad idea. "But I don't know the first thing about running a clinic. And I don't have enough money to build and—"

"I do," he interrupted.

"You do what?"

"Have the money to build and know a lot about running a business." He looked determined. And still angry.

"Running a business and running a health-care business are two different things," she said, trying to slow her heartrate. He wasn't listening. "We have to have insurance contracts and meet Medicare guidelines and file claims..." She sighed. It was seriously overwhelming to even think about. "I want to treat patients," she finally said. "I want to be a doctor. Not a claims specialist or business owner or practice manager."

"You can hire people," he said stubbornly.

She frowned. This was typical. He had to find a way for this to fit what he'd envisioned. "I don't want to hire people. I don't know what they need to know in order to be hired. And I'd be competing against Marty and AMP for patients, Luke. AMP is established in this area and now in Justice. By the time I'd get a practice up and running they'd be even more established."

"You'll just have to outdo him. And you can." Luke sat forward. "People will come to you. You can make this work."

He sounded supportive. He sounded like he wanted what was best for her. But she couldn't help but wonder—was it more that he wanted what was best for *him*? He'd been in love with Sabrina for years, but when she wanted to follow her dream to travel and try to make it in music he refused to go with her. He knew what he wanted and if she wasn't willing to give it... Kat didn't want to think about it, but it was very possible that he'd say *see ya* to her too.

She sat forward too, her temper rising. "I don't want to make that work," she said firmly. "I don't want to work for

Brickham, I don't want to work at the hospital in Alliance and I don't want to open my own clinic in Justice." She'd been willing to make the drive to and from Alliance forever, *for him*, until he insisted on her telling him what was *really* going on.

This was what was really going on.

He should have been content with the mega amounts of sex.

Luke just sat staring at her for a long moment. Then he sat back in his chair and gave her a huge grin.

What the hell? She poured another glass of wine.

"You definitely don't need to put up with any of that."

She drank half the glass of wine. "Yeah?"

"You deserve more than that."

Damn right she did. She narrowed her eyes. "What are you talking about?" They really needed to be on the same page here.

"You deserve the freedom to do whatever you want."

She did. But did he know what she wanted to do? "Like what?"

"Anything." He looked almost excited. "I can easily support you. You've already moved in. We'll sell your house. You don't have anything to worry about."

She drank the rest of her wine. Once she'd set her glass back on the table she tipped her head. "What will I do?"

He shrugged. "Pro bono work. Volunteer. Work at The Camelot. Nothing. Whatever you want."

"I could work at The Camelot?" she repeated. "Doing what? Washing dishes?"

He smiled. "No. You can bartend. Or hostess. Or nothing," he said again, reaching for his own wine. "You can be a lady of leisure."

"You want me to be a desperate housewife?" she asked. "We're going to need to put in a pool so I can get a pool boy. And a garden so I can have a gardener to mess around with."

He didn't pick up on her irritation. He grinned. "I'll come home for nooners so you won't have to worry about that."

He had to be kidding.

"Oh, well in that case, sure. I'll just stay at home. I'll just forget the ten years I spent in school, the fact that I love taking care of patients, the idea of doing meaningful work and feeling rewarded." She couldn't believe he wasn't kidding. Okay, pro bono work wasn't a *terrible* idea, but—

"Well, that brings up another fantastic option," he said.

She wasn't sure she wanted to hear it. "Oh?"

"We can start our family."

Kat just stared at him. He grinned back. She reached for the wine bottle.

Once she'd poured and drank again she said, calmly, "As in, I can get pregnant and then stay home with the baby because I don't have anything better to do?"

He frowned. "I want you to be happy, Kat. I want to give you something that means a lot to you, that you'll be great at, but that doesn't stress you out and make you feel like crap."

She understood what he was doing. He was fixing this. Or trying to.

That was what Luke did. He fixed things for people.

She'd come to him with a problem—hating her job—and he was making it so she didn't have to work at the job she hated.

But all of his solutions revolved around him still getting what he wanted—her in Justice.

"Babies are your solution?" she asked, sounding as exhausted as she felt.

"An option," he said quickly, finally picking up on her exasperation. "Off the top of my head. Without fully thinking it through before I opened my mouth and sounded like a chauvinist."

She actually smiled a little at that.

She wasn't ready for this fight. She wasn't ready to let go of him yet. The choice was clear—stay with AMP and keep Luke, or leave AMP...and Luke.

Kat stood and slipped into his lap. She looked into his eyes, then leaned in and kissed him, pouring her love into it. He didn't resist her for a moment.

When she pulled back, she saw the same love in his eyes. "That's for trying to fix things for me," she said softly.

Even the stuff that couldn't really be fixed.

She stood, took his hand and tugged him to his feet. "I need you," she told him.

Without a word, he pulled his wallet out, tossed a hundred dollar bill on the table, then took her hand and headed for the door.

Kat approached the door to the Camelot with an unexpected and unwelcome amount of anxiety.

She hadn't been there in over a month. And she hadn't really missed it. The month had confirmed that the appeal was Luke. She liked the people who came here, loved the food, usually had a good time. But it had been part of her daily routine because of Luke. Now she had him at home so she hadn't missed being at the Camelot.

On the few nights off Dr. Brickham had given her, she'd wanted to be quiet at home with Luke. Or loud at home with Luke.

But tonight was Luke's dad's birthday, so she was showing up.

She pulled the strap of her dress higher on her shoulder and breathed deeply.

This didn't feel right. She was incredibly uncomfortable. Which was crazy. The dress was a soft, flowing cotton, and was modest and tasteful.

Everyone was going to be shocked.

She was wearing yellow. Light yellow. No black. No boots. Her hair was soft and curly, her makeup was subtle and tasteful.

She was dressed exactly how Luke "Pillar-of-the-

Community" Hamilton's girlfriend should dress at his father's birthday party.

And she couldn't do it.

She felt vulnerable, extremely unsure of herself, definitely frustrated, even sad. Every bit of that would show. She needed to have everyone looking somewhere other than her eyes.

Turning on the heel of her conservative, comfortable, flat sandal she headed home.

In her closet ten minutes later, she reached for the skimpiest, tightest thing she had.

The black zip-front bandeau minidress would mold to every curve and show off plenty of cleavage. It would show off the swirls of silver body paint on her shoulders. It would look hot with her boots.

It would effectively distract everyone.

She wouldn't have to worry about any deep heart-to-heart talks or prying questions in this dress.

The men would be busy trying to pull their attention from her breasts and butt when they talked to her and the women would be busy hating her and regretting that they'd skipped the gym that morning.

It was perfect.

Twenty minutes later her makeup was nice and heavy and her hair was spiked and purple.

Much better.

She managed to stand in the doorway to the Camelot's main dining room for nearly a full minute before being noticed.

Sabrina was on stage and Marc was helping behind the bar, but Mrs. Sangle, Justice's high school biology teacher, noticed her just seconds before Luke did.

"Kat."

"Hi, Mrs. Sangle."

"It's nice to see you." The older woman's eyes traveled over Kat's ensemble and for the first time Kat noticed...and cared.

Dammit.

"How are you?" Kat asked, trying to ignore the irritation she felt. Besides, she couldn't decide if she was irritated with Dorothy Sangle or herself.

They were just clothes. Why did they have to matter at all? To Mrs. Sangle...or to Kat herself?

"Fine. Fine. No complaints. I wanted to ask you for some help, though."

Mrs. Sangle had trouble controlling her diabetes. "Of course. What's going on?"

"We're going to be raising funds to put an ice cream machine in at the community center. I was hoping you would cochair the fund-raising committee."

Kat stared at her. An ice cream machine. Seriously?

"I'm not sure I have time for anything like that right now," Kat said. She was sure she did *not* have time for that. If they'd asked her to do a presentation on managing high blood pressure or dealing with hormonal fluctuations she'd make time. But a stupid ice cream machine at the stupid community center? Really?

Luke came up beside her, slipping an arm around her, his fingertips brushing the bare skin at her waist. "Smile," he muttered with a big smile of his own for Mrs. Sangle.

Smile? He was concerned because she wasn't *smiling*? Well, she didn't frickin' feel like smiling.

"Evening, Dorothy," Luke said. "Thanks for coming."

"Hi, Luke." Mrs. Sangle glanced at Kat. "I'm sorry things are so busy, Kat. Maybe another time."

Oh, sure. The next time the town decided it needed to raise a few hundred dollars for something completely frivolous, Kat was sure they'd ask her to head it up.

"Just let me know when the preschool is ready to hear about the importance of physical activity or when the senior center wants to hear about how to keep their bones strong," she said. And she smiled as she did it.

Mrs. Sangle frowned. "I suppose Dr. Davidson will be

handling those talks now. But maybe you can get involved when we start planning the next book club."

Kat gritted her teeth, then opened her mouth.

But before she could respond, Luke broke in. "Thanks, Dorothy. Keep us in mind," he said as he turned Kat away and toward his office.

Once safely inside, he shut the door and faced her. "Bad night?" he asked.

"She wants me to raise money for an ice cream machine." Kat paced to his desk, then turned and paced to the other side of the room, full of angry energy.

"I know."

"That's ridiculous."

"Why? You're a great fund-raiser."

She stopped and looked at him. Was he trying to be funny? Push her buttons? She couldn't tell. And she wasn't going to try to figure it out. Just like she hadn't felt like smiling at Dorothy Sangle, she didn't feel like puzzling out what Luke was doing or not doing.

"I don't want to." She crossed her arms.

"Because you're busy and tired?" Luke asked.

"No. Because I don't like spending my time doing things that are stupid."

"You've raised money for stupider things than this. Like the potted silk plants they put in the church lobby."

She rolled her eyes. That had been stupid.

"Why did you do that?" he asked, coming toward her.

She averted her eyes, running her finger up and down the seam on her sleeve. She wasn't going to admit she'd done all of that to fit into his image of the perfect woman. No fund-raising event too trivial, no cause too inane.

"Have you ever noticed that they don't ask me to do anything serious?"

Luke tipped her chin up with one finger, making her look at him. "No, I've never noticed that."

"They ask me to do little stuff. Silly stuff." The realization was just dawning for her as well. She'd never been in the center of anything like Luke was.

"I don't think they—"

"Luke, I'm not who they want up in front of everything and everyone."

He started to shake his head, but she grabbed his face between her hands, stopping him. "I have purple hair. Or blue. Or green. I wear black leather. Often skimpy black leather. I have piercings. That's not who they want to shine the spotlight on."

"Everyone likes you," Luke insisted.

"They do," she agreed. At least, most of them liked her. "But liking me and wanting me as the image of the town are two different things."

"So, show them who you really are. Show them that this image isn't really you. Show them what's underneath." He swiped his thumb gently along the black line under her bottom eyelashes. The eyeliner came off on his skin. "I thought you were getting more comfortable being real."

She sighed and shook her head. "This is real. This is who I am here."

"But this is home. You should be most comfortable here."

He had a point. Home was where you could be yourself. Which made her heart flip, then ache.

Justice wasn't home for her.

"Then they shouldn't care what I wear. And my mistakes should be forgiven. And I shouldn't have to prove myself. I shouldn't have to be on every little stupid committee and fund-raise for every little stupid thing someone comes up with to fit in."

Luke didn't look surprised. But he did look disappointed.

She pulled away from him, not able to look at that. "I want to be real, Luke. I do. So I'm going to from here on out. And there's more to it than sweatpants versus leather." She took a deep breath, feeling like she was about to jump off the high diving board. "I don't like committees, I read the synopsis online instead of reading the last book club book, I pay Mrs. Jenkins to bake for me when it's bake sale time. And I'd rather watch football on your couch with a bag of potato chips instead of having a big fancy party with all our friends."

Or New Year's Eve parties, card parties, *American Idol* parties... Luke took any reason to get huge groups of friends together.

He was scowling now. "Is that all?"

"No." She'd come this far. She had to make sure he understood that she was not the right woman for him. In pretty much every way. "I want maybe two kids. Definitely not six. Definitely not more than six. And I don't want them for a while. My job is demanding and I won't be good at playing with Play-Doh, or reading Dr. Seuss four million times, or making science projects, or teaching them to ice skate."

Tears were threatening now. This hurt her, but she knew it hurt him too. He'd want to fix this and he couldn't.

"Anything else?" he asked tightly.

"Just..." She knew this answer was the only one possible. But once she said it out loud it would be real. Finally she managed to whisper, "I'm going to Rolland."

Several seconds ticked by. She couldn't look at him.

Finally Luke asked, "Stan offered you a job?"

She nodded, gathering her courage for one more question. She blew out a long breath and asked, "Will you come with me?"

He said nothing for a long moment. When she finally looked up she saw that he was clearly stunned. "Go with you?" he asked.

"Yes."

"Move to Rolland?"

It was too far for either of them to commute. "Yes."

"But..." He seemed genuinely confused by the proposal. Of

course he was.

This wasn't part of *his* plan. "What about the Camelot?"

"Hire someone to manage it."

He shook his head before she even finished the suggestion. "And my parents? Marc, our friends..."

Right. All the things that were actually way above blow jobs on his top ten list.

"What about us?" she asked quietly.

That made his frown deepen. "Let me think."

"Think?" He had to *think?*

"I'm sure I can come up with something that will work," he insisted.

Something that would work with his plans. Kat knew that was what he meant. Rolland wasn't even an option to him. Leaving Justice, sacrificing wasn't even on the table. For a month, all for *him,* she'd been working her ass off, putting up with all kinds of bullshit without a complaint while still putting out every night and now that it was his turn to consider what she needed he was still trying to manipulate it to work his way.

"I'm going to Rolland," she said again, her chin up.

"With or without me?" Hurt flashed in his eyes before it was replaced by anger.

She pressed her lips together and blinked hard against the sting of tears. Finally she said, "Without you, I'm guessing."

Luke took a deep breath in, staring at her. Then he nodded once, turned, pulled the door open and left the room.

Leaving her alone.

More alone than she'd ever been.

"Okay, let's do this."

Luke looked up from the paperwork he'd been pretending to do for the past hour to find Sabrina tossing her purse into one chair in front of his desk and dropping herself into the other.

"Do what?" He knew exactly why she was here.

She raised her eyebrows. "Really?"

He sighed and put his pen down. "Okay." She was here to yell at him. Finally. It had been two days since Kat had told him she was going to Rolland. Without him.

"So should I start with the obvious stuff or do you want me to go straight to the analysis?" Sabrina linked her hands over her pregnant belly and regarded him seriously.

He leaned back in his chair. "Give me something obvious." He needed a warm-up for the deep stuff.

He knew exactly what she was going to say too.

"You're an idiot."

Yep, word for word.

"She's the one leaving. I don't get why I'm the bad guy." His heart clenched like it had for the past forty-eight hours whenever he thought about the fact that Kat was leaving him. Leaving period. But definitely leaving him.

Sabrina tipped her head to one side. "Who said you're the bad guy?"

"Marc. Steve. Brad. Bill."

"My dad said you're a bad guy?" Sabrina asked with obvious surprise.

It was no secret that Bill Cassidy was one of Luke's biggest fans.

"Apparently the popular opinion is that Kat is perfect for me and I should do anything necessary to keep her with me."

Sabrina just looked at him for a moment. "So why aren't you?"

He felt the weight that had been in his chest since leaving Kat in his office grow heavier. "She has blue hair."

"Sometimes," Sabrina agreed.

"And piercings. And black leather boots."

"Always has," Sabrina pointed out.

"Do you really think that's what people want to see as the wife of their future mayor?" His gut clenched even as he said it out loud.

"Future mayor?" Sabrina asked. "I didn't realize that was on your to-do list."

He shrugged. He supposed on some level he'd just assumed he'd keep on serving Justice until he'd done it all. "I could get elected if I wanted to."

"You sound like an ass."

He knew that. "Yeah."

"I was actually talking about the thing with Kat. But yes, the mayor thing too."

He agreed.

But it was Kat's argument—that this was who she was in Justice and that wouldn't change. Which might be true. And maybe no one would take her seriously. Or take him seriously if she was beside him.

That made his heart feel like a block of ice in his chest—hard and cold. Kat was amazing and the idea that the town he loved couldn't see past the hair dye was painful.

"There's the kid thing too," he said. It wasn't just about her blue hair. She wasn't the right woman for him. She'd been very clear about multiple points that proved that.

"What kid thing?"

"She only wants two."

Sabrina said nothing to that.

"She doesn't want to play with Play-Doh." Kids needed to play with Play-Doh. They needed parents who would play with Play-Doh with them.

Of course, the Play-Doh was only symbolic of the bigger issue—she had a demanding job that she was great at and didn't want to give up, but that would make being a mom a challenge.

Sabrina sighed with obvious frustration and sat forward in her chair. "So *you* play with the Play-Doh. You'd love that."

"I..."

Sabrina raised her eyebrows, waiting for him to think that through.

Okay, he would love that. He'd also love to read Dr. Seuss four million times. And all the other things Kat might not be able to do. Being self-employed would make it very easy for him to be there for their kids.

"I'm really good with finger paints," he said.

"I have no doubt," Sabrina answered with a smile. "You're really good at almost everything. Except..."

He looked up with interest. "Except?"

"Knowing when a woman is right for you." She met his gaze directly, the obvious affection in her expression softening her words. "You were convinced I was right for you and I most definitely was not," she said. "Now you're trying to give me a bunch of reasons that Kat's not right for you when she's clearly perfect."

"She doesn't want Justice. She can't be herself here," he said, the misery of it hitting him square in the gut. Again.

"Then why do you want her to be here?"

"Because I'm here."

"Only because you've never imagined you could have the life you want anywhere else."

He sighed. "Are we to the analysis part already?"

Sabrina gave him a small smile. "The obvious you're-an-idiot stuff didn't take long."

He took a deep breath. "Okay, lay it on me."

Maybe it should have been weird to have the woman he'd proposed to twice giving him advice about another woman. But it wasn't. Sabrina knew him, cared about him, accepted him. She also knew, cared about and accepted Kat.

And he knew her. There was no way she was going to leave him alone until she'd said this.

Sabrina leaned closer.

"Your idea of keeping her is keeping her *here*."

He gripped the arms of his chair. Somehow he knew this wasn't going to be a pep talk. "It's killing me," he said tightly. "Wanting her, loving her, but knowing we can't be together...it's killing me."

Sabrina rolled her eyes, obviously unmoved by his plight. "Rolland would be even better for you than it would be for Kat."

"Excuse me?"

"You've spent your whole life helping this town. You've always been there, always been the one to count on. You know what Justice needs before anyone else does. You fix everything."

"And *this* makes me a bad guy?".

"Of course not. But it makes you...lazy," she said, meeting his gaze steadily.

"*What*?" He'd gotten up before dawn, sweated and worked and—

"Being a hero is easy for you here," Sabrina said with a shrug. "Heck, your cape and tights can be wrinkled and have holes in them and no one would care. But in a new place, a place like Rolland, you'd have to prove yourself again, wouldn't you? The hero title might even be taken already. By Kat even. So, it's a lot easier just to stay here and keep doing your thing."

He scowled at her. "I'm not staying here because it's easier than starting over somewhere else."

"Then why are you staying here?"

He couldn't believe this. "Because I love this town. And *most* of the people in it."

She shrugged again. "We're not going anywhere. Whenever you miss us or want to visit, just come back."

"You make it sound simple."

"No, you make it seem hard." She sighed. "Luke, you need to be a hero. That's not going to change. But you're not a hero because you're from here or because there's no one else or because we don't know any better. You're beloved here because of you. And that will be true anywhere you go. You don't have to worry about that."

It hit him that Kat had said something similar to him when they were on the road. She'd called him on the fact that he thought he needed to *do* things for people to like him, for them to want him around. She'd told him that people liked him for who he was.

Was he worried about that? Was that why he'd stayed in Justice? Why he was so bound to this town?

Very possibly.

Being liked always outranked not being liked.

He looked out the window again at the Main Street of the only place that had ever really been home.

"What about The Camelot?" he asked.

"It's a building full of tables and chairs," Sabrina said simply. "The feeling that's here, the reason that people come back, comes partly from you, Luke. That will happen wherever you are, in any building full of tables and chairs."

Another restaurant? In another town? Could he create this again?

He thought about it. He wouldn't have Marc full-time, but his friend would gladly come and train another staff and share his recipes. He wouldn't have the same crowd of people but... He thought of the people he'd met in Rolland, how welcoming and energetic and caring they'd been. It wouldn't be the same crowd, but the atmosphere of fun and acceptance and community wasn't exclusive to Justice.

It could be done.

"What about you guys? The baby? Mom and Dad?"

"Oh, for God's sake!" Sabrina exclaimed. "You're not moving to Africa. It's a few hours' drive. We have an RV. We can come visit. And vice versa."

It would be different. Strange. He said as much out loud.

"I'll tell you a secret," Sabrina said. "From someone who's been there—different and strange are scary. And being scared can be the best thing that ever happens to you. Getting outside your comfort zone makes you do one of two things: either change for the better, or make the conscious decision not to change because it's better to stay the same. Either way you're *deciding* what's best. It's too easy to get in ruts and not even think about what you're doing and why."

Well, it was a damned comfortable rut he'd been in all this time.

"So, you think I should go after her?"

"You've never gone after anyone before," Sabrina said with a soft smile. "Isn't your soul mate the perfect person to be the first?"

"Okay," he said slowly, feeling the weight in his chest lift. He grinned as a sense of rightness—and a new *plan*—coursed through him. "But I'm not giving you full price for the RV when I buy it from you."

Sabrina laughed. "There will be some negotiating on that."

"And there's no way I'd ever wear tights," he added as she got to her feet. "And certainly never with holes."

"But the cape?" she asked.

"Oh, I could definitely pull that off."

There was an RV parked in her driveway. Not just any RV either. It was *the* RV. The RV that had changed her life.

And it sitting in the driveway of the house she was renting in Rolland could only mean one thing: Luke was here.

She was torn between extreme happiness and incredible exhaustion. Happiness because she'd missed him and wanted to see him with an intensity that physically hurt. Exhaustion because she couldn't fight with him and send him away again.

He must have heard her drive in because he came out of the RV as she slammed her car door.

He looked great.

Maybe a little tired, but great.

She hadn't seen him in two weeks. She'd called Stan in Rolland the morning after Luke had taken her to dinner in

Alliance. He'd said she could start immediately. Dr. Brickham had appreciated her offer to give him thirty days' notice but had ultimately felt it was unnecessary. So she'd hired movers and had arrived in Rolland—and the rental house the hospital owned—four days after Luke walked out of the restaurant.

The two weeks had been...okay. She definitely liked her work better. She was busy and appreciated and welcomed. But there were a hundred things she missed about Justice—dinner at her mom's, the flowerbeds at the park, Marc's cheesecake, the fact that she could catch up on all the gossip with a stop at the post office.

And then there was the hole in her soul where her heart used to be.

And now he was standing in her driveway.

She'd been expecting it on some level. But she hadn't let herself expect it. Every time she'd started to wonder if he'd come, she'd squelched it.

"Hi."

One syllable and she wanted nothing more than to jump into his arms.

Instead she hugged herself. "What are you doing here?"

"It's my first night in Rolland. Where else would I be?"

Her heart thumped even as she held herself back from him. "It's not your first night. You've been here before."

"This is my first night living here, though. That's different."

Her heart thumped harder as her mouth dropped open. "What?"

"I need you. I want you. I have to be with you. So I'm moving to Rolland."

She stared at him. Was she dreaming? That would be a much better explanation for this than its being real.

"Have you been drinking?"

He smiled. "Of course not."

"Hit your head? Been diagnosed with a life-threatening illness? Been told an end-of-the-world prophecy?" She came to stand in front of him, just out of arm's reach—in case he had handcuffs.

He grinned, noticing the distance. "None of the above."

"So there's actually no good reason for you to move here?"

"You're here. That's more than reason enough."

That's what he was supposed to say, what she wanted him to say. If she'd scripted it for him that's what she would have written.

And instead of being thrilled, she suddenly felt like crying.

She'd wanted this, him, but...she really couldn't handle the almost-having-it anymore. He might move here. He might try it. But it wouldn't last. Or, almost worse, he'd stay but be unhappy. There was no way he would leave his friends, family, community and work for good.

She crossed her arms to keep from grabbing him. "You're not moving to Rolland."

"I am. I'm building a new restaurant."

"What?" she demanded.

"I'm building a restaurant here. Meeting with the real estate agent tomorrow morning to look at some lots. Don't know if I'll call it The Camelot or something else."

That sounded like something more permanent. Something to be more hopeful about.

Which meant a lot of squelching.

"I think that's a really bad idea," she said, starting up the sidewalk toward the house.

"No you don't." He started after her. "You love the idea for the same reasons I love the idea. It's something I'm great at and love to do and this town would love a place like The Camelot."

She opened the front door and stepped inside, letting the screen door swing back in Luke's face. He stopped it with his foot and followed her inside.

"You don't want a restaurant here." She tossed her purse and bag onto the first chair in the living room, then kicked her shoes off and continued to the kitchen.

"I want to be with you, you're here, I run restaurants, therefore I want a restaurant here."

She yanked open the fridge door and stared inside. She had no idea what she was looking for but she just couldn't look at him. This was all too tempting, too perfect—and it would last about two months.

"You'll never be able to stay here, Luke. This will never replace Justice." She moved some bottles and containers around, pretending to search for something.

"I'm not looking for a replacement."

"You shouldn't settle for a consolation prize either."

"Kat, look at me."

She was staring at the ketchup. She swallowed hard. "No."

"Why?"

"Because then you'll be able to talk me into this and it's a bad idea."

He chuckled. The next thing she felt was his hands on her hips. "I'm not looking for a replacement and this isn't a consolation prize. It's just something new."

She straightened and took a deep breath. "You don't do new."

"People can change."

She wished.

"I painted the lobby of The Camelot—the one in Justice—red."

"No way."

She felt one hand leave her hip. He must have reached into his pocket because he put his phone in her line of sight. With a photo of the newly painted Camelot lobby.

It was red.

She slowly turned to face him. "I'm scared."

"Me too."

God, she'd missed him. She wanted him.

But it would be worse if she had him again for a little while and then lost him.

"I can't make you move your whole life here when I know you're not going to like it, when I know you're going to eventually want to leave."

"You have to trust me. I love you."

She sucked in a quick breath. She wondered if she'd ever get used to hearing him say that.

"Tell me you love me too," he said. "I know you do. I know you're scared of what that means, but we'll work it out."

"I want you to be happy."

"I've never been as miserable as I've been the past two weeks without you."

"It's the sex."

He grinned. "I haven't been having any sex."

"That's what I mean." Maybe she'd overwhelmed him for a while. Maybe she was different enough from the other women that he was a little amazed. Or something. She'd accept that he felt something for her. Something big even.

But was it enough?

"I'm not here because of the sex, Kat." Luke cupped her cheek. "I'm here because you're here." He leaned in and kissed her.

It was soft, sweet, and full of promise.

"Tell me you love me too," he whispered against her lips.

She hadn't said it out loud yet. But he knew. "I love you too."

The smile on his face made her heart flip. He leaned in to kiss her again but she put her hand against his mouth.

"Which is why I can't let you do this. I love you. I want you to be happy. Go back to Justice."

He didn't look shocked or even a little surprised. He sighed in resignation. "I'm not going back to Justice."

"Maybe not yet," she said.

"But obviously I'm going to have to prove it."

"What do you mean?"

He let go of her and reached into his pocket again. "Here is a copy of the loan document from the bank. It's enough to buy the RV from Marc and Sabrina and to start building here. This—" he opened another folded paper, "—is the agreement between me and Marc for him to buy half of my half of the business. I'll stay on as twenty-five percent owner of The Camelot for now but Marc is the majority partner. And this—" he pulled one more piece of paper out, "—is the buyer's agreement from the couple who bought my house."

She took the papers with shaking fingers. "You sold your house? You sold most of The Camelot?"

"I did. I'm here to stay."

Oh, God. He was going to regret this. And it was all her fault.

"Maybe there's time to get it back. There's got to be time to change this. Marc will understand."

"I don't want it back."

Her eyes filled with tears and she took the step back from him that she needed to think clearly. "Maybe not this minute. But this is going to sink in and—"

"I'm staying." He turned on his heel and started toward the front of the house. Very much *not* staying.

"What... Where are you going?"

"To my RV. Where I'm going to live until the love of my life realizes that this is for real." He turned back to look at her from the front door. "And that it's for good."

He pulled the door shut behind him leaving Kat completely speechless.

And a little amazed.

Chapter Twelve

It only took her three days to learn that Luke's routine was to get coffee at the Pit Stop, the convenience store on the corner of Main Street, at seven a.m. And stay, chatting with the other men, until eight.

It wasn't hard to hear information about Luke. Everyone in town was talking about him, his move to Rolland, the fact that he was parking the RV—for free again—in the park until the restaurant was done and, of course, the fact that he was building a restaurant.

So it was easy to find out that he had already joined the men at the Pit Stop for coffee and donuts the past two mornings at seven.

Which was why she showed up there at seven a.m. three days after he'd left her house.

Because he hadn't showed up at her house again. He also hadn't showed up at the clinic. Or anywhere else where she was.

After the nights she'd spent tossing and turning, she needed the coffee almost as much as she needed to see him.

They made eye contact the moment she stepped in the door. Their eyes met over the bald head of the man Luke was talking to at one of the tables and, though his mouth kept moving with whatever he was saying, it also stretched in a smile.

He knew she couldn't stay away from him.

She sighed and headed in his direction. He got to his feet as she stopped by his table.

"Morning, Dr. Dayton," he said.

"Morning, Mr. Hamilton."

"Can I buy you coffee?"

"That would be great."

He took her elbow and headed for the self-serve coffee island where he proceeded to fill a cup and mix it with just the right amount of cream and sugar before handing it to her.

"I know what you're doing," she said.

He leaned in. "Do you?"

She nodded.

"Good. Pay attention." He lifted his hand and hooked the scooped neckline of her white sundress with his finger running it along the edge between the fabric and her skin. "I know what you're doing too."

Ah, he'd noticed.

Since coming to Rolland she was still wearing black but not *just* black. And not as much leather. And fewer kick-ass boots.

"What am I doing?" she asked, lifting the paper cup.

He dropped his hand. "You're starting over. You're taking the opportunity to be who you are now in a new place instead of letting how things have always been in Justice govern you."

She felt her mouth drop open. She wouldn't have put it quite that way but...yeah, okay. She was in a new place where she didn't have to keep up the façade.

"And that's what I'm doing too," he said, smiling at her look of amazement.

She frowned slightly. "How? You've always been a social butterfly, in the center of whatever's going on. How is this different?"

"It's a new place, a new start, a whole new town to win over and impress." He gave her a cocky grin. "Just what I need."

Yeah, just what he needed. *Two* groups of people thinking he could do no wrong.

She hid her smile behind her cup. Because he did need that. He needed to know that people loved him because of *him*. Not because he'd grown up in town, or because they loved his mother, or because he'd headed the town's Fourth of July celebration committee for the past five years.

"And so you know," he said, leaning in closer. "I'm building the restaurant, I'm having coffee, I'm filling in on the golf league because Conner's sick and I'm helping finish the roof at Sunshine Estates. And I like it. A lot."

Great. But it had been three days. They'd see how long that lasted. It wasn't The Camelot, it wasn't coffee with Bill and it wasn't golfing with Marc.

"Okay. Have fun. Just be sure to stick a note on my front door when you decide to move back to Justice," she said turning away. "Thanks for the coffee. Bye, guys," she called to the other men, giving them a little wave.

Conner wouldn't be sick forever and the roof would take another weekend at most.

Luke was trying to show her that he was prepared to make a life here for good.

She gave it another two weeks. Tops.

It was an unconventional seduction to be sure.

And it was taking a hell of a long time.

Luke watched as Kat let herself into the city council meeting through the door at the back of the school's gymnasium.

She was dressed in a black skirt, but her top was yellow, and her hair was curly and held back by a yellow headband. That was it. There were no streaks of color in her hair, no body paint visible and the only piercings were in her ears. She'd been dressing a little more conservatively since coming to Rolland. She hadn't completely given up her makeup, but she seemed to be hiding less behind her costumes.

Tonight, however, she was wearing kick-ass black leather knee-high boots.

An incredible sense of need washed over him. It was becoming familiar now. Whenever he bumped into her in town—

sometimes accidentally and sometimes not—the same powerful desire hit him. It was so much stronger than it had been in the beginning when he'd wanted her physically. Now he knew he was doing without so much more than just her incredible body. And he wanted it all.

But not yet. He was showing her that he was here to stay, that he *wanted* to stay. She had to believe that before they could move forward.

It had been six weeks since he'd been in her bed. It had taken him two weeks to get everything figured out in Justice so he could leave. Now it had been a month since he'd rolled into town in the RV.

Oh, he saw her. Quite a bit actually. They chatted at the post office, they'd worked together at Sunshine Estates twice since coming back, they got coffee at the convenience store every morning at the same time—which he knew was no coincidence—and she had to drive past the building site both to and from work every day. Also not a coincidence. Once he'd narrowed the build sites down to two, he'd easily chosen the one that would require her to pass him and the example of his commitment to this new life in this new town twice a day.

But every time he told her how much he liked it here, she rolled her eyes and said, "Okay."

Clearly he hadn't convinced her that he wanted to stay.

But the damnedest thing was, it was true.

He'd come determined to show her that he *would* make a life wherever she was because he wanted to be with her. But in the past month he'd learned that he wanted this new life too.

He took a seat in the front row even though she was in back. Bob Mason, the president of the city council, had asked him to make a few comments regarding the Fourth of July event next summer. He and Bob had gotten into a discussion about it while golfing last week and Luke had made some suggestions Bob really liked.

The council went over the usual business first. Old business included the grant for the new dirt and scoreboard at the baseball field, fees for renting the city center for personal events like wedding receptions, and planting more trees along the north side of the highway into town. New business included a revised trash pickup schedule and the appointment of the Fourth of July celebration committee.

"Ladies and Gentlemen, I know that you've all met Luke Hamilton over the past month," Bob said as an introduction to Luke's comments. "I think you would all agree when I say that he's full of enthusiasm and it's a pleasure to have him here."

There was applause at that and Luke felt his wide, stupidly pleased grin.

"I know he's new and Steve Schroeder did a great job with the Fourth celebration last year, but I've given this a lot of thought and I would very much like to appoint Luke Hamilton to be the chairman this year."

Surprise rumbled through him as the audience applauded again.

"Luke, will you come up here, please?"

Bob waved him forward and Luke got slowly to his feet. He'd never been truly appointed to anything before. In Justice they'd either assumed he'd do it or he'd jumped in and offered.

"I don't know what to say," he told Bob as he joined him on the short stage.

"I know you have a lot going on with the restaurant. But we really want you involved. Just say yes, son," Bob said, clapping him on the back.

"I..." Luke shrugged. "I'd love to."

He looked out into the audience, searching the back row for Kat.

Just in time to see her leaving through the back door.

Dammit. What was that about?

"Tell everyone a little about what you're thinking," Bob said.

"I, um..." Luke tried to focus back on the audience in front of him. But something gripped him. A take-care-of-this-right-now urgency. "I'm sorry, but I have to go."

"Go?" Bob asked. "But..."

"I have something I have to take care of. Right this minute."

He bounded off the front of the stage and jogged up the center aisle. Pushing the door open hard enough that it banged against the concrete wall, Luke searched the immediate area, hoping Kat was just taking a phone call from a patient.

She was nowhere.

He scanned the parking lot just in time to see her car pulling out onto the street.

He ran to his car and followed her, speed-dialing her cell number.

She didn't pick up.

Now what? Had the hospital called? But she took a right instead of a left at Jackson Street.

He followed until she turned into the park and pulled up next to the RV. He watched, a bit dumbfounded, as she got out of her car and started toward the RV, shrugging out of her jacket as she went. Then she let herself into the RV without sparing him even a glance. Okay. Well, this was...hell, he didn't know *what* this was but he knew what it was *not.*

She was *not* going to tell him to leave again. She was *not* going to tell him she was leaving. She was *not* breaking this off. In fact, he was done with the no kissing, no touching...

He stomped into the RV and promptly stepped on the yellow shirt she'd been wearing. He looked up to find her in the door to the bedroom dressed in a pink lace teddy and the boots.

"What are..." he started as all the blood pounding through his body quickly rerouted south.

"Marry me, Luke."

He stared at her dumbly. "Huh?"

"Marry me."

"But I... Are you... Back there..."

"Back there I realized that it had really happened. You are part of this town. You're here to stay."

"Just now?" he asked. "I've been here for a month." He locked the door and headed for her.

"Yes, but you've been having coffee and golfing. Temporary things. The Fourth of July is nine months away. And you're taking on the whole thing. You've committed to being here at least until then. You'd never tell them you'd do it if you weren't *sure* you were going to stay."

"I'm building a restaurant. That's a pretty big commitment." He stripped off his T-shirt.

"I saw that you finally got the foundation in this morning." Her eyes roamed over him hungrily.

"So, that proves that I'm staying, right?"

She shrugged. "Maybe. But now you're making lasting commitments to *people*, like the committee. For you, that's bigger."

"That's all I needed to do?"

"That's all you needed to do. You aren't Luke without getting involved, doing stuff, fixing stuff. Now I know you're really putting down roots."

He unbuttoned his jeans and she licked her lips.

But she went on, "I've been in this town, with these people, taking care of them, working with them for six weeks now. They're amazing. If you stay another nine months you will definitely think so too and never be able to leave."

He liked the sound of that. He also liked the way she was watching him take his pants off.

"And now," she said. "They've proven that they're smart enough to put you in charge of things around here. They love you and they want you to stay too. That makes this the perfect town. We'd be stupid to leave."

He was now in boxers only and stood directly in front of her. "Well, I've been telling you for a long time just how smart I am."

She smiled and started untying the tiny bows that held her teddy together. "Yes, yes you have."

As she peeled the pink lace away from her body, Luke swallowed hard. “And we’ve definitely made progress here.”

“Oh?” The teddy dropped to the floor.

“I have you in this RV and there’s not a pair of handcuffs to be found.”

Kat gave him a seductive smile and reached behind her. “Who said that?”

Epilogue

Kat watched Luke holding Sabrina and Marc's new baby girl. He had his elbows propped on his thighs, the baby cradled in both big hands, nearly eye to eye with him. If she was awake, that was. Still, he was staring at her as if he'd never seen something so fascinating.

Marc had petitioned for naming her Guinevere, but Sabrina had rolled her eyes and filled the birth certificate in with Abigail. After Marc's late mother.

Abby.

She was perfect.

Sabrina's labor had been just long enough to allow Kat and Luke to get there, Kat to get into her scrubs and into position to welcome her goddaughter into the world.

Abby was six hours old and only now had her father gone to take a shower and her mother was napping.

Kat arranged the last of the flowers and gift baskets that had been delivered then crossed the room to sit on the arm of Luke's chair.

"You know that whole have-my-babies-and-stay-home-to-raise-them offer you made me?" She brushed the soft hair off the baby's forehead.

"Yeah?" Luke asked, eyebrows up.

"I think I'd like to do half of that."

He gave her a grin. "Want to start work on that right now?"

"You'd have to put the baby down," she pointed out.

His eyes went back to Abby. "Yeah, well then it might have to wait."

Kat laughed softly. "I've already lost you to another female."

He looked up at her quickly. "Never. She's just..."

"Adorable," Kat filled in with a little sigh.

"I'll give you six if you've changed your mind about wanting only two."

"Ah, sweetie." She leaned over to kiss his cheek. "Don't be ridiculous."

Just then there was a knock on the door. "Dr. Dayton?"

Expecting a nurse with some paperwork Kat looked up. Then froze.

Julie Martin, Tom's wife, stood in the doorway.

"Um, Julie, hi." She scrambled to her feet.

"I'm sorry. I know you're here with Marc and Sabrina. This is probably very inappropriate, but I had to take the chance to talk to you."

Oh, crap. What was she supposed to say. Or do? Should she have her lawyer here? But she didn't want to have her lawyer here. That didn't feel right. She wanted to talk to Julie.

"Sure, Julie, it's fine."

Kat didn't look her best. She barely looked like herself. Not only was she in scrubs, but she had no makeup on, no jewelry on and white tennis shoes on her feet. She felt the lack of armor more now than she had in all the time in Rolland.

"You okay?" Luke asked under his breath.

"I think so." She gave him a quick smile. "Be back soon."

Nothing Julie could say could change that Luke loved her and vice versa. That was the most important thing. It also wouldn't change her place in Rolland. She loved her job, her coworkers, her patients—and it was mutual. Plus, Stan and the rest of the physician team had her back.

But Julie could hurt her. Kat acknowledged that on her way to the door. Julie could hurt her because she still cared.

"Did you come over here just to talk to me?" Kat asked. "You could have called."

"Some things should be said in person," Julie told her. "And yes. We're staying here in Alliance right now while Tom undergoes more rehab and when I saw the post on Facebook that Sabrina and Marc were here having the baby I knew you'd be here too."

"Well, I'm glad you came to find me. If there's something you want to say, I'm glad you have the chance." Even if it was bad, Kat told herself. Julie had the right to tell her whatever she was feeling or thinking.

Julie stood before her, pressing her lips together, her arms crossed tightly over her stomach.

Kat just waited. It was all she could do.

"I um..." Julie trailed off, then laughed lightly. "This is a little awkward."

Well, *that* she could do something about. "Julie, I don't blame you and your family for turning my name into the licensure board. You had a legitimate concern. I'm *very* sorry to have caused that concern. But I'm not angry."

Julie's eyes got a little brighter. "That's incredibly gracious of you, Kat. And this probably sounds cliché but I have to say it. We didn't want to. We were encouraged to do that."

"By Dr. Brickham?" Kat knew the answer even before the other woman nodded.

"Yes. He insisted it was the correct procedure. Just like he insisted we sign paperwork for AMP to launch an investigation."

Kat was really trying not to be defensive but it was damned hard. "In many ways I'm glad they did the investigation. They found no wrongdoing which means everyone can sleep better at night."

Julie nodded but she still looked upset. "I remember being so surprised by how adamant Dr. Brickham was about all of it."

Kat shrugged. "Your husband is a longtime patient of his. He felt that he was doing what was right for all of you."

Julie crossed her arms tighter. "That's what I thought at first. But when we got back from Denver I found out..."

She trailed off and took a deep breath.

"What did you find out?" Kat asked.

"That you'd been asked to leave the Justice clinic and that Marty Davidson was taking it over."

"Dr. Davidson is a good doctor, with more experience than I have. It's a good decision."

Julie frowned. "Maybe that's all true, but Dr. Brickham didn't ask him to move to Justice for those reasons."

"What reasons did he have?" Kat asked, feeling her heartrate pick up.

"He wanted to get Marty out of Alliance. He was having an affair with Dr. Brickham's daughter, Ashley. Ashley's married with two little girls, Marty's married with kids too—Dr. Brickham wanted to avoid any scandal or problems, so he moved Marty away."

Kat took in the information with a strange combination of surprise, confusion and interest. "Wow. I had no idea."

"I'm just so sorry we were the excuse to get you moved out of Justice. And now you've moved away completely," Julie said. "We know it was a mistake, Kat. We don't blame you."

"Thank you, Julie." Kat took the other woman's hand. "I can't tell you what that means to me."

"Well, I also wanted to tell you that if you want to pursue getting your job back in Justice, I'd be very happy to tell what I know to...whoever needs to know it. You weren't really moved out because of Tom."

More surprise vibrated through Kat. She could get her job back? She probably could. If it became public that her reassignment actually had nothing to do with her professional skills, then it wouldn't be hard to get the town of Justice to rally behind her and strongly encourage AMP to put her back in the clinic.

She could move back to Justice.

Luke could move back to Justice.

They could have that life back.

"Thanks, I appreciate that."

Julie nodded. "Of course. I don't know if I'd go to the Board for AMP or..."

"That won't be necessary."

Kat swung around at the sound of Luke's voice behind her. He came to stand next to her, pulling her up against his side. He smiled down at Julie. "Thanks, but no thanks."

"Did you hear?" Kat asked.

"The whole thing," he confirmed.

"We can move back home," she said.

He shook his head. "Going home doesn't require a move. We're home in Rolland."

"But..." Kat started. Then she stopped. She didn't want to leave Rolland either. Justice was their hometown, where they visited, where they had a million fond memories.

But Rolland was home. Where they were going to make two million new memories.

She looked at Julie. "Never mind. It's not necessary."

Julie looked skeptical but she nodded. "Well, let me know if you ever change your mind."

They watched Julie get on the elevator with a final wave, then Kat sighed and hugged Luke.

"Let's get married here before we go back to Rolland," she said.

She knew he was going to say, *But what about our new friends?*

"But—"

She grinned. "Then," she interrupted, "we'll get married again in Rolland."

They started back for Sabrina and Abby's room. "Yeah, that's probably a good idea. You might scare the nice folks of Rolland if you showed up in the black wedding dress, veil and boots you have planned for Justice."

She laughed and watched Luke head straight for the bassinette as soon as they stepped into the room.

But she wasn't so sure about the black dress and veil for

Justice either. Because some days a girl needed kick-ass boots...but some days she didn't.

Some days turned out just fine in white tennis shoes.

About the Author

Erin Nicholas has been reading and writing romantic fiction since her mother gave her a romance novel in high school and she discovered happily-ever-after suddenly went a little beyond glass slippers and fairy godmothers! She lives in the Midwest with her husband who only wants to read the sex scenes in her books, her kids who will *never* read the sex scenes in her books, and family and friends who say they're shocked by the sex scenes in her books (yeah, right!).

For more information about Erin and her books, visit:

www.ErinNicholas.com

www.ninenaughtynovelists.blogspot.com

www.twitter.com/ErinNicholas

www.groups.yahoo.com/group/ErinNicholas